Inkdrops

IN
THE
Rain

ASHER M ISRAEL

Copyright

Dedication

Dedicated to the memory of my dad,
James Francis Lansdowne – who lost the battle –
but remains to this day, the kindest person I've ever known.

To all those who taught me the hardest lessons – Thank you.

Quote

O benefit of ill! now I find true
That better is by evil still made better;
And ruined love, when it is built anew,
Grows fairer than at first, more strong, far greater.
So I return rebuked to my content,
And gain by ills thrice more than I have spent.

William Shakespeare – Sonnet 119

Chapter One

Alice rubbed her father's back as he vomited – for the third time – on the kerb outside Abbey Wood train station. Families scurried by like ants trying to make the most of the London sunshine. Some paused momentarily to watch the young child scuff her pink trainer – newly covered in vomit, against the concrete. Others just bustled past in a rush.

Christopher's plan was to take his daughter to the mechanical theatre; just as they did sometimes on an impromptu whim. He knew it was one of Alice's most treasured places where she could escape into the wondrous fantasy and illusion that was a far cry from her own life. He winced at the realisation that he was the reason she needed an escape in the first place.

While he crouched on all fours, waiting for the next wave of spew to empty from his stomach, he played over Alice's excited squeals from last year's visit to the special place:

"Look at this, Daddy!" She'd dragged him by the shirt to look at a painted wooden mechanical bird pecking at poisoned birdseed before falling over dead; its little yellow beak moving at the mercy of the commanding levers and pulleys. "Daddy, this way!" Alice had ordered, pulling her father to the carved woman with curly wire hair in 'The Nightmare'. The woman jolted awake from her peaceful slumber at the realisation that a monster was leaping through her window. At this climax, the calm light changed to blue and white thunderous flashes, and the little wooden figure rubbed her eyes as the monster disappeared from sight. Christopher had watched and smiled as his daughter screamed with glee, he'd watched her analyse the delicate cogs and gears, intermingling and working together in perfect harmony.

Now, he watched hurried, careless feet passing by his face, and a splatter of brown and orange on his daughter's white-frilled sock in his line of sight.

Three hours earlier, there was no choice for Alice but to accompany her father to The Black Horse Inn. The waif had looked up at him with doubtful eyes, her persistently knotted, dark hair strewn about her shoulders.

"You have eyes as big as saucers," was the only response he gave to her look of questioning. He used to say that in reference to the line from one of their favourite stories 'The Tinderbox' by Hans Christian Andersen. He had read her all the tales from the weathered, red-covered book when he was sober. When he read to her and saw her light up, he felt like a proper father – not the excuse of a dad he was right now, clutching on to the cold concrete, hands trembling with sick dripping down his chin.

Christopher knew Alice could see through him; he was as transparent as the liquor glass that was often in his hand, but still, he kept up the charade. They both did. She was a smart kid, and he regularly broke his heart over the

2

thought that she was probably clinging on to the hope of him changing; becoming what she needed him to be.

"Let's go back now, Daddy," Alice soothed her father after the waves of vomit stopped. He nodded and wiped the remaining moisture from his mouth on to his sleeve. They began the short walk over the grass in a direct line to Christopher's house. It hadn't been Alice's home for four years, and she was glad of that. She didn't even like being at fifty-two Blackley Street for short periods of time. It was a large and unfeeling Victorian house, always draughty, with the smell of damp and rotting wood. Painful memories from number fifty-two had been ingrained in the young girl's subconscious, just as they had also become part of the fabric of the house.

As they walked, Alice spotted a blackbird from the corner of her eye, floundering by the stump of a tree. Only one wing was open and the creature was hopping around hopelessly in circles. "Look, Daddy, that bird is ill – can we take him with us?" She pointed to the wretched creature with concern. "We can give him that medicine I have to take when I'm ill."

Christopher looked over to where the bird was hopping about.

"Oh dear, poor thing – let me find something to carry him in." He found a newspaper in a nearby bin and fashioned it into a little carrier. The scared little bird tweeted desperately as Christopher nudged it into the paper cone. Alice carried the speckled creature carefully all the way to the front door, not taking her eyes off the bird once.

"Happy birthday, sweetie!" a voice called as they approached the house and Alice looked up, shocked. Her mother, April, stood by the front door with a flimsy smile painted on her lips. Her blonde hair was curled into tight tendrils and she carried a birthday cake in the shape of a pink fairy, eight candles protruding from the surface.

"What on earth are you wearing?" April asked, her happy tone disappearing as she assessed Alice's outfit: a hand-me-down jumper that was two sizes too big and a checked, pleated school skirt teamed with trainers.

"Look what me and Daddy found!" Alice told her mother, "I'm going to look after it until it's better."

"Alice, those things are full of diseases," April wrinkled up her nose. "Put it down."

"But Mummy, I…"

"Put it down, now!"

Alice stood with her head down, looking at the helpless creature in its little cone, and held on tighter.

"I said now!" April commanded. Alice obeyed the order and carefully placed the bird under the hedge in the front garden, crouching just in front of it in a spot where the leaves were sparse and she could spy on her parents. She saw her father approaching her mother – *this meant trouble*, she thought.

Christopher staggered over to his ex-wife.

"What are you doing here?"

"It is our daughter's birthday, it's customary to have a cake," April replied shortly. "Your mother grudgingly told me you were taking her out for the day. I came on the off-chance I might catch her."

Christopher looked down sheepishly.

"Oh, okay."

April wafted her hand in front of her face as the smell of alcohol and vomit hit her nose.

"You're a useless shithead, do you know that? You're drunk and look at the state of her. Those clothes don't even fit. No need to guess where you've been!"

"Oh, fuck off April," Christopher replied. "You think

you're so fucking superior? You're thirty and living in a bedsit. There's a reason Alice doesn't live with you."

April's face tightened and her cheeks flamed a shade of magenta. She put the cake down on the wall so she wouldn't lose control and throw it in her ex-husband's face.

"She doesn't live with you either, thank God," April spat in return. "At least I *have* a fucking job! You're no better than a dosser. This house is all you've got left and you won't have that for much longer. Alice will be living with me soon enough, where she belongs!"

"Ha! You are kidding, right?" Christopher questioned, "good luck trying to get her from my parents. They'll fight you to the bitter end. They love her and she's got a good life there. You know that your social life will suffer if you have to look after your own child all the time. Kids aren't fashionable at parties, you know! I know what I am, April, and I know I could be doing better, but I will not let you ruin her. And for the record, I had to leave work through stress, because my wife left me struggling trying to run a house, look after a child, and hold down full-time employment!"

"Oh yes, blame someone else like you always do, Chris!" April fired back. "It's only a matter of time before your family finds out that you live on fucking cans of special brew. They may not have listened to me, but the truth always comes out."

"I do not!" he spat at April.

"Well, let's ask our daughter, shall we?" April turned, accidentally knocking the cake from the wall. The pink fairy toppled and hit the ground, face down, with a smack.

Alice knew her cue to leave when the arguments reached a certain level of anger. She ran indoors, not forgetting to take her precious blackbird inside its cone.

W hen they had lived together as a family, Alice's parents' arguments assaulted her ears on a daily basis, echoing around the house thick and fast like the rattling of a tommy gun. Relentless.

There was a spattering of good times dotted on an otherwise gloomy tapestry; there was happiness and laughing once, somewhere in the depths of her mind. Alice sometimes played a fond memory over and over so much that she'd forget whether it was real or if she'd imagined it. She remembered crawling into bed with her parents during the night – she would often do this and feel safe in between the warmth of their bodies. They loved each other once; Alice pictured the feeling of 'love' in her head like rays of sunshine.

One morning, when Alice was four, she came down the stairs to see that her mother's bookcase was as bare as a winter branch. April had moved out; no-one had told Alice, and within her subconscious mind it had registered as abandonment.

In the months that followed, her mother visited once per week, and Alice could sense her dad's tension and anger towards April like a knife hanging in the atmosphere. Once a week, when April was made to leave, the four-year-old girl screamed and pounded on the cold windows as she watched her mother's figure become smaller and smaller in the distance, until she was just a dot in the night. Her father turned off the bedroom lights and shut her in the dark, alone, until she cried herself to sleep. Sometimes the crying would last thirty minutes, sometimes more. The smell of the musty yellow duvet on her bed filled Alice's nostrils, and it was always as cold as ice.

She watched her breath as she lay there, night after

night, staring at the peeling paint on the windowpane. There were never sheets on the old, stained mattress and the buttons used to press into Alice's back when she rolled over.

"It's okay, Mathilda. We'll feel warm when we go to sleep," she told her stuffed companion. Mathilda lay there with her sewn-on smile and one orange and black eye missing, the stuffing now poking through. Mathilda had bald spots where Alice had cuddled the fur off, but she loved the toy more because of her defects. Alice used to stick a forefinger in each of Mathilda's ears to block out the sound from the alcoholic rapture that inevitably exploded downstairs, directly beneath her bedroom. It was always men's voices shouting, sometimes there was smashing glass; sometimes erratic laughter and the smell of burning food.

"Don't worry, we'll be okay – I promise," she would soothe Mathilda, "I mean a real promise, not one of Daddy's promises."

Alice lay there with her stuffed toy and poked her head out from beneath the covers just long enough to wind up her musical jewellery box on the bedside table. Auntie Jane had given it to her on her last visit. There was no jewellery to adorn the red felt lining, only a little faceless ballerina twisting around in circles, again and again.

"There, there, little bird. Don't worry, I'll take care of you. I didn't really forget about my birthday, but I didn't say anything because I knew Daddy didn't have any money," Alice stroked the bird's wing and began busily constructing a nest out of a box and some newspaper just as April burst into the bedroom.

"Oh, thank God! I thought you'd run away somewhere," her mother held her hand to her chest. "How did you get in?"

"There's a key under the plant pot," Alice replied matter-of-factly, not taking her eyes from the construction that was underway.

"You're coming with me today," April said, "Daddy isn't feeling very well."

"Did you give him some medicine?"

"No, Alice. We don't have the medicine that Daddy needs."

"Can I bring my bird?" Alice looked up at her mother.

"No!"

"I want to stay here, then. He's ill and Daddy is ill, I'll have to stay here to look after them both," Alice reasoned.

"But it's your birthday," April said, her voice cracking with the threat of tears.

"It's okay, Mummy, I want to stay here."

April stood there for a long while, expressionless, watching her daughter screw up bits of newspaper. She huffed like she always did when she didn't get her own way – Alice recognised this 'huff' all too well.

"Okay, fine," April said eventually, then stalked out of the cold house. Alice peered at her mother through the bedroom window, watched her light up a cigarette, and heard the click of her red stilettoes get fainter as she walked away.

After Alice had completed the nest and her little bird was resting safely inside, she tiptoed over the floorboards to see her father, her bare feet cold. He was sitting on the armchair in his bedroom with a glass of brown liquid in his hand.

"Don't drink that, Daddy," Alice said, staring at him with large, sad eyes.

"It's okay, Alice," he said with a weak smile.

"But you can't be thirsty anymore – you had those drinks in the pub," she pointed out.

"You're right, baby, I'm not thirsty." Christopher's red-rimmed eyes stared at the floorboards of his room while he drained his third glass.

"Mummy said you weren't well. Are you feeling better yet?" Alice asked.

"I'm starting to sweet pea. I'm starting to."

Alice sat on his knee until he began snoring. She pulled the duvet over from the bed and placed it over him gently, the pungent odour of stale sweat enveloping her.

She was glad to get back to her grandparents' house that evening, courtesy of a ride from her Grandad Bill in his bottle green Morris Marina. Alice noticed that her dad always managed to be on form – or at least, awake, when Grandad Bill was coming to collect her. Not a lot of conversation went on between Bill and Christopher; that was the way of things.

"How was your birthday, darling?" Bill enquired once Alice had fastened her seatbelt.

"Good," she replied. "Can I have hot chocolate when we get home?"

"Of course you can, kid," Bill chuckled, "You can have whatever you want."

Chapter Two

It was the sort of day where the sunlight filtered through the trees, dappling the grass beneath with its natural beauty. Alice had no desire to enjoy the outside, much preferring to stay inside the shade of the home she shared with her grandparents. She stared at herself in the mirror for a while, analysing her thick eyebrows and looking at the way her cheeks moved when she smiled. *Was she pretty?* People used to tell her that she was – she wasn't sure if she believed them.

After Alice had finished scrutinizing her face, she peered out of her bedroom window. Her bedroom was at the front of the house, and she liked to be able to watch who was coming and going. She had watched for her dad's visits from this window many times, waiting for him to walk up the path – sometimes he arrived, sometimes he didn't.

She watched the local kids riding their bikes and climbing trees in the precious moments before their parents called to them to start making their way to school. Alice did not want to climb trees, or ride her bike – she only wanted to read books. Beatrix Potter's talking animals were her favourite, especially the Tailor of Gloucester's little mice who sewed through the night with teeny tiny stitching. Alice felt safe in her insular world, she felt safe in the shadows; she felt safe within the walls of her grandparents' home.

The house was a terraced, three-bedroomed building where everything largely remained unchanged, from the carpets in garish shades of brown and orange to the floral curtains. It wasn't a hoarder's house, but it was a house full of stuff – there were knick-knacks and thingamabobs everywhere. A roll of sticky tape could be found almost anywhere, which was handy for Alice's cardboard box craft projects. Alice counted five magnifying glasses dotted about the place and lots of lamps. Bill used these last two items for reading.

According to her granny Hetty's wartime mentality, they could run out of supplies at any moment. The cupboards and drawers were brimming with tins of food, packet sauces, toilet rolls and soap. Alice made a point of counting these last two items once when she was bored – there were ninety-six toilet rolls and twenty bars of soap.

Alice had a quick rifle through Hetty's dressing-table drawer; one of her favourite pastimes. She piled three sets of old false teeth on top of each other, balancing them like a delicate tooth-tower. She set out four one-armed pairs of glasses around the tower, which she decided would be the wall that kept intruders out.

"Come and eat your breakfast, Alice," Hetty called from the foot of the stairs.

"Coming," Alice replied, and she quickly set out some disused powder puffs and lipsticks on the dressing table that she planned to come back to later. Today, the shade

'Jelly Roll Pink' took her fancy, she decided she would apply some of it to her lips later.

Alice made her way down the narrow staircase to the kitchen and ate her regular sugary cereal in silence. It gave her a tummy ache, but she swallowed it anyway.

"We're leaving in exactly eighteen minutes," Bill told his granddaughter. He'd always been a stickler for time keeping and routine. He walked Alice to school dutifully every day, and every day Alice dreaded entering the doors of Mrs. Hillary's class.

Mrs. Hillary had meticulously neat tight brown curls on top of her head and a pock-marked face. She was a woman who rarely smiled and often intimidated the impressionable youngsters in her care. Alice wondered why she ever became a primary school teacher in the first place; she didn't seem to like children much.

Alice was well aware that Mrs. Hillary disliked her, for reasons she did not know. She could feel the dislike reaching towards her like an invisible hand and hitting her in the stomach. Mrs. Hillary's face reminded Alice of a toad's, and she was glad that the teacher was not beautiful on the outside – she was far too ugly a person underneath to show any prettiness anywhere else. Alice had learnt quite expertly at a young age how to hold in her desire to cry. She found she was much more accepted when she did this.

Bill walked Alice into the playground outside her class-room, planting a small kiss on her forehead before leaving. She made a beeline for a heavy-set boy called Ben, who was cowering behind one of the weather-worn school sheds, waiting for the class doors to open. Alice had met Ben in the middle of the spring term last year. He'd been moved from another school on account of being bullied for his weight. He was a distinctly round boy who was snubbed by most of his classmates – but not by Alice. She'd befriended him a few weeks after he'd arrived and the pair became thick as thieves. Ben was kind, and Alice watched the way his eyes would disappear into a crinkle when he smiled. Every lunchtime he fetched her black and white patterned lunchbox, and they ate their lunches in a corner somewhere, away from everyone else.

"What are you doing behind here?" she asked. Ben didn't answer, but his eyes darted over to where Richard was standing.

Alice followed his gaze. "Not Richard, he's a little weed!" she scoffed.

"He's mean," Ben whispered.

"Don't worry, I'm here now," Alice smiled, and sat down on some bits of twig and dirt. Ben did the same.

"My mum says that your dad is a drunk. I don't really know what a drunk is," Ben said unexpectedly. Alice was silent for a moment.

"It means he forgets what is important."

"Oh," Ben replied on autopilot – he was writing his name on the back of the rotting wood of the shed with a pencil from his pocket.

"What do you think it's like when you die?" Alice asked him.

"I think it would be scary. Like, imagine you died, but you weren't really dead and you got buried alive."

"I wouldn't be scared," Alice replied, and began etching a coffin into the wood with a sharp twig-end she'd found. She could say anything to Ben, pose any weird question or scenario, and he never judged her. They had found a symbiosis in their friendship that made school bearable. It was as if their souls were friends long before their bodies were.

The pair's favourite pastime was the 'what if' game.

Alice piped up then: "What if you were starving to death on a desert island and I died first – would you eat me, and what would you eat first?"

While Ben contemplated his answer, a shadow was cast over the pair by a blonde-plaited, freckled girl called Katie. A small, smarmy boy named Richard tagged alongside her.

"Look, it's *Wednesday and Pugsley*," Katie drawled, smirking. The pair laughed and began to sing the Addams Family theme tune – poor Ben was too overweight to get a school uniform that fit him, so his mother used to put him in a white and black striped T-shirt for school.

"Okay, *Barbie and Ken*," Alice replied casually, and a sour look came over Katie's face. Ben laughed.

"What are you laughing at, Fatty?" Richard taunted. Ben coiled up like a snake going into itself, trying to hide the tears welling up in his eyes.

"Don't call him that again you *shithead*!" Alice didn't mean to say it, but the word just popped out of her mouth. She felt a forbidden sense of satisfaction at having dumbfounded Richard, who'd never been called a shithead before. His mouth crumpled into a small wrinkle as he attempted to think of a comeback.

"Say something, Richard!" Katie demanded, nudging him harshly on the arm, but Richard kept his wrinkled mouth shut.

"Well, your parents must hate you – they sent you to live with your grandparents, probably because you're so weird," Katie spat at Alice.

The words stung; even Ben came out of his coil to witness the exchange. He stepped forward then, about to speak, but the words seemed to dry up on his tongue. Alice willed herself not to cry, her face felt hot and her head pounded with the exertion of controlling her emotions.

"Go on, cry!" Katie demanded. Alice eyed her for a long moment. The girl's venomous words snapped something in Alice's head and before she knew what she was doing, she grabbed Ben's pencil from his hand and jabbed it into Katie's arm. A small spot of blood appeared from a ring of graphite on her skin and the girl ran crying to Mrs. Hillary, Richard trailing behind her.

Three days later, Christopher and April were preparing for a meeting at the headteacher's office at Foxgrove Primary School.

Christopher looked at himself in the cracked mirror, combed his brassy hair back and straightened his tie. He couldn't remember when he'd last knotted a tie; he had to think carefully about the movements. When he was a teacher, he used to do it on autopilot without a thought. He had a routine back then; it seemed a lifetime ago now.

He'd taught music at the local comprehensive and the kids would call him Sir. They respected him. No-one respected him now, he accepted that. Christopher knew he didn't deserve it. At one point the world was in his hands, only for him to discover that it was as fragile as a sand sculpture. He watched it disintegrate and slip through his fingers until nothing was left. Well, nothing except Alice, that is. His faded eyes moistened as he thought of all the negative space in his life.

He thumbed his gold St. Christopher pendant through the gap in his shirt, took one last look in the cracked mirror and shook the emerging memories out of his head before they could grip him again. He glanced at the bottle of vodka sitting teasingly on top of his decrepit piano, picked up his keys and left the house. He was going to keep a promise just once.

Alice and her mother sat outside the office of Mr. Braithwaite: the headmaster of Foxgrove Primary School. He was a kind man in his late fifties with steel grey hair that was coarse and spiky. He wore silver-rimmed round glasses, his ice-blue eyes shining through, magnified. Alice liked the way Mr. Braithwaite always pouted when he was considering an answer. She liked the fact that he never shouted and always reasoned with his pupils – even the youngest ones. He told stories in assemblies that he claimed were true, but Alice thought they were too fantastic to be genuine. Her favourite was the one he told about his neighbour stealing his milk from his doorstep, and Mr. Braithwaite putting chilli sauce in it one morning very early before the neighbour was awake. After that, he said his milk was never stolen again. Alice didn't care if his stories were made up; they made her feel happy nonetheless.

She kicked her feet against the chair leg as they waited, and April shot her a look of annoyance. Five minutes before they were due to see the headmaster, Christopher arrived and Alice ran over to him, much to April's dismay.

"I didn't know you were coming, Daddy!" she sang, and Christopher lifted her up and hugged her tightly, kissing her on the head before putting her back on to her feet. Alice wished he could be like this all the time.

"Of course I was going to be here, sweet pea!"

April looked like she was chewing on a wasp and glared at her ex-husband as Alice bounced back to her seat. Christopher sat down next to his daughter, trying to avoid eye contact with April.

"Sober, are we?" April commented, tapping her long red nails on the small table beside her.

Christopher replied without looking at her: "You know; you don't always have to be a B-I-T-C-H."

"I know what that says!" Alice piped in. "What does sober mean?"

"Never mind," April and Christopher said in unison, just as Mr. Braithwaite opened the office door. He invited the three of them inside and they all sat opposite him – Alice seated in between her parents. The door opened again and Mrs. Hillary took a seat next to the headmaster. Alice's heart sank. She surveyed the rows upon rows of books sitting on shelves behind Mr. Braithwaite's desk. His office smelled of books and coffee; one day she'd have an office that smelled of books and coffee, she thought. She started counting the books from left to right and was up to number thirty-six when Mr. Braithwaite started speaking.

"So, I understand that Mrs. Hillary telephoned you about an incident that occurred with young Alice here." Mr. Braithwaite addressed them in a friendly but firm manner. "Now, you're one of my best pupils, Alice – I was very surprised to hear about what happened."

Alice smiled shyly while Mrs. Hillary rolled her eyes.

"You know there's no excuse to hurt another pupil, don't you?" Mr. Braithwaite continued.

Alice nodded and then piped up: "It was Katie and Richard's fault. They came over calling me and Ben names and Richard said that my parents hate me."

"Oh, what absolute rubbish!" Mrs. Hillary interrupted. "This girl has such a vast imagination, if only she put it to good use! She spends half of her time in my class doodling and the other half looking miserable!"

One of Mrs. Hillary's tight curls had come loose from its uniform place and was hanging just above her eyebrow. She kept trying to toss it aside with a jerky head movement that Alice found comical, though she kept her amusement hidden.

"Miserable? What makes you feel sad, Alice?" Mr. Braithwaite's voice was as soft as a feather now.

Alice suddenly felt everyone watching her, her parents' eyes telling her to keep her mouth shut – she could feel them dreading her response. Alice looked at Mr. Braithwaite's kindly face, her eyes wide.

"Nothing," she replied eventually, quietly, and she felt the tension melt just a little between her parents. They weren't going to be found out – not today.

***

A few weeks after the meeting, Alice stopped seeing Ben in her class, or at school at all. She learnt later that Ben's mother had moved him to St. Ambrose Primary School. No-one had bothered to tell her; he was just there one minute and gone the next. It echoed the separation of Alice from her mother, and the feeling squeezed unpleasantly on her heart.

Alice and Ben had been friends for one year and one month. She refused to cry, crying never did any good. Instead, she packed up her feelings and placed them in the little space in her heart where her best friend used to be.

Chapter Three

Two years passed; adding more painful notches to the post of Christopher's existence.

He walked through the fog to the top of Eltham Hill, South East London. The air was cold and unforgiving to Christopher's solemn face as he made his way through the graveyard, reading the epitaphs of the souls who had passed. There was something peaceful here; no sound could be heard other than a slight wind blowing the branches of the towering fir trees.

Stopping at some of the gravestones, he gazed upon the old and worn ones with barely legible names. The stones were grainy with moss growing over them, some stood straight and a couple leant at angles under the pressures of time. He noticed how many of the headstones bore three or four family names: mothers, fathers and children – all resting together. He squeezed his eyes shut at the thought, trying to quell a sudden emotion that had risen up in him. Christopher looked up at the grey sky veiling the winter sun and tried unsuccessfully to pray.

He often tried to pray for forgiveness, for hope – for an

end to his suffering in whichever form it might take. Somehow, he always felt like he was doing it wrong, as though he was just whinging to the Almighty. He didn't expect a hand to descend from the clouds offering a cupful of hope, but if he didn't believe his own prayers, what was the point?

The ground was frosty and Christopher could see his breath in front of him; he was the only warmth amongst the cold, dead things. He liked to visit the graveyard early in the morning so that he could be alone, finding comfort in the solitude and lack of life there. As he walked further up the hill, Christopher reached the yard that housed the new gravestones. The shiny black-and-white marble with etched gold lettering was much different from their weather-worn counterparts.

There was a certain sadness in contemplating the recent dates recorded on the graves. Emotions would still be raw, families would be suffering their losses and crying themselves to sleep. A tear formed in the corner of Christopher's eye and it remained there for a time before it fell on to his cheek. He could hardly bear to walk past the children's graves, never mind read them. Some of them bore pictures of the child; teddy bears and ribbons adorned the epitaphs, and Christopher felt a deep anger that their young lives had been robbed from them so soon.

He held three flowers in his hand, always the same three: a lily, an iris and a snowdrop. As the rows of gravestones came to an end, there was a clearing with a small church in the middle. The stained-glass windows were protected by metal grids but other than that, it was quite a modest building with an arched dark wooden door and black iron doorknob. Christopher could see the illumination of candles through the coloured glass, which he thought was unusual for such an early time in the morning.

He turned the iron doorknob just to see if it would shift, and surprisingly, the door creaked open.

Christopher walked gingerly down the aisle, broken pieces of mosaic crunching underfoot, unsure if he was allowed to be in there. He felt like he was intruding, but continued to the front of the church, where there was a table and an enormous candlestick holding three flickering candles. Christopher had always liked the smell of churches; frankincense mixed with musty wood.

"Hello," came the voice of a man behind him. Startled, Christopher spun around to see who was addressing him.

"I didn't mean to scare you," the man said gently, "Do you need any help?"

The voice was soft, and the compassion Christopher felt radiating from this stranger tipped him over the edge. Suddenly, tears started falling fast down his cheeks.

"Come now," the stranger said, and guided him to one of the wooden pews, "I am Father Oakley. Tell me your sorrows, let your worries go to God."

Father Oakley was small in stature and wore half-moon spectacles. Christopher thought him to be around sixty and noticed his weather-beaten face. The priest had a short, trimmed grey beard and eyes that looked like they were smiling, even when his face was expressionless.

"God let bad things happen," Christopher spoke, finally. "He is still letting bad things happen. Why won't he help me?"

"What are these bad things?" Father Oakley enquired.

"I have been ruining my daughter's life for years. I drink, and it ruined my family. I let her down all the time, and she always tells me it's okay. But it isn't okay, and I can't stop," Christopher confessed. "It's like an invisible force takes hold of me and I need the drink. It makes me forget the past, because I can't live with the pain."

"What is your name?" the priest asked.

"Christopher," he replied quietly.

"Addiction is an illness, Christopher. There are places that can assist you in dealing with addiction. Have you been to any of these places?"

"I've been to Alcoholics Anonymous, I've been on anti-depressants, I've had counselling and tried various thera-pies. I've even been to a clinic where I stayed for three months. I was fine when I was there, but when I come back to my life – my shitty, ruined life – I go back to my old ways. Tell me how God can exist if he will not heal me."

Father Oakley paused for a moment, looking as though he was in deep thought.

"God is not like people imagine, Christopher. They often describe God to me as a 'he' like *he* is a person with all this power, deciding who does and who does not deserve good things in their lives. In truth, God is you, and God is me. God is the living force within the trees, plants, birds, flowers and animals. God is not outside; God is inside us all. It is easier for us to place the blame for the condition of our lives on to an outside influence, we do not have to take responsibility for ourselves if we do that. We can just blame God, and that is that. But, if we are God, all of us, then the ability to heal is inside ourselves." His words were calm and measured, they gave Christopher a sense of security amidst his uncertainty. "The problem is that we, as humans, have forgotten that we are divine expressions of life. We have forgotten that we *are* God, and we have forgotten that the power is within us, in our own minds and in our thoughts and beliefs."

"Then why can't I heal myself? If I am God, and I

want to be happy, why can't I make it happen?" Christopher looked at the priest desperately.

"Imagine your heart is like a ray of sunshine, and this sunshine is healing and loving energy," the old man responded. "This is how we are all born, no-one is born with fear in their hearts. But as life unfolds, we encounter unpleasant experiences that are there to help us learn and push past our boundaries. Each sadness or painful emotion is like a raincloud that blocks our ray of sunshine, and we forget our loving kindness and our divinity. Then all we can see is grey clouds because they are blocking the healing energy within us."

"That's all very nice, Father, but if I can't move the rainclouds, then I am at a loss."

"Let love be the force that outshines them, Christopher. You said you have a daughter – I assume you love this daughter very much?"

"Of course, she's the best part of my sorry existence."

"Then use that love to motivate you. Love is the greatest healing energy on earth and in Heaven. Use it. Focus on that instead of your past pains. We cannot change the past; we must forgive ourselves for whatever part we played. If we choose to live in the past, we will never be happy."

Christopher took stock of the priest's words. "Thank you, Father. It makes sense, but it is not that easy." He got up from the creaking wooden pew before Father Oakley could say anything else.

Father Oakley watched him and called behind him: "I'll pray for you."

As Christopher walked out of the building and to the edge of the clearing, he suddenly realised he'd left his three flowers on the pew inside the church. He turned on his heel and backtracked the short 100 yards back to the building. When he reached the door, he turned the iron knob and pushed, but the door did not open. He rattled it a few times, but the door was locked. Christopher walked around to the windows, which were now dark – no lights shone from inside and there was not a soul to be seen. He stood there for a moment, confused. He'd only walked to the end of the clearing and back. It was barely enough time to blow out all the candles and lock the door.

Just then, a bent-double, elderly priest approached with a key to the church door.

"Oh, hello," Christopher greeted him, "I've left some flowers inside, would I be able to go and fetch them? I was just speaking with Father Oakley, but he must have locked up for some reason."

"Oh," the priest said, sounding surprised, "You're welcome to go and look, but I'm afraid Father Oakley passed away last month."

Christopher stood there for a long moment, nonplussed.

"I was speaking to him, only a few minutes ago. Is there someone else here?"

"It's just me now, I'm afraid. I open up and lock up. He was a lovely man, Father Oakley. He is greatly missed by the congregation."

"Oh… I see," Christopher replied absently.

"Are those the flowers you mean?" the priest asked, gesturing to Christopher's left hand. He looked down and there in his hand were the lily, the iris and the snowdrop.

"Yes…they are. Thank you." Christopher backed away from the church, unsure of what had just happened. He played the conversation with Father Oakley over in his head. He had been as real as the flowers that had somehow found their way back to his hand.

Christopher was stone cold sober and wondered briefly

whether he was going mad. He continued to walk until he found the three precious nameplates in the garden of remembrance by the crematorium. He wiped each one with the end of his coat until they were shiny again. The sun had broken through the cloud and fog to make a beam of light that glinted on the gold of each nameplate.

"God?" Christopher asked, almost silently, as a sudden gust of wind blew over his head. He lay each flower in its designated place and prayed. His prayers reminded him of his Catholic schooling; he could not remember the last time he'd said a proper prayer and believed it. Christopher felt that something important had happened there that day, although he did not quite know what.

A few hours later, Bill had been attempting to sit down for ten minutes before his wife realised he was having a rest and set him back to work on a needless task. Alice, meanwhile, was looking out of the living room window, watching for her dad to come walking up the pathway.

She had her swimming towel packed in a black and white embroidered bag and wore her swimming costume underneath her clothes for ease of getting ready when they arrived at the local baths. She and Christopher had arranged the excursion last week, and she was excited for the trip. Sometimes, Christopher bought her a powdery sugar doughnut afterwards, or a bun with lemon icing on the top; she looked forward to that, too.

"You haven't done the vacuuming yet, Bill. Look at you, taking it easy. You're good to yourself, aren't you?!"

"For goodness' sake, woman, is a man not allowed to sit down in this house?!" Bill replied, his tone harassed. He was met with a tense stare from Hetty that told him with all certainty that he was not. He got up from his chair, tutting as he went to plug in the vacuum cleaner.

"Here's your hot chocolate, Alice." Hetty handed the steaming cup to her granddaughter, using a much kinder tone than she'd used with Bill.

"Thank you, Gran," Alice replied quietly, still fixated on the pathway beyond the window.

Alice enjoyed the years that passed at her grandparents' house – mostly. It was a visit from Alice's auntie Jane, just before she'd turned ten years old, that finally opened Hetty and Bill's eyes to what was going on with their son.

Jane lived in India, and Alice sometimes spoke to her on the phone. Alice recalled the visit; the adults sat and talked in the kitchen with the door closed for what seemed like hours. She'd tiptoed on the middle stair and peeked through the glass at the top of the kitchen door to see what was going on. She couldn't hear much, only the dulcet tones of her calm auntie Jane, who had always been the kind sort.

After that night, something in the atmosphere changed. There was a little more fear in the air, and the intensity of the atmosphere squeezed Alice's bones just a little tighter

---

"What time did Dad say he'd come today?" Alice enquired.

"You know your dad, he's not a very good timekeeper. I'm sure he'll be here soon, love," Bill said, uncertainty in his voice.

Alice always remained hopeful that her dad would arrive when he said he would, sometimes still looking out of the window for hours after he was due to arrive. She knew it was hit or miss, but she kept watch for a while anyway, just in case.

Eventually, hours later, acceptance set in. "I'm going upstairs," Alice said with a sigh. She took her bag upstairs, unpacked her towel and got changed out of her swimming costume. Alice sat in her little box bedroom and drew a picture of a woman bound with ropes around her wrists and ankles. The same dark-haired woman always featured in Alice's pictures, always wearing a pained expression. Some of her figures were tied up, some were impaled on spikes in a macabre bloody scene, others were simply crying. She kept these private drawings of unfortunate women in a box under her bed – they were her secret.

Three miles away, Christopher was entering a much different doorway. As he walked into the room, he took a seat in the circle comprising twelve other people.

"Let's start," the leader said, and looked directly at Christopher's seat, gesturing for him to get up and start speaking. Christopher looked around tentatively. Some of the faces were looking back at him; others were staring at their hands or at the floor.

"My name is Christopher and I'm an alcoholic." He paused and took a deep breath in. The room fell silent as Christopher began telling the group what happened fifteen years ago, on the fateful night that had changed his life forever.

Chapter Four

8 years later

Will McAvoy changed into the ironed shirt, tie and trousers he'd prepared the night before and quickly drank a too-hot espresso shot which burnt his tongue, making him wince. He picked up his keys from the sideboard, ready to leave for Hartley Manor – the place he'd taught GCSE and A-level English for the past three years. Just before he left, he caught himself in the mirror by the door; smart, but with a few more grey hairs than he remembered. He frowned, his forehead overly lined, and remembered what his mother used to tell him: 'such an ordinary face, my boy, but the prettiest brown eyes I've ever seen.' A sudden sadness passed over him as quickly as it had begun. He ran his fingers through the sandy waves of his hair in an effort to neaten it. He'd neglected to cut it for some time, but decided it looked quite dashing, something along the lines of *Mr. Rochester* from his favourite classic novel – *Jane Eyre*. He laughed at this ridiculous thought, *dashing* – who was he kidding? He stopped his finger-comb midway through as it dawned on him that today was his thirty-third birthday.

Will frowned at himself for a second time; he'd never liked birthdays, but he'd never forgotten his own before. His eyes darted to the annoying blink of the red light on his answer machine indicating a message which he had no intention of listening to.

When Will arrived at work that morning, his A-level English class were sprawled about on tables, waiting for the bell to signal the start of class. There was no urgency about the students, and he remembered when he was eighteen, how nice it was not to feel a sense of urgency about anything. A memory played briefly in his mind of him and his friend Tyler buying orange sodas at the mall in Johannesburg after school. They would spend hours in the mall, doing nothing in particular, talking about nothing in particular. It was a gift, Will realised, that he'd taken for granted at the time.

With anticipation, he scanned the room to see who was absent. He felt a sense of relief, as always, when he saw that Alice was there, occupying her usual seat. She wouldn't look at him, she never did unless he addressed her directly; a curious pattern he'd noticed about her. He dumped his pile of papers and books on his wooden desk, placing his keys and bag in the deep drawer underneath. The students were getting their last-minute chatter in until Will's deeply accented voice filled the room. He watched them take their seats as soon as they heard him speak.

He liked the heavy workload in the economically deprived area of South East London. It stopped him from thinking about all the painful things that lurked within his memory. Things that could not be rectified. Things that kept him awake at night.

The fledgling adults he educated now knew what the

rough end of life felt like. His job was more than teaching them pronouns and how to analyse prose; he was a pillar of safety and continuity that some of them needed. More than once he had involved social services when it came to his students' situations. They needed him as much as he needed them.

The stark contrast with Will's own silver spoon experience was not lost on him – that was part of his driving force to dedicate so much to his profession. That, and the element of escapism. Here, he could do something meaningful, he could make a difference. *He wouldn't let them fall.*

"Okay, time to settle down class," Will's voice was effortlessly loud and authoritative. He handed a pocket tissue to a girl with big earrings and mascara-streaked tears running down her cheeks.

"He's not worth it," Will told her in a low voice, having just overheard the conversation of Big Earrings' boyfriend kissing another girl with tongues.

He addressed the class as he walked around the tables, giving out copies of *The Glass Menagerie* by Tennessee Williams.

"That South African accent is so sexy, it wouldn't take long for him to cheer me up," Big Earrings muttered to her friend, and the pair descended into giggles. Will raised his eyebrows at them, his face unquestionably serious.

"Would you like to share your thoughts with the class?"

"No, Sir," the girl replied, face flushing at being caught out.

"Open your books up to page three," he continued, approaching the desk where Alice was sitting. He could see only a fraction of her face, like a chink of light amid the dark strands shrouding her. He pulled a chair around to the other side of the desk and sat facing her.

"Is there anyone under there?" he asked, lightly

sweeping a piece of her hair aside. Alice tucked her unruly locks behind her ear and gave him a timid glance of acknowledgement. "Ah, there you are, Alice-Bug," he said.

"Hi McAvoy," the words left her mouth delicately and quietly, like the seeds of a dead dandelion blowing in the breeze. Will noticed that she kept her eyes firmly rooted to a spot on the desk in front of her. She was painfully shy, that much he'd learnt, and although she smiled, there was an unspoken sadness behind it. Will had thought more than once about asking her if she was okay, but he didn't – it wasn't his place, and besides, it is such a general question to ask that he knew he wouldn't get the information he sought.

"Where's your other half?" Will asked, gesturing to the empty seat beside Alice. "All you girls come in pairs, usually."

"Louise is late, I think," Alice replied softly. Will noticed her cheeks flush the colour of light rose, and just then, she lowered her head so that her hair shrouded her face again.

"Louise, late? Never!" Will said sarcastically. Alice laughed and Will felt satisfied that if he could make her laugh or at least smile, he'd done his job.

Alice's delicate hand slid an envelope ever so gently from underneath her workbook and pushed it over the desk to her teacher. As she did so, her fingers touched his hand, and she pulled them away immediately as if she'd received an electric shock.

"Happy birthday, by the way," she said quietly, eyes still firmly focused on the desk.

"How did you remember?" Will smiled, touched that someone had remembered his birthday, but not just anyone – Alice. Alice had remembered. He looked down at the cream envelope in his hands.

"I guess I've got a good memory," she replied.

"You are something else, Miss. Wilde. Thank you," Will said, having never meant the words 'thank you' more in his life than he did right now. He found it intensely difficult not to reach out and hug her, but he knew very well that such an action would be considered inappropriate, and so he did what he had done for the past three years he had taught Alice – kept his distance.

When he looked at her, all the happy memories played over in Will's mind of him and his sister Victoria, playing games outside in the South African sun. They played tricks on Gregor, their gardener, a thickset man with skin, dark from working outside and constant beads of sweat on his bald head. They watched him get into a tizzy, moving his shovel and fork when he had gone off to get the hose, then giggling behind the large oak tree that dominated the centre of the garden. They watched him look for his tools in confusion.

The last time Will had cared about his birthday. It was his twelfth. The sun had beamed through the tall windows of the house where he grew up in the most affluent part of Johannesburg. He and Victoria had been asking their parents to take them to Gold Reef city, and it was all arranged – he still remembered the anticipation of going on all the theme park rides. They'd talked about it at length, how they would go on everything at least twice, and the first one to throw up would have to do a forfeit.

Their father had broken the beam of light that morning, restlessly stamping across the floor, making wild hand gestures while Will's mother stood nearby, crying. His mother and father were yelling at each other; Will watched through the bannister spindles from the landing.

"I can't Jacoline, you don't realise how important this

deal is – if it falls through, we are in the shit, do you understand that?!"

"What about Will?" his mother asked, clutching at her husband's shirt sleeve.

"You can take him – do I have to do everything in this God-forsaken household?!"

"You know I can't, Scott – you know I can't go out of the house!"

Jacoline swallowed some coloured pills she'd been prescribed and Scott stormed out of the house. She had pills for nervousness, depression, hypochondria and agoraphobia. She suffered, and her hands often shook.

In the end, Will and Victoria had spent most of the day talking to Gregor. Gregor used to tell them folklore tales of his culture, all the while pretending that he was bothered by the two sprightly children, but in reality, Will could tell he liked the company and treatment as an equal which he didn't get from his white employers. The children had grown to love him like family.

"Okay, I tell you one story, just one. Then you go," he would say in his thick Zulu accent. But he never told just one.

One day in the height of Summer, Gregor stumbled over in the garden and couldn't get to his feet. Will noticed how frail he had become, how much less animated he was when he told them stories – which had become a rarity in the last months. Then came the day that Gregor died, Will and Victoria cried together in secret at the loss of their friend, and carved a letter G into the bark of the large oak tree. Victoria picked some small blue flowers and placed them on the dirt under the carving. It was a strange experience – one day he was there, the next he was gone, and that was that. Jacoline had comforted the distraught children with her limited maternal capacity, but made sure to tell the children not to let their father see them crying.

"It's just me and you now, Will," Victoria looked over to her brother, a tear rolling down her cheek.

"It's okay, Vic, I'll take care of you," he put his arm around her and squeezed her shoulders.

"And I'll take care of you," she replied, resting her head on her brother's arm.

They sat there for a good while by the tree until the sun had started to sink in the sky.

A few days later, Sam arrived – Gregor's replacement.

Business and money mattered to the McAvoys. People did not.

Will sometimes wondered what made the penny drop for some people. What singular event or conversation happened in their lives to make them realise just how lonely the world could be. For him, it was the time of Gregor's death. The man's body, ravaged by AIDS, showed Will how cold-hearted and callous his father was, and how weak and scared his mother was. He wondered why the fuck they'd chosen to have children in the first place – maybe it was an accident. At least that's how it felt. It was him and Victoria against the world. They didn't have sibling rivalry or petty squabbles like other brothers and sisters. It was as if she was born to be his soulmate in the lonely world created for them by their parents. From the day she was born, he loved her; a squashy and screaming baby with not a hair on her head. When their mother couldn't cope with the crying, young Will would rock his sister back and forth in his chubby toddler arms. Soon enough she would be soothed and silent, and all would be well with the world.

Years later, the day came that he never thought he

would see – the day Victoria took her last breath; the day he lost his best friend.

———

"**A**re you okay, McAvoy?" Alice's words jolted Will from his thoughts and he shook his head slightly.

"Sorry, I was miles away. How are you getting on with the book I gave you?" he asked, needing a distraction from the wave of pain just brought up by his memories.

"Jane Eyre? It all seems a bit moody and serious – a bit like you," Alice said as she giggled and Will gave her a look that was only reserved for her: one that questioned how she always managed to make him laugh. "I thought you didn't laugh?" she continued, finally looking at him.

"Well, I only allow it three times per year, so I'm nearly at capacity – don't be making me laugh again, Miss. Wilde, you're ruining my street cred."

"Street cred?" Alice questioned, raising an eyebrow.

"Now, Alice-Bug, don't start," he joked, "look after that book, won't you? That was my own copy from when I was studying, back in the days when I was a young 'un."

"I will. I've nearly finished it, I'll return it next week," she promised.

"Keep it. Don't say I never give you anything," he told her, getting up from his chair to return to the front of the class.

"Hey, Sir – does anyone else get a look in?!" a girl called Ariana called out brashly. "We're on page three now, we're waiting for you to teach... or something!"

"Yes, yes, slavedriver," he joked as he commenced the lesson, feeling a little happier for having received Alice's card.

Alice recalled the first time McAvoy had called her

Alice-Bug. It was two years ago. He'd asked her to help him carry some sets of books from the store cupboard, promising it would only take ten minutes of her lunch hour. Alice jumped at the chance to assist him, though she never let her eagerness show.

The hallways were bustling with students rushing to get to the lunch queue before all the 'good stuff' was gone. Alice didn't mind about this. She would happily give up a 'good' canteen lunch to spend more time with McAvoy. She walked a few paces behind him, noticing how well fitted his clothes were to his body. She stared at the nape of his neck; slightly tanned with the glistening of golden hair just visible in the sunlight glaring through the hall window.

"You can walk next to me, Alice, I'm not that bad," he told her, turning to face her for a moment. Alice felt a mixture of embarrassment and excitement that he'd invited her to walk alongside him. She knew people wouldn't understand why these small moments with her English teacher meant so much to her; the truth is, she was hopelessly in love with him. It wasn't an infatuation from the young adult, nor a lustful desire. It was simply just love; purest deep care for him, and it was her most closely guarded secret.

They walked the length of the busy hall together until they reached the store cupboard – the very last door along the corridor. McAvoy unlocked it and held it open for Alice as she entered the small space. He pulled over a short stepladder to stand on and reached up for some books on the top shelf.

"I'll pass these down, are you ready?" he asked, and at that moment they both heard the door slam shut, followed by giggling and footsteps running down the hall.

He got down from the step and pushed against the wooden door which was locked from the outside. "Shit.

We're locked in." He banged on the door to attract attention. The hallways, which were a stampede just a moment before, were now silent – everyone was at lunch. Alice stood there awkwardly, feeling small, clutching an armful of books.

"Hmmm. We might as well take a seat," Will said, and they both sat down on the hard, grey floor. "Sorry, Alice. This is all my fault. I should have known better than to leave my keys in the door."

"I think that's what you'd call a fail, McAvoy," Alice replied with a half-smile, finally finding her voice.

The teacher laughed and looked at her in an amused but perplexed way. "Y'know you're funny. You don't speak for ages, and then you come out with something that makes me laugh. I'm not that easy to make laugh by the way, in case you hadn't noticed."

Alice didn't dare look at him. There was only half a metre between them, though to her, it felt like an entire ocean.

"Thanks," she murmured in reply, running her forefinger down the spine of one of the books in her grasp. She could feel McAvoy looking at her; she did not look up.

"Do you like it here? In England, I mean," she piped up suddenly.

"Well, yes. I can't say I miss it back home," Will admitted. "I mean, it's not really home now. There's lots of stuff I was glad to leave behind. My home is here now."

"I'm glad you're here," Alice said, regretting the words as soon as she heard them leave her mouth. "You're alright, I mean," she corrected quickly, blushing.

"Alright, eh? I'll take that as a compliment," he smiled at her.

Alice felt like there were a thousand little hooks in her teacher's eyes, drawing her in. "Sorry, I didn't mean to stare," he apologised. "You remind me of someone, that's all."

Alice smiled shyly, turning her attention to some stacks of paper on the shelf beside her. She took one and folded it diagonally, ripped the paper along the crease and made a square. She proceeded to make purposeful folds as McAvoy watched with fascination as the little paper square came to life. It was an origami bug, and Alice pushed down on its paper back to make it jump. "Is there no end to your talents?" Will asked, fascinated by the little bug. "Could you show me how to make one?"

"Sure," Alice replied, feeling nervous energy surface once more. "Fold this into a diagonal," she instructed, handing him a piece of paper. He followed the directions as he was told. At times, Alice had to guide his hands correctly. Her skin was pink from blushing and she prayed for him not to look at her.

When he'd finished making his bug, Will smiled and held it up between his thumb and forefinger.

"Very good," Alice said. "You won't beat me at a bug race, though."

"Wanna' bet?" McAvoy replied, taking a pen out of his pocket and setting it on the floor. "This is the finishing line."

Alice and McAvoy crouched beside each other, shoulders touching, and placed a finger on the backs of their paper bugs.

"Okay, Sir, are you ready? Three, two, one – go!" They advanced furiously, both trying to make their bugs jump the fastest without veering off at an angle. Both were rapidly approaching the blue biro finishing line, but Alice's bug got there first.

"Well, you have certainly earned the title of Alice-Bug, congratulations!" McAvoy knighted her with an imaginary sword and Alice could barely hide that she was beaming inside, she couldn't remember a better moment in her life than this one right now.

Just then, Mr. McCabe, the headteacher, turned the key and opened the storeroom door. He did a double take at Alice and McAvoy crouched on the floor together.

"Bug race," Will explained feebly, holding up his paper insect.

"I see," Mr. McCabe answered shortly. He jangled the keys in the air. "I assume these are yours?" he said, handing them to the teacher before turning to Alice. "You'd better get to lunch, young lady – there's only ten minutes left."

Alice nodded and hurried out of the storeroom, secretly pocketing the two paper bugs.

That evening, Will sat in his flat, alone, apart from his cat, Heathcliff. The black and white animal had just knocked the bag of cat biscuits off the side of the kitchen counter and let them cascade all over the floor. Will couldn't be bothered to get up and clean the mess. He rolled his eyes and took a drink from his glass of whiskey and coke. "Happy birthday to me," he muttered dully. Will looked over to the side table where he had put up his solitary birthday card from Alice. It bore a picture of an abstract watercolour cat under a huge moon. He gazed at it for a long moment, a smile touching the edge of his lips.

Will's thirty-third birthday had passed unspectacularly, but what else did he expect?

"Fucking failure, Buddy, I think that's what they call it," he spoke his thoughts aloud to the cat, but Heathcliff only purred and closed his eyes. Will's alcohol-addled mind wandered to thoughts of Alice. He felt the need to protect her, but he didn't know what he was protecting her from. He realised that his caring had started creating a personal issue for him. Somehow, Alice had managed to bypass the wall around his heart that kept intruders out. She had unwittingly found her way into his closed affections, like a gradual process of osmosis.

"I won't let anything happen to you," he muttered, mentally addressing Alice. The alcohol got the better of him, and he joined Heathcliff in a well-needed slumber. The only activity in the room was the red blinking of the answer machine light; a tiny red dot in the darkest corner of the room.

Chapter Five

Christopher fingered the clear glass knight before moving two squares forward and one square to the left. He considered momentarily what an odd pattern of movement that was. Today, he was visiting Alice at his parents' house. He looked across the populated chess board to his daughter's face, full of concentration, planning her next move with the frosted army waiting in anticipation.

Christopher's hair was slicked back, drawing attention to his new gold-rimmed glasses, behind which his blue eyes danced just a little. It had been a month since he'd had a drink. He'd given up on and off over the years, even achieving six months of sobriety before now, but the alcohol had a way of finding him again. His Victorian house had eventually been repossessed when Christopher found himself unable to get back into work due to his mental state. Part of him was glad the unforgiving house was gone; he hoped the sadness within it had disappeared, too. He now lived in a fifteenth floor high-rise council building twenty minutes from Hetty and Bill's. People rarely visited him, and he couldn't blame them.

Now that he'd been alcohol-free for a time, he had blitzed his flat and cleaned all the mould off the walls. He'd treated the damp, thrown away ten bin bags full of clutter and even joined a beginners' computer class. He was basking in the new energy. Alice seemed to have a spring in her step, too.

"So what's new, sweet pea?" he asked, as she moved one of her pawns forward.

"Not much," she shrugged.

"How's college?"

"Good." She kept her eyes on the board.

"Good? Not just okay?"

Alice broke into the ghost of a smile.

"Oh my God, that's almost a smile − hold the front page!" he called through his hands, which he'd cupped around his mouth into the style of a megaphone. "Alice is almost smiling!"

"Oh, you're so funny Dad, you should be on TV," she commented, rolling her eyes.

"I know; I've been saying that for years. I'm too good, you see, they can't afford me!"

Alice stifled a giggle as they resumed play.

"Ah, I've had enough of chess, let's go for a walk," Christopher suggested.

"Hmmm, okay. It's only because I'm winning, though," his daughter replied, smirking while pulling on her ankle boots and coat.

They took a walk to the familiar abbey ruins, which led into sprawling woods that were nearby Christopher's parents' house. Alice and her father had come here often over the years, exploring the ruins and digging for sharks' teeth in a special part of the place.

"Have you seen Mummy this week, sweet pea?" he asked his daughter as a conversation starter.

"I'm staying tomorrow night. You do know I'm eighteen, don't you? And I haven't used the names Mummy and Daddy since I was about ten?!"

The tone was light between them. It was a pleasant exchange and Christopher smiled to himself.

"Ah, look! The magic pond; just where I left it!" Christopher exclaimed with theatrical triumph.

"Magic my arse," Alice replied while her dad made a face of mock disdain.

"Now, Alice, darling, light of my life, dear one… You're never going to find a husband if you go around talking like that."

"Er, are we in Pride and Prejudice?" she responded. "I don't want a husband. So *arse arse arse arse arse!*"

They both giggled and sat down by the magic pond. Christopher had named it so, explaining that sometimes it disappeared and sometimes it was visible. In truth, sometimes he just couldn't find it, but Alice played along anyway.

For a while, neither of them said anything, they just sat in comfort with the steady earth beneath them. The sky was just beginning to turn dusky and a slight breeze had blown ripples towards them on the pond. It stirred up the dry winter leaves that had settled on the ground. Alice batted one from her face.

"I wish it was always like this, Dad," Alice turned to her father, but he didn't look at her. He couldn't. He was crunching a brown leaf between his fingers and letting it blow away in crumbs.

"I know. I'm trying."

"I know you are," she said.

"You know when you mention that Mummy is angry a

lot? She wasn't always," Christopher said, his gaze fixed on the magic pond. "Maybe that's my fault. I could never be the husband she wanted. I ruined it all." His throat suddenly felt thick and dry as a bone, he'd never really spoken to Alice about this sort of thing before. Alice was looking at him, waiting for the continuation of the story.

He took his gaze away from the pond and looked into her face. "Eyes as big as saucers," he told her.

"You always say that," Alice half-smiled.

Christopher continued: "I ruined everything for us, it wasn't Mummy's fault. I wasn't the person she thought I was. I wasn't attentive…"

Alice cut him off: "Well, maybe she should've looked a bit more closely. It's never only one person's fault, is it?"

"I know I've let you down, Alice, I'll never forget that. You deserve so much better—"

"Dad, don't," Alice cut him off.

"I'm sorry I've been a bad father. I'll always love you, you know? I'm weak. I wish I wasn't," Christopher's blue eyes became bloodshot with welling tears.

"Dad, don't say that. I love you too. Don't cry," she gave him a hug and wiped his eyes.

"Perhaps it's time to head back now, sweet pea, don't want to be late for dinner," Christopher said finally, Alice nodded and the pair walked back in silence to Hetty and Bill's.

"I've got coursework to do," Alice announced as they stepped through the door and she disappeared upstairs to her bedroom, tiny even by box-room standards. Alice didn't really care that it was small, it was her own, and Hetty and Bill let her put posters and stickers anywhere and everywhere – even when the adhesive ended up ripping the wallpaper. She sat on the familiar dusky rose carpet in the small square of space on the floor, which was edged by a wardrobe, a radiator, a chest of drawers and a row of books she kept in a line just showing under the bed. The room had old-fashioned faded rose wallpaper – Alice had begun tearing it a little at a time, years before, when she'd first spotted some of the edges peeling.

She treasured this time alone, she would sit and think about McAvoy; a ritual she did every day after college. She would close her bedroom door and drift off, replaying the things he had said to her that day. She could hear a perfect replica of his voice in her mind, and she wondered what he would be doing right now at this very moment. Over the past three years she had built up a picture of his life, threading together the snippets that he'd told her about himself. She knew he drank too much coffee, which he sometimes put a sneaky spoonful of sugar in. He did a long cycle ride once a year for a mental health charity, and shared a home with his cat, Heathcliff – named after the *Wuthering Heights* character. Alice knew that he didn't really watch television, preferring to read, and that he almost became a lawyer instead of an English teacher. It was common knowledge in the class that McAvoy was single. Such information does not get by a group of young women, most of whom are testing their newfound sexuality on anyone within a five-mile radius. Alice saw them shamelessly preening themselves, trying to get noticed by anyone who passed them by. She spied some of the girls in her class flirt with McAvoy from time to time, and she used to giggle to herself when they realised he was having none of it and told them to get on with their work.

Alice took out her drawing pad and a tin of graphite pencils, which she kept in her bottom drawer. She picked out a moderately hard lead pencil and began to sketch McAvoy's face; she knew it so well it was effortless for her to do so. She drew the angled shape of his jaw first and pencilled in the soft curls that framed his face. Next, she lined his evenly set lips and the tip of his nose. She chose a softer lead pencil to add the stubble on to his chin and above his top lip; shivering, a little at the desire that rose up in her to feel it brush against her face. She continued with his eyebrows, feathering in their fairly straight shape, arching only a little. Lastly, she sketched and shaded in his almond-shaped eyes the shade of darkest honey, adding each long eyelash painstakingly with the tip of her pencil. God, he was beautiful. Why did she have to love him? How could loving him make her feel so trapped and at the same time set her free? She shook her head at the perfect image on her page and squeezed her eyes shut.

Alice was flustered, trying to resist the surging hormones in her young adult body. She was meant to begin her essay but was too distracted to concentrate.

She decided to take a cold shower to quell her confusion, as well as to cool her flaming cheeks and the recent stirrings in her body, which made her feel uncomfortable. She peeled off her jeans and the white vest top that stretched snugly over her bare breasts, stood in front of the mirror and surveyed herself. Alice removed her black knickers and left all her clothes in a pile on the floor. She looked at the reflection of her pale womanly body and ran her hands over her jutting hips and shapely thighs. She wondered if she was attractive, unsure of this, and confused about her feelings for McAvoy.

The next day, Alice and her best friend, Louise walked arm in arm down the school hallway at lunch time. Alice wasn't really listening to her friend's chattering; her mind was too preoccupied, although she did interject at regular intervals to show that she was at least pretending to listen. In truth, she was feeling utterly deflated. McAvoy had barely spoken to her in that morning's class. It wasn't like him. He'd never acted *off* with her, and she wondered what was wrong. Her stomach flipped as she heard his deep voice shout her name from behind. The pair both spun around to face their harassed teacher just outside the assembly hall.

"Alice, come and see me after your last lesson." McAvoy didn't acknowledge Louise at all, his face serious.

"Okay," Alice replied quietly.

"Good," he said, and stalked off down the hallway.

Once McAvoy was out of view, Alice turned to Louise with a worried look on her face.

"What an arrogant prick," Louise said. "He's so bloody rude," she added, in a poor imitation of his South African accent.

"What have I done wrong?" Alice asked, puzzled. "He did seem a bit stressed in class this morning, didn't he?"

"Yeah, so he's in a bad mood. He's probably not getting enough – if you know what I mean. Maybe that's why he wants to see you after school," Louise laughed at her own teasing.

"Don't, Lou. It's not funny." Alice was genuinely distressed about why McAvoy wanted to see her, and why it seemed like he was in such a bad mood.

"Don't worry, chick, it's only McAvoy. What's the worst that could happen? He could bore you to death I suppose."

"He's not boring," Alice said, instantly regretting giving Louise the additional teasing ammunition.

For the rest of the day, Alice could hardly concentrate on anything in her afternoon classes. Her stomach was violent with butterflies, and by the time the last bell rang, she was a bag of nerves.

M cAvoy sat very still with his elbows on the desk, his fingers interlinked, which made a resting place for his chin. He was trying to remain calm, but the anticipation of seeing Alice was making him uneasy. She knocked almost inaudibly on the door a moment later, and Will got to his feet, gesturing for her to come and sit opposite him. She obeyed and waited for him to speak.

"So," he started, and exhaled loudly. He could see all the different shades of green in her questioning eyes, which for once, were looking at him directly. Will wasn't sure how to start the conversation, but the pause was now becoming a defined silence, and so he just spoke.

"Are you okay?" he asked, finally. *Fucking good one, Will – could you think of a more generic question?* He mentally punished himself.

"Erm, yes, I'm fine. Are... are you okay?" Alice replied.

"Yes. Well, not really. I'm just dealing with a few things at the moment that are unfamiliar to me." *Like that I care about you so much I only feel content when I know you are in the same building as me.* He was starting to feel like he had multiple personalities with all the things he wished he could say, compared to the clipped speech that was actually leaving his mouth. At that moment, he was thankful telepathy wasn't really a thing. Christ, he'd be in trouble if it was. "I realise that I was rude this morning, I'm sorry," he said.

"It's okay," Alice responded.

"It's not okay. I'd just had a shitty night, that's not your fault. If I'm honest, I worry about you, Alice. You look sad, even though you smile. I've seen a similar look before, in my sister's face. You remind of her."

Alice looked at him, expressionless for a few moments. "I didn't check up on you this morning, and it's bothered me all day," Will continued.

"Don't worry about me, I'm okay," she smiled reassuringly. "I thought I'd done something wrong."

Will laughed and the tense atmosphere melted into something altogether nicer. "I've known you for three years, Alice-Bug, I'm not sure you are capable of doing anything wrong. You're the only person who really makes me smile. How do you do that?"

Alice's cheeks reddened, and she tucked her hair behind her ear, looking shyly down at the desk.

"Erm, I don't know McAvoy, but I'm glad if that is the case," she told him.

"I can't remember how old I was when I stopped smiling, but then it was only my sister who could ever get me to, and now you," Will shook his head slightly, trying to refocus his thoughts which had become fuzzy at the edges. "I'm sorry, I must sound like a crackpot going on about you and my sister being similar. I just wanted to try and explain why I feel the need to check you're okay."

"That's really nice, McAvoy, and I don't think you're a crackpot at all. I think you're very caring and that you always try to do your best for your students – you're not like most teachers," she replied.

"Could I ask you something personal, Alice?" he said.

Alice looked a little surprised at the question. "Okay," she replied.

"You're a lovely and intelligent girl; why do you always look so sad?"

Will looked her directly in the eyes, and in them he could see Victoria. The same pain, like a silent scream masked by a smile. He waited for her to speak, the eye contact so piercing, he felt that if he sat there long enough, he would get any answers he needed just by looking into her.

"Um… things aren't really straightforward at home."

"You live with your grandparents, don't you?" Will asked.

"Yes," Alice replied.

"And your parents – do you see them?" he continued.

"Yes, on and off. My dad has some problems," she answered.

"Ah, I see. It's difficult. I also don't speak to my father much; he has issues too. Perhaps we're not so different, Alice-Bug."

There was an understanding between them, Will wondered if mutual pain was the reason, but dismissed it. It was more than that.

"He's an alcoholic," she continued. "My mum is pretty angry most of the time. My grandparents do a good job of looking after me though, but I don't feel free. Maybe no-one is really free."

Will wrinkled his brow in concern for the pessimistic opinion of freedom from a girl who had her whole life ahead of her.

"That's an interesting viewpoint. I guess we are all trapped by some feeling or circumstance. I'm sorry things are so unsettled for you. If it gets too difficult at home, please will you promise to come and speak to me? I am your pastoral tutor as well as your English teacher, remember? It's my responsibility to make sure you're okay." He wanted to reach out and touch her, he wanted to shake the people who were hurting her, he wanted to give her comfort. Impulsively, he reached over the desk and held her small, fragile hands inside his own. Alice didn't flinch. They looked at each other for a long moment, then Alice looked back to the desk. Neither of them spoke or moved for what seemed like an hour, but in reality it was less than a minute. It was one of the most important almost-minutes that had happened to Will in the last few years.

When Alice arrived back at her grandparents', April was already waiting outside in the car for their bi-weekly visit. Alice could see from her mother's expression that she wasn't happy. Alice greeted her grandparents quickly and then left, getting into April's red Escort. It was only a short drive to her mum's small flat, but Alice could feel the daggers in the atmosphere already. She crashed out of her blissful state and back down to earth: her reality was now, here in this car, with a woman who was ready to have a go at her about something – anything.

"How was school?" April asked, shortly.

"It was okay. I had art, Miss. Penny liked my sculpture."

"What sculpture?" April questioned.

"I told you about it ages ago. I did a sculpture of a woman impaled on spikes— a Romeo and Juliet theme with a twist," Alice answered.

"Alice! For fuck's sake, why do you have to be so morbid? Juliet didn't fucking mutilate herself!"

"I said it had a twist," Alice replied quietly.

"Don't get smart with me, Alice Wilde," her mother sounded dangerous.

"I wasn't being smart."

"Why are you still answering me back, then?!"

Alice knew better than to reply again. Her insides were churned up and her chest burned with anger. Repression was the order of the day when Alice was with her mother, she got yelled at for what she did and for what she didn't do, and she certainly wasn't allowed her own opinions.

Alice looked down at her hands while April had a full-blown muttered conversation with herself. Just an hour ago, Will McAvoy's hands had been there around hers. The thought of it sent a spike of nervous energy through her body. Alice wasn't paying any attention to her mother now; she stared through the car window and saw a home-less man by a lamppost when they stopped at the traffic lights. He was in torn denim clothes and had a dirty white beard. He picked a lit cigarette end off the ground and smoked the last remaining puffs. He looked up then, straight into Alice's eyes for a split second, before the traffic lights turned green. And for a split second Alice knew that he wished he were in her place, and she wished she were in his.

When they arrived at the flat, April switched on the TV as usual and lit up a cigarette. Swirls of smoke soon filled the oppressive space they were to share for the next thirteen hours. Alice attempted her homework with the television blaring in the background, sighing with frustration. April looked up sharply, as if someone had just thrown a bucket of water over her.

"What?!" she scowled.

"What?" asked Alice in response.

"You're fucking huffing and puffing over there, what's your problem?"

"I don't understand this homework. Don't worry about it, I'll get help with it tomorrow," Alice replied.

"It's homework, that means you are supposed to do it at home!" April's tone was shrill; she was gunning for a fight. "Let me see that," April grabbed the worksheets and eyed them briefly before throwing the papers all over the floor. Alice scrambled to arrange them and shoved them back into her bag, heading for the door. "Where the fuck do you think you're going?!" April screeched after her.

"Away from you! You're a fucking nasty bitch!" Alice's anger had finally boiled over. She'd never spoken to her mother that way before and immediately regretted it.

They assessed each other, unmoving for what seemed like an age: a lion and a springbok eyeing one another before the inevitable happens. As if in slow motion, Alice saw the ashtray hurtling towards her, old ash and cigarette ends decorating the carpet as it came into contact with the side of her head. The next thing she felt was a tremendously sharp pain and a warm trickle down her forehead. There was a crunch of smashed glass under her shoes as she stumbled backwards.

April stared open mouthed at her daughter and the splash of red on her white skin. The shards of glass glinted on the floor like diamonds. Alice felt blank, emotionless. The only feeling she was aware of was the pain.

Not another word was spoken between them afterwards, and Alice walked back to her grandparents' that night. She made an excuse for returning – that she needed space to do her work – arranged her hair neatly over the head wound, and Hetty and Bill were none the wiser.

She wouldn't see April for a while now. Whenever her mother had done something wrong, she never confronted it; instead, she wrapped it up and tucked it away in a drawer where it could not be seen – a drawer that was bulging with unresolved issues.

Alice thought of the precious minutes she had spent with McAvoy that day –the connection between them, the tangible event that wasn't just a longing in her head. She escaped into him as her head throbbed and was sore to the touch. Even the thought of him was her salvation; it was healing. At that moment, it was everything.

Chapter Six

The next day, Alice barely spoke to anyone – not even to Louise, who sat next to her for most of the day at college. The bell was about to go, signalling the end of their final class. Alice would go back to her grandparents' as usual and pretend everything was fine, just as she had for most of her life. The only thing keeping her going was the replaying in her mind of McAvoy's desire to protect her, holding her hands like she belonged to him, making her feel safe. She had been so happy that day until the encounter with her mother; is that really how fragile happiness can be?

Alice leaned her head on her hand without thinking and quickly removed it as she felt the pain slicing through her scalp, followed by a dull throb. She'd managed to cover the emerging bruise on the side of her forehead by parting her hair differently.

On autopilot, she watched McAvoy from her desk, looking for his glasses which were on top of his head amongst his sandy curls. She smiled an unnoticeable smile at this habit of his; it was the only smile she'd managed today. She noticed he looked thinner than usual, his face a little more angular and his eyes a shade more tired.

"Hey, are you okay?" whispered Louise. "Why don't you come and stay at my house tonight? My parents won't care."

"I might, I'll call you later," Alice said, packing up her pens as the bell sounded.

Louise turned Alice's face to hers gently and Alice surveyed the freckles on her friend's tanned nose; the familiar afro hair that always smelled of cocoa butter, and always the biggest, widest smile waiting for her. She kissed Louise on the cheek, feeling a sudden surge of love for her.

"Call me. I will worry if you don't," Louise said earnestly. "Listen, your mum was bang out of order for what she did. Are you sure you don't want to tell anyone?"

"What's the point?" Alice said quietly "It's done. She's made her bed, let her lie in it. I won't be staying with her anymore for a token night or two a week, she can lick her wounds and stay away from me."

Louise squeezed her friend as they both joined the queue of students filing out of the classroom at 3.30 pm that day. Alice could feel McAvoy's eyes on her, but kept her head down as she walked. For once, she didn't want to converse with him, to pretend she was okay, because she knew her words wouldn't fool him when he could read her face so well.

"Alice, a word please," McAvoy's deep voice almost made her jump. Louise gave her a sympathetic smile before following the rest of the students out of the room.

He pulled the chair out for Alice to sit down opposite him at the table. She obliged, noticing the flecks of grey in his hair and the throbbing pulse at the side of his neck. Her eyes darted to his mouth as he spoke and she spied his rogue tooth, beautifully out of line with the rest. He kept his eyes on the stack of exercise books that he'd started to mark and didn't lock eyes with Alice until the last student had left the room. They both heard the self-closing door bang shut and Will looked up at his student.

"You're not yourself today; I'm sorry if I crossed the line yesterday. I mean, I probably did cross the line," he told her.

"It's not that, McAvoy," came her short reply. She knew she couldn't hold her tears back if he started questioning, and she anxiously pressed her nails into the palms of her hands.

"For God's sake, Alice. You've barely spoken to me or even looked in my direction today. That's not the Alice I know." He leaned over the desk, shortening the gap between them.

She traced a scratch in the wooden desk with her fingernail. Her mind awash with confused feelings; anger and sadness mixed with the excitement and anticipation she felt now her body was only twelve inches away from McAvoy's.

"Look at me, Alice-Bug," his voice took on the gentlest tone she'd ever heard. She obeyed his request, keeping her head down but locking eyes with him just for a moment. Alice lowered her eyelids again to focus on the brown desk in front of her, knotting her fingers together for want of something to do. She felt his hands in her hair then, and he tenderly fingered the inch long wound of dark dried blood which was only just visible in her hairline. Her eyes filled up with tears, it felt unfamiliar to her as she saw them drop on to the wooden desk. Crying never helped anything. The halls seemed eerily quiet, like the world was on pause. That perhaps there, in that classroom, they were the only two people who existed.

Alice noticed the lines of worry on McAvoy's face

deepen as he surveyed her injury. He pulled his chair over to sit next to Alice and folded her up in his arms. Alice's head rested just underneath his collarbone and moved rhythmically with each breath he took. She let her long fingers settle on his ribcage and sobbed silently; her tears becoming a warm relief. The scent of his familiar after-shave comforted her. She could feel the heat from his hand, which seemed big and protective on the back of her skull as he rocked her ever so slightly.

Alice was aware of her breathing; it seemed fast. Her tears were warm on her face and she did not ever want to move from McAvoy's arms enveloped around her. She could feel a slight pull as he gently gripped a handful of her long hair and let it slide through his hand to where it ended just by her waist.

"Who did this to you?" McAvoy asked.

Alice did not answer for a while; she did not want to break this moment with words.

"I'm okay. It won't be happening again," she said softly.

"I should report thi –" McAvoy started, but Alice cut him off.

"No, please. I'm fine, honestly," she pleaded.

McAvoy let out a large sigh but did not loosen his firm hold of her.

"I can't just let this go. It's my job to look after you," he told her, planting a small kiss on the crown of her head.

"It was a one-off. Please believe that. I'm not in any danger. It isn't your job to look after me McAvoy, as kind as that is," Alice said.

"It *is* my job. It is," he replied with an undertone of something troubled.

Alice's eyes were welling up again and tears started to fall onto her teacher's white shirt. She pulled away and stood up to leave, feeling embarrassed all of a sudden. McAvoy got up from his chair and faced Alice, tilting her chin to guide her gaze towards him.

"Teaching is a strange deal you know," he began, "they expect you not to care too much about students, they expect you to care enough but not too much – sometimes that's not possible. I'm here for you, is what I'm trying to say."

Alice smiled sadly, constant tears making two streams down her cheeks and falling from her chin. Will dried them with the end of his silk tie.

"Thank you," she whispered, his caramel eyes hooking her in.

McAvoy very gently swept the backs of his fingers across her cheekbone.

"Are you safe? If you go home, are you safe?"

"Yes, I'll be safe, McAvoy. I'll see you tomorrow," she replied, her face shiny with tears.

W ill hardly remembered the journey back home. He'd packed his marking stack into his backpack and walked the twenty minutes by the river to get back to his flat. He pondered what had happened; he wanted to protect Alice, to make whatever was hurting her better. He battled himself in whether he should report her injury to the authorities, eventually he found peace with the fact that he would keep a close eye on her, that his gut instinct was right all along and she did need protecting from something, from *someone*. He stood still for a moment, looking deep into the swirling water of the river by his home. Will had never given anyone the opportunity to get close, and even now he hadn't: Alice had stolen it. *When people get close, someone gets hurt*, was the thought that surfaced from some-where deep in his brain. Will took a deep breath of cold, fresh air. For the first time in years, he felt something. Something about his connection with Alice warmed him to his core.

Holding Alice had mentally transported him back to the day he and Victoria learned of Gregor's death. That night, his sister had crept into his bedroom, teddy in hand, and sobbed. He'd held her tight for about an hour until she'd stopped crying and fallen asleep on his bed. He'd covered her up and made a bed for himself on the floor next to her but hadn't slept a wink that night – instead, he versed all the stories that Gregor had told them over the years, feeling his own tears welling up, which he'd swal-lowed back down.

He entered his flat on autopilot, dropping the blinds a little, the street light now dissecting the partially darkened room. The only other illumination in the corner of the darkness was that little red light again – blink blink blink – relentlessly tormenting him. It demanded attention he was not willing to give.

Will was about to rip the cord from the wall when the phone starting ringing, making him jump. He answered it gingerly just before it rang off and heard his father's voice on the other end. The feeling of Will's renewed sense of life slowly faded away and was replaced by a feeling of shock and adrenalin. After a few minutes, Will let the phone slip from his hands and hit the floor. Then, in a sheer moment of rage he ripped the answering machine from its resting place and brought it down with an almighty crash. His polished tiled floor was now covered with the innards of the machine, its red light slowly petering out until it was dead.

Chapter Seven

The day passed by painfully slowly at college that day. Alice's heart sank when she saw Mrs. O'Grady sitting in McAvoy's place, the very spot where he had held Alice so tightly only yesterday. She'd learned that McAvoy had called in sick that morning. This made Alice uneasy, as she knew he hadn't called in sick for the three years he'd been her teacher. She wondered if it was something to do with her. Maybe he thought he'd crossed a line, maybe he was actually sick. Alice couldn't bear not knowing, or the thought that he might be unwell and alone.

When she arrived home, Bill asked enthusiastically about her day, as he always did.

"Did you say you'd started The Canterbury Tales, love?" he asked, not taking his eye from his magnifying glass over a section in the paper.

"Yes, it's hard," Alice replied, disinterested in English for a change. Her mind was too tied up wondering whether McAvoy was okay and toying with the idea of going to see him.

"Words and books are so important, I'm so glad you

are doing English," Bill said, gazing out of the window for a moment, smiling. He had always been a bookworm, and the house was full of shelf after shelf packed with books on all sorts of topics, as well as encyclopaedias, dictionaries and magazines.

"I've got all the Tales upstairs somewhere, it'll be under C for Chaucer," Bill said, springing up to go and find them.

"Sit down!" boomed Hetty's voice from the kitchen, which was well within earshot of the living room. "Dinner is ready as soon as your dad gets here, Alice – your granddad can go and look at books afterwards."

Bill returned to his seat. Opportunities for little slices of freedom had to be taken on the sly. Sometimes he gave Alice a knowing wink when he was doing something he shouldn't – like tinkering with some of his beloved gadgets.

Half an hour passed and there was no sign of Christopher.

"He's not coming," Alice stated unemotionally. She figured he was caught up in his addiction again. She was no longer surprised by his absence; she no longer cared much, either. Six months sober was nothing new, things could always be undone with just one single drink. Besides, Alice had more important things on her mind than whether her dad turned up for dinner or not.

"I'm dishing up," Hetty announced. Alice's head throbbed from the concealed wound on her head, and she managed to force down one of Hetty's staple meals: mince and mashed potatoes, under the matriarch's watchful eye. She was a strict woman, not very tall, with a grey wave of hair and blue eyes, like Christopher's. Although strict, Hetty was as maternal as they come. She took Alice in all those years ago without a second thought. Alice knew she was loved and wanted at her grandparents' home, and although she suffocated under the weight of her grand-mother's overprotection and love, she was grateful Hetty and Bill had been there to rescue her.

"I'm going out about six o'clock, Gran," Alice said delicately, waiting for her grandmother's resistant answer.

"Where? And who with?" came the enquiring response.

"Just Mum's for a few hours," Alice lied, but it was a necessary lie. In truth, she was going to visit McAvoy to see if he was okay. It was a bold decision that made her nervous, but she felt drawn to checking that he was alright. His address was etched in her mind from when it had come up in conversation a while back – filed away ever so carefully into her memory bank. She couldn't tell her gran the truth – Hetty would have given the Gestapo a run for their money. Her grandparents were still unaware of the incident with her mother; thankfully, her fringe provided the perfect cover for the purple-ish bruise just below her hairline.

Hetty tutted and carried on eating.

Alice couldn't wait to disappear upstairs. She needed to think without any distractions, except that she'd promised Bill they'd do some work on the Wife of Bath's Tale. After dinner, Alice fulfilled her obligation for forty-three minutes. She did not want to ruin what was probably the highlight of Bill's day.

"Middle English, eh?" Bill chuckled as he carefully placed a bookmark where they'd finished and closed the book.

"It's hard, but I understand it a bit better now. Thanks Grandad," said Alice.

At six pm exactly, Alice left the house wearing jeans, a casual white t-shirt and a white coat. She knew Hetty was watching her from the door, as she always did until she disappeared down the street. She could feel violent butter-flies in her stomach, and she wished she had not eaten a whole plate of food earlier.

As she approached the bus stop in wait of the number fifty-three, Alice discovered nobody else waiting: she was alone. She was glad of the space to just sit in the cold air for a time, by herself, and breathe. Her brown hair blew gently in the December breeze and the tip of her nose reddened in the cold air. She closed her eyes and pictured McAvoy opening the door and letting her in – she could almost smell his aftershave even now.

W ill cleared the steam from the bathroom mirror with a wipe of his hand and looked at himself. He noticed the dark circles beneath his sleepless eyes. He wiped away the water dripping down his face and walked across the shiny floor, leaving wet puddles as he went.

The broken answering machine still lay in pieces where it had landed the night before. Will dropped back into his bed and wound the duvet around his body, like a snail in its shell. His head was pounding. There were two empty vodka bottles lying on the floor by the bed, the blinds had been down all day and there was a half-empty packet of cigarettes on the side table. Will had not smoked for ten years until last night. Heathcliff was the only semblance of something familiar and constant in Will's life now that everything suddenly seemed to be crashing down around him.

A gentle knock at his door caught Will off guard and he clambered out of the bed to pull on some jogging pants. His mind was a swirl of emotions that all mixed horribly into some sort of poisonous concoction. He walked tentatively and suddenly lightheadedly towards the door and opened it an inch to see who was bothering him – he never had visitors. A jolt of shock ran through him to see Alice standing there clutching a plastic bag. He glanced from Alice's face to his disgraceful apartment. Everything stank of cigarettes. There were cat biscuits all over the floor, empty bottles and clothes strewn about. He couldn't let Alice see him living like that. He thought of what he must look like, and what he must smell like: an alcoholic, just like her father.

"Alice…" was all he could mutter, "What are you doing here?"

"You're not okay, are you?" she asked quietly. Will just looked at her standing there. He was lost for words for a moment.

"It's not a good time, Alice. I'm sorry," he managed, and pushed the door closed, but it was met with resistance from his student's foot. Uncharacteristically, Alice pushed her way into the dishevelled place. She placed the plastic bag on the countertop, unpacked bottles of Lucozade and flicked the kettle on.

"Mrs. O'Grady said you weren't well," Alice said as she busied herself cleaning up cat biscuits and the contents of an ashtray, tipping both into the bin. "I've never known you to have a day off sick in three years, I was worried about you."

Will watched her cleaning up pieces of his broken life from the countertop and floor as if it was second nature to the eighteen-year-old.

"Please go," Will's voice cracked as he balled up his fists and sank to the ground. His hair was curly and looked dark where it was still wet from the shower; he was cold, but he didn't care. Desperate tears escaped from his tired eyes and he let out a primal shout – it was a noise of fear, sadness, guilt and hopelessness all rolled into one. "You can't see me like this, Alice – please," he pleaded, but she continued to clean up the mess from the previous night and start pouring two cups of coffee.

"I think you could use this," she said, as she placed the steaming cup on the tiled floor next to him.

"I'm supposed to be the one who looks out for you, not the other way around," he said, staring at the floor.

"Someone needs to look out for you, too," Alice replied. She sat opposite her teacher, cross-legged on the floor. "Talk to me."

He sat, shirtless, with goosebumps protruding from his skin. The hairs on his arms stood on end and all he did was look at the floor while the coffee went cold. Alice waited until he spoke, and she listened.

"I've mentioned my sister to you before, of course, because you remind me of her so much. We were thick as thieves, she and I. Mum and dad were complete failures as parents, always too wrapped up in themselves to even notice they had kids. We only had each other to rely on. When Victoria was six, she lost her first tooth. She was so upset because she thought it would never grow back again. I told her to put it under her pillow and the tooth fairy would pay her a visit. You should've seen her glee in the morning when she found a shiny coin under her pillow that I'd put there from my own money box. Mum and Dad didn't even notice she'd lost a tooth until a few weeks later. That's how things were: the dysfunctional family unit we were born into is what we recognised as normal. I've never spoken to anyone about what happened to Victoria, I never knew how desperately dark life could be until she died." Will rubbed his forehead. He looked at Alice as if he needed her approval to continue, she nodded.

"She struggled as a teenager, how could she not? –

having a mother who was comatose on pills most of the time. She started dabbling with drugs – just marijuana at first and then coke and pills. She was trying to block it all out and I could see what was happening, but I couldn't stop her. One day she'd gone to a house party not far from where we lived. One of her hairbrained friends had had the sense to call me to come and pick her up, they told me she was out of control. When I arrived, Victoria was standing on the balcony, laughing one minute and crying the next. She was walking up and down the ledge, almost losing her balance more than once. I tried to reason with her to get down but she was too out of her mind on drugs – she said she knew better and that she didn't need me to look after her anymore. She slipped. I lunged forwards somehow managing to grab her hand.

The look someone gives you just before they know they are going to die can never be adequately described. I'll never forget it as long as I live. It was sadness, regret, pain, fear and so many other things I cannot paint a picture of. I couldn't hold her – I let her fall." Will grabbed his hair in angry fistfuls.

"We all heard the thump of flesh on concrete. Dark red blood was oozing from the back of her head and dripping off the verge. Then I heard screaming, so much screaming. In a matter of seconds, Victoria was not Victoria anymore – she was just a body." He sobbed and put his head in his hands. Alice moved towards him, stroking his hair while he cried without measure.

Twenty minutes passed and not another word was spoken between them. Alice held her broken teacher, her long arms delicately wrapped around his bare skin. In this moment, he needed her. He wished he didn't. He liked her skin against his and felt ashamed for realising it.

"It wasn't your fault, McAvoy," she told him eventually.

"You can't blame yourself forever. Is that why you want to help me? Because you think if you do it will make up for what happened with your sister? I'm sorry I remind you of her, but please don't punish yourself. I can't bear to see you suffering. You don't deserve it."

Suddenly, Will jumped up, wiped his eyes and went to find a t-shirt to put on.

"Thank you for stopping by Alice, but I'll be fine," he said without feeling, as he walked over to the front door, opened it and invited Alice to leave. Her brow furrowed as she walked uncertainly to the door. She looked at her teacher, his hair still slightly damp and his skin still covered with goosebumps. Will would not look her in the face, instead choosing to focus on the Converse All-Stars she wore on her feet. Alice left without another word and he gently clicked the door closed behind her.

Will went over to the window, not taking his eyes off her for a second. She looked up and for a gut-wrenching moment he thought she had seen him, but she hadn't. He watched her figure become smaller as she walked away; she put her white hood up as it began to rain. Will did not leave the window until Alice was no longer visible to him. He was rooted to the spot, churned up inside with guilt.

The wind whipped around outside, the tops of the trees swaying savagely in unison – their swinging branches just visible under the dull glimmer of the streetlights. Will's mind was numb from thinking and feeling. He had opened up his darkest vulnerabilities to the girl who needed protecting from her own circumstances, who only yesterday was cradled in his arms, crying, because someone had injured her. He felt irresponsible that he had let her take the role of caring for him, and sick at himself for enjoying the feeling of her being so close to him. He knew what he had to do.

Chapter Eight

Monday came and went, as did Tuesday and Wednesday. Alice's English class was absent of McAvoy, and the days for her were agonising. Her brain was on a permanent overload of needing to know what was going on. She chewed over a million thoughts. How many days would pass until he reappeared, and what would he say to her? Alice's brain hurt; her eyes hurt from the tears that all of a sudden seemed to come to her readily when she had spent so many years blocking out her emotions. Surely the college would have to tell them something; they couldn't just leave them hanging for another week? The thought of another week of not knowing was unbearable.

As if someone had just read Alice's mind, Mr. McCabe, the head of school, appeared at the door of the English class as the bell sounded. The usual flurry of packing up, talking and trying to get out of class as quickly as possible was quelled by the tall, grey-suited figure, who was waiting for all eyes to be on him before he spoke. Mr. McCabe was a respected figure at the school; he had the natural authority necessary to be in charge of one thousand or so pupils.

He nodded to the languages teacher who had been covering the lesson and cleared his throat before addressing the small class of only ten A-level students.

"Class. As you may have noticed, Mr. McAvoy has been absent this week."

Alice was waiting with bated breath. She could barely wait for the next words to come out of his mouth.

"Regretfully, and so close to exam time, I'm here to inform you that Mr. McAvoy will not be coming back to Hartley Manor due to personal reasons. He has returned to South Africa, and I'm afraid I can't tell you any more than that."

There was a gasp among the students, some muted chattering and sounds of shock. Will McAvoy had been well-liked by the class – with the exception of Louise.

"I'm sorry to be the bearer of bad news, I am working on a suitable replacement to get you through the exams. Mr. McAvoy will be missed, of course," Mr. McCabe gave them a brief smile before exiting the room, leaving the students to hypothesise the reasons as to why their English teacher was not returning.

Louise looked at Alice, who was staring straight ahead at the whiteboard. She could make out some of Will's writing on the surface that had not yet been rubbed out. Her eyes traced the loops and flicks of his letters, matching it in her mind to the way he'd written notes on some of the pages of the Jane Eyre book he'd given her.

"Babe," Louise called to her friend, "are you okay?" Alice continued staring straight ahead at the board.

Louise's question remained unanswered, and she led her silent friend by the arm, following the rest of the gossiping class to join the sea of others trying to cram out of the doors as quickly as possible.

"I'm taking you to the coffee shop, babe," Louise told her friend.

By the time they'd got to Bean and Cup – one of their regular haunts – Alice had still not spoken. She stared at the milk patterns in the latte Louise had bought for her, milk froth spilling over the edge of the glass mug. The synapses in Alice's brain connected the smell of coffee with McAvoy; he often had the smell of coffee and mints on his breath. It was pleasant – it was him. She hadn't known that the last time she'd smelled coffee on his breath would be the last ever.

Alice's brain couldn't handle this new information. She felt like she was watching a film, like she was an observer of her own life. She didn't like this version of reality. She wondered if she might wake up and realise she'd been in an altered state of consciousness all along; perhaps someone had spiked her drink with a hallucinogenic drug and none of this was really happening. Maybe she would go back into college tomorrow and there McAvoy would be, standing at the front of her English class like he always had. She knew she was kidding herself, even as she her mind tried desperately to cling onto any flimsy hope it could muster.

"Look at me," Louise said, and this time Alice obeyed, her eyes almost full to tipping point with tears.

"South Africa," Alice said. "He's gone."

Louise held Alice's hand and looked at her. "I knew you had a soft spot for McAvoy, but I didn't know it was this bad…he could come back, Alice, you never know what could happen."

"He left, and he didn't even say a word, no goodbye or

explanation. I meant something to him, Lou – I know I did. He told me I did."

"What are you talking about Alice, did something happen?" Louise said with a perplexed look on her face.

"I went to McAvoy's place yesterday. I wanted to see if he was alright."

"Why?" Louise asked, surprised.

"He never calls in sick, and he wasn't okay when I got there."

"What did he say when you turned up? How did you even know where he lived?" Louise questioned eagerly.

"It doesn't matter; I just knew from a while ago. He was surprised to see me at his door, of course. He wasn't in a good way, and he started telling me about his sister and how she died. He was crying."

"So, then what?" Louise asked.

"I told him it wasn't his fault, and I just sat with him for a while. Then he turned cold and asked me to leave when he'd just opened up and told me all that stuff. I felt as if I had done something wrong."

Louise looked at her friend sympathetically, waiting for her to continue speaking.

"I don't know what to do," said Alice numbly. She versed a quote from Jane Eyre in her head, over and over:

'I have a strange feeling with regard to you. As if I had a string somewhere under my left ribs, tightly knotted to a similar string in you. And if you were to leave, I'm afraid that cord of communion would snap. And I have a notion that I'd take to bleeding inwardly. As for you, you'd forget me.'

She wondered how many times Will had read that underlined paragraph in the copy of the book she had – his book, the only piece of him she had left.

What happens to the string in real life? Does it snap, or just become agonisingly stretched? Her mind was like a jumble of puzzle pieces, except that they were all pieces from different pictures. Nothing made sense; all the security she had built up around herself had been castles in the sky. She was a piece in the glass menagerie that had fallen to the floor and shattered.

Alice didn't drink the coffee. Louise was reminding her of all the positive things she could think of, but her voice sounded muffled, like they were underwater. Alice felt like she was about to be swept up by an enormous wave and was powerless against it.

"I've got to go," Alice said abruptly. "I need to clear my head, or something."

She was suddenly desperate to be on her own so she could sob until she had nothing left. Reluctantly, Louise let her leave with the promise of a phone call to check in later on.

Alice walked for hours, her head swimming with confusion. Her face was red and wet with a constant stream of tears. It rained heavily; the clouds shrouded the light, and the sky was now a menacing shade of gunmetal grey. Alice had on a light jacket that was completely soaked through to her skin, as were her trousers and shoes. Her dark hair was plastered to her head in strips. The rain and her tears mingled, and she found herself standing outside McAvoy's apartment, her eyes hot from crying and her skin cold with the winter wind and rain. Alice did not care that she was wet and cold; in fact, if she had the option of being wetter and colder, she would choose it. What did it matter now? Will was her salvation, and he'd disappeared without a word. Ghosted her.

Alice climbed up the first step to the rail that separated the high pavement and the river below. The water tossed and swirled fiercely; it did not need to apologise for its erratic nature, it was accepted as the wild thing that it was. Why wasn't she? Alice questioned. Her whole life she'd had to make herself palatable for other people. Then there was McAvoy – beautiful, stoic, mysterious McAvoy, who seemed to accept her for what she was: damaged goods. Maybe she was too damaged for him after all.

Alice felt the pain of rejection deep in the pit of her belly, and she sobbed again, as much as was humanly possible. She climbed on to the next rung of the black metal barrier and leaned over it, the sound of the fervent river filling her ears. She imagined what it would be like to plummet into the water, hitting the river's surface with a hard smack. The icy water would destroy the heat in her body until it couldn't function, and hypothermia would set in. Her eyes were stung with the cold wind and she imagined McAvoy coming home now, seeing her and taking her inside to talk to her and make her feel warm and okay again. But that wasn't going to happen. McAvoy was six thousand miles away, and she was here, in England, leaning over the barrier, flirting with desperation.

After a time in the desolate street, staring into the depths of the river, Alice decided to go home. The rain was coming down in sheets, there was not another soul in sight. The streetlamps' light reflected from the drenched concrete pavements and provided the only colour against the grey landscape.

By the time Alice reached the front door to Hetty and Bill's she was exhausted; emotionally and physically. Hetty was waiting for her as she turned her key in the wooden door.

"Alice Wilde, where have you been?!" Hetty asked frantically.

"I was walking, I lost track of time," Alice replied.

"God help us, look at you, you're soaking! Anyone could have run off with you, Alice. The world is a dangerous place," Hetty scolded.

"Sorry," Alice whispered.

"Your dinner is in the oven. Bill, go and run her a bath," Hetty ordered, and Bill obeyed immediately. Hetty brought a towel from the radiator and wiped Alice's face and hair.

"You silly girl, you'll catch your death of cold," she said as she rubbed Alice down. Alice stayed still, like a statue. She let Hetty push her head from left to right with the towel and agreed with what her grandmother was saying to her. She didn't even know what she was agreeing to; the words sounded garbled among her swimming thoughts.

Alice made her way up to the steaming bath and peeled off her sodden clothes, leaving them in a wet pile on the floor. Her skin was goose-pimpled all over as she stepped into the steaming bath water, which scalded her, the pain providing some sort of release as she gradually lowered herself in. Everything from her stomach down was pink with heat.

She lay there for a time, looking at her feet with their blue painted toenails. The tears were building up again, hot behind her eyes, and Alice's jaw ached from trying to hold them in. She couldn't fight the sensation any longer; hot, furious, sad, disappointed tears spilled down her face. There would be no more conversations and no more secret looks. No more person to care about her who wanted to know her for what she was, no more possibilities and no more having something to look forward to – someone who made her happy. Now, there was nothing. No salvation, just a black abyss where once there was him.

Alice didn't clean her body in the water, she just lay in it, unmoving, until Hetty called to her to go and eat her dinner. Eat? How was she supposed to manage that? She stepped out of the bath, making a puddle of water on the floor, and wrapped herself in a towel. Alice pulled some pyjamas on before venturing downstairs to face her meal.

Hetty and Bill had already eaten, so Alice was left on her own in the kitchen with a plateful of fish, potatoes and broccoli that she knew she couldn't eat. She was thankful for small mercies that she was by herself and didn't have to explain anything to anyone. Alice wrapped the potatoes up in a piece of kitchen roll and carefully put them in the bin underneath some other rubbish, then proceeded to do the same with the fish. By the time Hetty had come in to check on her, the plate was empty.

"Good girl, you'll feel better for eating that. I'll make you a hot chocolate."

"Okay," Alice replied, knowing there was no use refusing the drink. Just then, she heard the front door open and close, and then Christopher's voice – slurred and loud. Her stomach clenched as the smell of layer upon layer of alcohol wafted in. When she was young, she knew this smell well, but she didn't identify it as alcohol until many years later. Her father flounced into the kitchen in his theatrical, drunken way.

"Hello, sweet pea!" he bellowed. Alice looked at him. He had a new cut on his face and his hair was dishevelled, his denim stonewashed jeans undone.

"Do you want dinner?" Hetty asked him, as if this was totally acceptable, as if he hadn't gone AWOL for the last week because he'd been off on a bender.

"Oh, yes please Mummy," he replied, making Alice cringe. Whenever he was drunk, he called Hetty 'mummy'. Christopher sat down at the table next to Alice, the pungent stench of booze knocking her sick.

"I've got homework to do," she lied and got up from

the table. Hetty called her to come and sit down, but Alice ignored her – she needed to get out of the oppressive space as quickly as possible. Suddenly, Alice felt a handful of her hair being grabbed and she screamed like a caged animal. Hetty was dragging her back into the kitchen, "I said sit down! Your dad has come to see you, I don't know what's wrong with you, Alice!" Hetty released her hair as Alice complied and sat down on the chair furthest from her dad. She made herself as small as possible, crossing her arms against her chest and pulling her knees up to her chin. Hetty continued plating up the food for her son.

"What is going on?" enquired Bill, who had come in from the living room to see what all the shouting was about.

"Nothing. Go and sit down and I'll bring you a cup of tea," barked Hetty at her husband.

"No, I will not. Why did Alice scream?" Bill enquired firmly, and was met with silence from both Hetty and Christopher, who were behaving as though everything was perfectly fine. Bill looked to his granddaughter, who had folded herself up like a little piece of paper.

"I just wanted to go upstairs," Alice's voice was barely more than a mumble.

Bill took her by the hand and led her out of the room. "Go upstairs, love."

Alice was glad for Bill rescuing her, and she darted upstairs into her bedroom, wedging a chest of drawers against the door so that no-one could get in. She heard an argument break out downstairs. Alice couldn't hear much except for the odd word, but Bill was putting up a good fight by the sound of things. Eventually, all went quiet. She hadn't heard Christopher for a while; maybe he had gone. She hoped that he had.

Alice was a ball of adrenalin after the ruckus with

Hetty. It had brought her out of her exhaustion when all she'd wanted to do was sleep so that the day could be over. Hetty had never done anything like that before. Alice wondered what had pushed her over the edge – the desperation to have a falsely happy family, perhaps.

Christopher's voice sounded outside her bedroom door, and the dread that Alice so often felt when he'd been drinking spiked through her body. He tried to push the door open, but Alice's blockade was doing its job.

"Alice, can you lend me twenty quid? I've got to go, apparently I'm not welcome." Alice put her earphones in to block out Christopher's drawl.

"Fuck you," Alice muttered under her breath, not caring whether it was heard or not. Claire de Lune was filling her ears now; she was trying to find calm in the storm. She picked up a piece of plastic that was lying on the floor, it had one sharp end. It had snapped off one of the coat hangers the other day. She rotated it between her thumb and forefinger for a while and then, as if guided by an invisible force, she pressed it into the skin on her arm. It felt nice.

She dragged it next, making a pink line on her pale skin. As Alice got lost in the music, she repeated the dragging motion again and again until little blood spots started to appear. A sense of relief washed over her and she licked the wound; the metallic taste of blood on her tongue was the most nourishment she'd had all day. She let the pain take her away from the bundle of thoughts that had been bouncing violently around her skull. She went delightfully numb, and for a while, was able to detach from the worst day of her life.

Chapter Nine

Alice stood in the middle of her newly decorated bedroom and surveyed the bubblegum pink shade of paint on the walls and the flowery border halfway down.

"So, what do you think?" April asked with enthusiasm.

"Oh, it's um… great!" Alice said, trying to summon up something that sounded like gratitude. She hated pink. And flowers.

"We're going to have such a good time; we should have a party!" April's excited trills rang through Alice's brain. The last thing she felt like was having a party.

Alice pulled her hair up into a ponytail as she prepared to move some more boxes. She noticed her mother clock the mark on her head, which had healed to a medium shade of pink. April rubbed her ear with her thumb and forefinger and moved over to the nearby table, picking up a shiny ornament and placing it down again before declaring that she was going to make some tea.

A few weeks after the furore at her grandparents', Alice had decided, reluctantly, to call her mother and ask if she could move back in. She didn't know if it was a wise idea, but felt that it was the only choice she had. There was no danger of her dad dropping in drunk there, and there would be no interference from Hetty to contend with. There would, however, be April's passive aggression and unpredictable behaviour, but Alice reasoned it was probably still the best option. At least she would have some freedom. She never told her mother what Hetty did.

"Listen, I have to pop over to my friend's. I'll be back a bit later, okay?" Alice called to her mother in the kitchen.

"Oh, okay," came the response. There was a hint of disappointment in April's voice, "I guess I'll see you later then," April said in a sulky tone.

Alice had operated on autopilot for the last few weeks, a mere ghost of herself. Louise was now the only brick stopping her wall from collapsing completely. Alice was relieved to arrive at the familiar blue door on Epstein Road, giving three quiet knocks. Louise opened the door and the pleasant smell of jasmine wafted out, bringing Alice immediate comfort. It was a smell that she associated only with Louise's home, the source being the essential oil burning in the hallway.

"Hi babe, come in," Louise gave her a warm hug. They disappeared up to her bedroom and as soon as the door was shut Alice burst into tears.

"I can't cope," Alice blurted out. "I can't cope with this; I don't know what to do. Help me."

Louise put her arm around her friend, a tear in her own eye. She lulled Alice and held her while she broke into pieces.

"You're at your mum's now, aren't you?" Louise asked gently. "I know it's not great, but at least your dad won't be messing your head up every five minutes."

"I don't even care about them, Lou. All I can think about is McAvoy," Alice whispered through her tears.

"It's gonna be okay," said Louise comfortingly, handing Alice a mug of ginger tea brought in by her mother.

Eventually, Alice calmed down enough to have a conversation with her friend. For what seemed like hours, she filled her in on all the details of the words and feelings exchanged between her and McAvoy. The situation, her body and even her voice felt surreal as she spoke, like she could be in a dream within a dream.

"I just feel so alone, and so stupid," she finished.

"Hey, you're not the stupid one, Alice – he is. What was he thinking anyway, getting so close to you?" she asked.

"I don't know; I will never know. That's what's killing me – that, and the fact that I never thought it was possible to miss someone this much."

Louise's brother Tom barged in without knocking.

"Oi!" Louise barked.

"Hey, what's wrong with her?" Tom said, noticing Alice's red face.

"None of your business, get out!" Louise scolded.

"But I wanna borrow your Radiohead CD!"

Louise exhaled in annoyance and threw the CD at him, ordering him to leave.

"Bitch," Tom laughed as he walked out of the room, then all was silent.

"Sorry about him, babe. Boys are dickheads when they're fourteen; fucking immature."

"No, it's okay," Alice laughed. "Actually, that's the first time I've felt like laughing since McAvoy left. Normal is good, I don't get a lot of that."

"I know," Louise replied with awareness. "Well, think of us as your second family. Any time you want an irritating brother around, just drop by."

Alice smiled at the genuine kindness in Louise's brown eyes.

"I don't know what to say about McAvoy," Louise said. "I know you don't want to hear it, but you need to try and get over him. You can't let him rule your life."

"I can't get over him," Alice replied, her voice cracking. The tears started falling again from her tired eyes. "He was my direction; he was the person who made me happy without even doing anything. I guess I didn't realise how much he had become intrinsic to who I am, and now that he isn't here, I feel completely lost. I don't know what my life is about anymore."

"He really meant the world to you, didn't he?" Louise responded. "I believe you, I believe whatever you two had was real. I used to notice the way he looked at you; it wasn't the way he looked at everyone else. That's why I used to take the piss. Sorry," she looked down at her hands.

"It's okay," Alice said, rubbing Louise's arm. "It makes me feel better that you noticed, it's a reminder that I'm not just delusional and making it more than it was. I keep thinking I see him when I'm out. Any person with the same build, same hair, and I do a double-take. As if he's just going to be walking around and I'll magically bump into him. I need to stop it, but I don't know how."

"I know," Louise said. "You'll get there, and I'll be here. How's it going at your mum's?"

Alice rolled her eyes: "She wants to have a party."

"Hmmmm. Does she know about McAvoy?" Louise asked.

"God no, are you nuts?!" Alice replied.

"How about we go job shopping tomorrow? It'll take your mind off things." Louise suggested.

"What the fuck is job shopping?" was the surprised response.

"Looking for jobs, obviously," Louise replied, throwing a cushion at Alice.

"Oh. Yeah, okay," Alice agreed, although she had no inclination to look for jobs, or to do anything, in fact. She would go through the motions for Louise; she would behave like one of the mechanical theatre spectacles, moving because it had to, because someone else was pulling the levers. If it was left to Alice, she would not move again. She would stop dead.

"Are you sure you'll be okay though? I'm going to worry about you," Louise asked, her face concerned.

"I don't know," said Alice, honestly. "I'll be fine, I guess. I miss him, Lou."

"I know you do, but maybe he isn't the man you thought he was. Whatever reason he had to leave, he could have told you somehow," her friend reasoned.

"Yes, I know. Maybe he didn't think I was important enough," Alice said quietly. They chatted for a while, but Alice felt vacant and decided to go home.

She made her way down the stairs of Louise's house, feeling the seeds of doubt in her belly about her interpretation of what had seemed so genuine between her and McAvoy. Why hadn't he let her know what was going on? Louise was right, he could have left a message somehow. If he had cared as much as he said he did, why would he have left her in the misery of wondering what had happened?

"Hi Mum," Alice called when she got home, but there was no answer, only a note by the phone:

"Met Tracey for drinks, didn't know what time you'd be back. See you later. Mum x"

Alice was pleased to have some privacy. She ran herself

a bath with just the hot tap; she needed to try and burn the memory of Will McAvoy away. She undressed and lowered herself into the bath slowly; it was burning hot, but she needed to feel the intense heat on her skin again. She lay back, acclimatising to the water temperature as steam filled the room, obscuring her vision. The heat made her dozy.

Alice examined the lines on her left arm: there were three little scratches she'd made the other day with a safety pin. As she surveyed the scars, Alice felt her sense of desire grow: her needs had surpassed scratches; they weren't enough. Alice picked up a razor from the side of the bath and held it an inch away from her eye, examining it closely. Two shiny new blades winked at her. She rested the razor against her red skin and it provided a cool relief. As the sharpness pressed into her arm, two pink lines appeared. Alice closed her eyes and pushed the blades in harder, this time sliding them across her arm, slicing her flesh. A little blood oozed out, and she plunged her arm into the sting of the hot bath. The blood dispersed into a pink cloud in the water and she closed her eyes again.

"Alice!" came April's shrill voice, jolting Alice awake. She became acutely aware that she was cold and wet, soon realising that she was still in the bath, having fallen asleep. The water was still and slightly pink.

"Uhh, yes, I'm in the bath!" she shouted back, clambering out of the cold water and wrapping a towel around herself. Alice raced to her bedroom, keeping her arm firmly down by her side, and wrapped herself in the duvet to get warm. She shivered and felt goosebumps prickling all over her body. The new lines on her arm were dark red; the skin around each wound was trying to form a scab but had remained soft and malleable from soaking in the water. She pulled on a long-sleeved top and pyjama trousers before going to greet her mother mechanically.

"So, did you have fun at your friend's house?" April asked.

"Um, yes – it was okay," Alice replied.

"Louise, was it?" her mother continued.

"Yes, Louise," Alice confirmed.

"What class were you in together, English?" April asked. *English*, the word seemed to echo in Alice's brain. She had just managed to numb herself, space out for a while, and now April's words had brought her right back down to earth with a painful bump.

"I'm really tired, Mum, I think I'm going to have an early night," Alice yawned, and walked to the stairs. She needed to be away from her mother; away from all people. She shut her bedroom door behind her, closed her eyes and slid down to the floor, crumpling like a piece of burning paper. Will's copy of Jane Eyre lay on her bedside table; she smelled its pages every night. Some of them had started to ripple in places from the moisture of her tears.

"How could you do this to me, McAvoy?" Alice whispered. "I've got nothing. I am nothing." She had read in a book about spirituality that every thought and action affected every other thing that happened – even on the other side of the world. Alice wondered if those words she'd uttered would make something happen somewhere else – something she'd never know about. Maybe in Iceland or Japan her dismal words had made a tree fall down or caused a car accident. She remembered a line that read: *'We are all connected by an energetic force that runs through us all'*, but Alice didn't feel this connection. In fact, she'd never felt less connected to anyone or anything. She was small and alone on the huge face of the earth.

Her thumb and fingers casually rolled up her sleeve, and she dug her nails into the wound that was trying to heal itself. She couldn't block out the feelings of rejection and loneliness. McAvoy knew her life was full of pain, and he'd still chosen to leave without a word. The balance had shifted and Alice had well and truly toppled. As her name-sake fell down the rabbit hole, so Alice was falling into a much darker place.

O ver the next six months, the earth kept turning; the days continued to pass, and long nights came and went in Alice's desperate life. Her cutting habits were now a daily occurrence, and she'd look forward to the end of the day when she could shut herself away and be alone. She'd pour herself a glass of wine, light a cigarette, and experiment with various sharp tools; sometimes razors or scalpels, or even just safety pins. Her arms, wrists and thighs were adorned with cuts from sorrowful blades. She hid her scars well, always wearing long sleeves with bracelets or wrist bands. April noticed that her daughter didn't seem happy, but dismissed it as teenage angst. She didn't seem to mind Alice's sudden penchant for smoking and drinking; they shared wine and cigarettes some evenings until Alice could escape once more to the solitude of her bedroom.

The hours of each day seemed to lapse by so slowly until evening arrived, when Alice could kill her emotional pain and cry herself to sleep thinking about Will. She saw Hetty and Bill once or twice a week – the hair-pulling incident had been brushed under the carpet; the status quo was maintained by all.

. . .

At around seven pm one Friday night, the doorbell sounded. April had gone out for the evening and Alice didn't appreciate this unexpected interruption.

"Hello, baby!" Christopher stood in the doorway, in his hand a blue plastic bag with something inside. Alice noted the dried blood on his nose and the familiar sickening stench of booze.

"What are you doing here, Dad? You know you're not allowed here," Alice said.

"I'm seizing an opportune moment. Mummy has gone out, hasn't she? I didn't see her car," he slurred.

"You look like a tramp," Alice said blankly.

"That's a nice way to speak to your daddy, isn't it?!" Christopher barged past his daughter and made himself comfortable in the living room.

"What the fuck are you doing? Get out!" Alice was livid, she didn't want him there. She wanted to be alone, not babysitting the excuse for a father she hadn't seen for months. Christopher produced a gin bottle from the plastic bag and started swigging from the bottle.

"Fine. Kill yourself, I don't care anymore!" Alice blasted before returning to her bedroom, slamming the door in rage and locking it behind her.

Anger boiled inside her; Alice clenched her fists and pursed her lips into a hard line. She turned up the music playing on her stereo and threw her wineglass against the wall. The blue glass broke into pieces, splinters ricocheting away and landing on the carpet. Alice grabbed her hair by the roots and pulled until it hurt. Sobbing, she sank down to the floor, picked up a broken piece of glass and started dragging it desperately along her skin, from the inside of her wrist up to her elbow. Thoughts came into her mind of the recurring dreams she'd had her whole life, of silent screams that refused to leave her mouth. And then Alice had a sudden moment of clarity.

She began to feel calm; the brain fog lifted. Alice moved over to her bedside table and retrieved some razor-blades that she'd bought and stashed away in a drawer, unwrapping one carefully and looking at it for a while. She picked up her phone and texted Louise: *'I'm sorry. I love you x'*. Alice switched off her phone and started cutting into her wrist with no hesitation – short sharp flicks. The blade made easy work of producing blood and it trickled down the side of her wrist and fell in small puddles on to the carpet. Alice was numb; a greater power had taken over. She welcomed the thought of dying, wondering if McAvoy would ever find out. Would he be upset? Would he care at all? Christopher was silent next door; Alice figured he'd probably passed out.

She cut deeper and deeper until there was a half-inch deep gash on her wrist and the subcutaneous layer of tissue was showing yellow fluid with a neat red slash where she'd gone over the same line. The blood dripped faster, pooling on the floor beside her. After a while, exhaustion washed over her and she needed to close her eyes. The last thing that registered in Alice's brain before her heavy eyelids shut out the world was McAvoy holding her hands within his own – the happiest day of her life.

Chapter Ten

Will managed to get the bowl over to his mother's bedside just before she vomited violently. He placed it on the floor and rubbed her back. Jacoline retched for the next hour, unable to keep food inside her body. She had grown steadily worse in the time since Will had arrived in Johannesburg all those months ago.

The cancer had spread from her liver to her bones and Will had finally given up any optimism of hoping she would survive, deciding instead to make the best of the time they had left together. The doctors had advised them to start a course of treatment for palliative chemotherapy in a bid to prolong Jacoline's life. As he looked at her, lying helplessly on the sodden bed sheets, Will wondered what the fuck there was to prolong. Scott had insisted on it, though, and Jacoline, as always, went along with her husband's wishes. Scott looked in on her in the evenings when he got back from the office and did little else. Will knew she was going to die but his father wouldn't accept it; he thought that if he threw enough money at the doctors, they would save her.

The wave of vomiting had ceased for now and Jacoline fell back, exhausted, against the pillows that were propping her up. Will adjusted them and she gave him all the crease of a smile she could muster as she closed her eyes and let sleep take her while it could.

He watched her for a while. She wore a bandana decorated with blue flowers to hide the patches on her scalp where there was no longer any hair. As his mother drifted into the only place where she had peace, Will could hardly hear her breathe. Her mouth was slightly parted, her skin waxy and tinged with yellow. If he'd walked into the room now and seen her as she was – lying there, devoid of her life's essence, he'd have believed she'd just died. He kissed her on the head and returned to his room, where he spent most of his time now. He'd become his dying mother's live-in carer, drafted in so that his father wouldn't have to deal with his wife's deteriorating condition himself.

Will was tired, so tired. He barely slept, nor did he eat, getting by on a few morsels a day. His stomach seemed permanently knotted from stress and dark shadows had appeared under his eyes. He no longer recognised his reflection. Along with the pain of seeing his mother's life ebb away each day, was the pain of leaving Alice the way he had. He couldn't forget that the last time he saw her, he'd more or less thrown her out. After that, he'd booked the first ticket he could to South Africa and left, hurriedly leaving Heathcliff with a neighbour in his building who was fond of the friendly cat, along with a few boxes of possessions he didn't want to lose and his flat key to sort out with the landlord. Upon leaving his boxes with the fifty-something auburn-haired woman, with whom he'd only exchanged minimal pleasantries in passing, he regretted not having made more of an effort to be nicer to his neighbour, or to people in general – he hadn't even learnt her name. He left all his furniture and packed one suitcase of essentials to take with him. Will thought about leaving a letter for Alice, or trying to get a message to her, but when the time came, the ink in his pen would not form anything legible. Nothing he could say sounded good enough.

Upon his departure from the UK, Will had thought a clean break would probably make for a better healing process – although now he doubted this. He was used to cutting people off, but this time he couldn't quite sever the connection. Every day he felt an empty space that he hadn't quite realised Alice was filling for those three years. Every night he lay in bed not sleeping, thinking about how she had looked after him in his hour of need – with tenderness and care.

The heaviness of guilt tightened in his chest like a vice. Will had noticed an increase in palpitations in the last few months, like his heart was unsure what it was supposed to be doing anymore. He wrote to Alice in his journal; letters she would never read, but somehow, it eased him slightly.

D*earest Alice,*

Mum has been really sick today, sometimes she has good days, but today she looked like death had come for her. Life here is very solitary. My days are long and full of sadness. I'm watching my mother die.

I often wonder what you are doing. You'd like it here – the homes are big and there are sprawling landscapes. We have a great view of the city as our house is on a hill; I stand outside at night and look at all the lights twinkling in the darkness. Sometimes I pick one and imagine that you are there. And although I can't see you, it seems like you aren't thousands of kilometres away. You could be just around the corner.

I wish I could see you and check you are okay. I tell Mum about you when she is asleep. I tell her that I've never met such a pure-hearted person. I feel sorry for the way I left.

You are missed – indescribably missed.

The smell of ink rose from the page and Will breathed it in deeply. Whatever happened in the world, there would always be ink on paper, keeping records of thoughts for time immemorial. He found a small comfort in this as he closed his precious journal and placed it on the desk before him; his old desk, in his old room. Besides a laptop, journal and pen, the only other item on Will's desk was the card Alice had given him for his birthday. He didn't know if it made him feel better or worse having it there but kept it like an epitaph of what he'd lost.

Will leaned back in his chair and spotted the familiar pair of crystal onyx bookends, each propping up the weight of eleven books. He pondered thoughtfully that bookends need to be split up to fulfil their function – they are meant to be apart. Some things just work better apart than together. His eyes fell to the shelf underneath, where there was a tin of paint. His memory processed the paint tin and traced it back to when he was fourteen and had painted his room sky blue. Then he thought of Gregor.

Gregor had always worn the same clothes: a checked shirt and khaki dungarees with rips and stains here and there. He walked with a slight limp on his right side, which he told Will was due to a bad dog bite on his ankle that never healed properly. By the time Will was ten and his sister Victoria was eight, the three had developed an unspoken yet undeniable bond. The brother and sister would sit agog in fascination as Gregor told stories of the

Tokoloshe: a feared creature that supposedly stole lives while everyone was asleep.

"The only way the Tokoloshe doesn't get to you is to sleep high," Gregor's thick accent was still as clear in Will's mind now as it had been back then. He looked at the shelf again, remembering that Gregor had told him that he slept with each leg of his bed propped up on paint cans so that he would be protected from the mysterious life-stealer.

"They come and bite off your toes while you sleep. Suck your soul out. Then dead," Gregor traced a line across his neck with a finger. He became more animated every time he told the story, his dark, bloodshot eyes bulging as he maintained a deadly serious expression.

"You white kids don't know. But I know," he would say, and wag his finger.

Will and Victoria would watch intently while Gregor ate bread and pilchards for lunch with a can of coke to wash it down – the same meal every day.

"Why do you come and sit with me always?" he had asked once, as they sat in the garden during the school holidays with the sun beating down on them.

Victoria was twisting blades of grass around her fingers. "You make us laugh," she piped up.

Will thought for a long moment and adjusted his cap before answering. "Because you're real," he replied, watching the beads of sweat forming on Gregor's forehead.

Suddenly, Gregor burst into rapturous laughter and declared: "Yes! I am real!"

He continued to laugh as he picked up a spade, shaking his head. "Go now, I've got work to do," he chuckled.

The children's father never saw their exchanges with Gregor, he was always working. Their mother was too caught up in her own mental struggles most of the time to notice what was going on, so they largely did as they pleased when they weren't at school.

One cool spring day, Will noticed that Gregor seemed thinner than usual. In fact, now that he thought about it, Will realised that Gregor's stature had diminished significantly – but when? As Will looked on, he saw that the old man's movements seemed to lack the animation they'd previously had.

That same day, at nine pm, Scott came home from work and unwrapped the dinner that had been left for him by the maid. Will sat at the marble breakfast bar in the kitchen, circling his finger around a cup of milk.

"Hi son. Have Victoria and your mother gone to bed?"

"I think so," said Will.

"Ah. Did you eat?" his father asked.

"Yes."

Scott pressed the button on the coffee machine while he waited for the food to heat up in the microwave.

"Dad, did you notice that Gregor doesn't seem well?" Will asked his father, his brow furrowed.

"Yes, Will. He's dying." Scott positioned the cup so the coffee stream would hit the middle of it, and the microwave pinged to alert him that his food was ready.

"What?" Will asked in shock.

"AIDS. You know it's rife with these lot," came the response.

Will didn't speak for a while, silently watching his father eating the plate of food and taking sips of coffee every once in a while.

After a few minutes, he found his voice.

"These lot? You mean black people?" Will said finally, feeling irritated.

Scott gestured vaguely in response.

"Weren't you going to tell me?" Will questioned.

"Why?" was his dad's simple response.

"Because, he's been here for…"

"Fourteen years now," Scott confirmed. "It's a shame. We'll have to get a new gardener. Gregor is a good worker. Damn shame." He shovelled a forkful of potato into his callous mouth.

Will looked at him in disbelief. "Is that it? Don't you care?"

"I care about you, your sister and your mother, okay? I don't have room to care about everyone," Scott replied, in a matter-of-fact tone. "The more people you care about, the more opportunities there are for people to hurt you. Gregor is a good worker, I'm sorry he's dying, but getting upset about it won't change the fact."

Will got up from the breakfast bar and left his father to eat the rest of his meal alone. He went upstairs to bed, wrapped himself up in his white duvet with blue wavy lines, and cried himself to sleep.

Gregor died one month later.

Nineteen years on, and Will was once again wrapping himself up in the same duvet of his childhood, trying not to cry, and wishing for sleep.

The next day, Scott left early for work, haphazardly mentioning to Will on his way out that he had a big case on with Richardsons: a pharmaceutical giant whose corruption kept Scott firmly in employment. Scott had acted as their lawyer for the last thirty years and did what he had to do to prevent them from being liable for any of the harm they caused through their experimentation with drugs and chemicals.

Will had always hated what his father did for a living;

even at a young age, he knew it wasn't all above board. Richardsons had afforded them nice cars and a big house with a pool – Scott had earned a reputation as the best lawyer in the city. He was cold and clinical, analysing facts and knowing exactly which documents to hide and how to twist any situation to make it favourable for his clients. Now that Jacoline was dying, Will saw his father throw himself into his work even more.

Will went into his mother's room and opened the curtains. A flood of bright morning light came in and made Jacoline squint.

"Morning Mum. How are you feeling?"

"Okay, I think," she answered softly. "Will you take me out today, into the garden? I want to see outside."

Will smiled at his mother's request.

"Of course I will. The nurse will be in soon and then we can go, okay?" He went downstairs to make some breakfast, more out of habit than hunger. There was a buzz at the gate and Will pressed the entry button. "Go on up," he told Nurse Elizabeth as she walked into the grand entrance to their home.

Coral-coloured pillars flanked the central double staircase that bowed in the shape of an arc. The floors were marble and pristine, with one large salmon and gold-coloured silk Isfahan rug laid between the staircases. Everything in the house was expensive, from the curtains to the teacups. It was one big status symbol that Will had been glad to get away from when he'd moved to London.

Will made a filter coffee and walked outside to survey the impressive gardens maintained by Sam, their faithful gardener, who had come in to replace Gregor all those years ago. Will took a deep breath: the day was beautiful; deathly cold, but sunny. The trees had tired of their leaves and stood waiting for a burst of life and renewal. Perhaps it was a little cold for Jacoline today, he thought. Will ran his hand through his ever greying hair and rubbed the remaining sleep from his eyes. His face was gaunter than it had been in previous months. He sat on the step outside with his coffee steaming in the chilly air and his skin protesting against the cold: he felt goose bumps along his arms and his hair bristled. Will sat there for a long while, deep in thought, as his coffee cooled in its cup.

"Okay, all done," Nurse Elizabeth popped her head around the door and waved goodbye. "She said she wants to go out in the garden today – just make sure she doesn't get too cold."

"Oh, thanks. Bye, see you later," Will replied absently. He went upstairs, washed and pulled on some casual clothes before returning to his mother's room. "It's really cold today Mum, are you sure you want to go out?"

"Will, I've been cooped up in this room for too long. I want fresh air in my lungs and some daylight on my face," she instructed firmly. The nurse had washed and dressed her, administered her morning dose of medication, and Jacoline was ready to venture out.

"Alright then, let's do this!" Will said – Jacoline laughing at her son's feigned enthusiasm.

Jacoline's wheelchair was waiting at the bottom of the stairs and Will helped her fragile body down the vast staircase slowly, and ever so carefully. When she was comfortably seated in her chair, Will pushed his mother out into the crisp breeze, every part of her wrapped up in a bundle of woollen materials, other than her face. As Will pushed his mother in her wheelchair, Jacoline took large gulps of air, drinking in the elements as if they were sacred nectar.

"You're a good boy, Will. I know it wasn't always nice for you growing up."

"That doesn't matter now," he said.

"Yes, it does. I was so wrapped up in myself that I never realised how much I was hurting my precious boy. Or Victoria, God rest her," Jacoline's eyes squeezed shut at the mention of her daughter's name. "I have been coming to terms with my own demons in the last few months," she continued. "I wish I could have dealt with them sooner, but instead I let them devour me all these years."

Will could feel tears pricking in his eyes, like they were burning in the brisk air.

"I loved you and your sister William, but it was always like I was looking at life through grey mesh – I never saw clearly until now. Things seem so bright out here: vibrant and joyous. I feel peaceful my boy."

Will stopped pushing the wheelchair and bent down in front of her, holding her gloved hand.

"It's okay Mum, I know there were issues and I forgive you. You did your best."

A tear escaped from Jacoline's sallow eye. "I hear you, you know. I hear you talking about Alice – dark hair and green eyes. She's important to you."

Her words tipped Will over the edge and he broke down with his head on his mother's knee. His hands covered his face and his body convulsed with emotion. Jacoline rubbed his back. "There, there, my boy. It'll be okay. I'm only sorry that it's me who has complicated things."

"It was already complicated. Besides, I wouldn't have left you here with only Dad for company." Will's sorrow intermingled with sudden anger.

"Listen, don't be too hard on your father. I know he's difficult to understand. But he's always loved us. He's always done his best for us the only way he knew how. He can't bear to see me like this, that's why he's thrown himself into work," Jacoline reasoned.

"Well, he should try harder! How can you be so forgiving?" Will asked, genuinely.

"I've got no anger left in my body, William. A great sense of clarity came over me and I can see everything the way it is with no judgement. He creeps in to see me in the middle of the night you know, he thinks I don't know," Jacoline's smile was sad. "This girl you speak about, William. You need to find peace with her, whatever that means. Don't let something unresolved eat away at you for the rest of your life like I did."

"It's too late," Will said. "I let her down, the same way I let Victoria down."

"It's never too late, William. What happened to Victoria wasn't your fault, you know? You were like a parent to her, and I'm sorry I couldn't see it. I'm sorry you had so much pressure put on top of you. If I could turn back time, I would, believe me," she paused and took a deep breath in.

"I don't have long left, son. I'm on the last chapter. I don't want to put this on you, but I need you to help me get some affairs in order – my funeral. Dad is in denial; he thinks I'm going to recover. Don't cry, William, it's okay, I'm happy. I'm ready to go." A peaceful smile crossed her lips: "Perhaps we can go back inside now, I'm very tired."

Will nodded to his mother's request, his emotions reaching capacity.

Chapter Eleven

Alice sat in the white painted waiting room at the end of a long row of seats with her head leant back against the wall. This was her first visit to Green Haven mental health facility, April sat in the chair next to her, tutting and sighing at their lengthy wait. Alice ignored her and stared blankly at the notice board, which was littered with posters about counselling, checking your medications were up to date and one that read in large type 'THERE IS ALWAYS HOPE'.

Hope? Alice questioned inwardly. Her mother had discovered Alice in a pool of blood streaming from her cut wrist and taken her to hospital the same night. Alice didn't remember much of the ordeal, although she had heard about it every day since (with a side-helping of guilt from April.) – Christopher had been AWOL ever since.

After Alice had been assessed, she'd been referred to Green Haven, and she'd duly obliged; there was no fight left in her. She couldn't forget Will, or how much her heart hurt. Whatever she had shared with her English teacher, it was gone – as temporary as a dewdrop in the morning sun.

April went off to complain about the waiting time, and Alice was glad of the space. She sneaked a look over to a black guy in his late forties sitting two seats away. He wore a leather jacket and matching leather hat; he had some grey stubble on his face and lots of lines under his round, fish-like eyes. The man caught Alice's glance and moved into the vacant seat next to her, closing the gap between them.

"Alright? I'm Clarence," he introduced himself, holding out his hand to be shaken. Alice took his hand out of politeness and greeted him.

"You're a cutter, I see," he said, grabbing Alice's wrist lightly. "That's nothin' love, take a look at this," Clarence pulled up his leather jacket sleeve and showed her some old healed scars all along his wrist. They were vast and jagged at the edges, though the middle was smooth and shiny. Alice smiled at Clarence's matter-of-factness. He was a cutter, and she was a cutter. That was that.

"This your first time?" he asked. "I've been coming 'ere for years. They keep changin' my meds. Said until I don't wanna kill myself, they'll keep increasin' the dose. Fuckin' twenty-something silver-spoon graduates got no idea, not a day's depression in their lives; you can tell by the way they talk to ya. I've been on the streets since I was fourteen, bet they've got rich Mummy and Daddy payin' their way through school!"

"So, why do you cut?" Alice asked him with interest.

"Probably the same reason you cut – relief and escape. I'm right, ain't I?" he answered, and Alice nodded.

"Look love, you're a pretty girl. It ain't too late for you to get out. It's too late for me now. But you still got a chance. I got a daughter your age, she don't talk to me now. I fucked everythin' up, see? Can't go back now. You've got a chance," Clarence took Alice's hand in his own and squeezed it hard, staring at her intensely. Alice saw a lifetime of regret in his eyes. A distant voice called out at that moment, and Alice was aware of a figure just beyond the waiting room.

"That's me," Clarence said, getting up. "Gotta go now, love. You remember what I said."

"Bye," Alice called, but Clarence was already halfway to the psychiatrist's office.

She could've cried for Clarence; he was too far gone. She wondered if she'd be coming here when she was Clarence's age. The thought alarmed her.

"Who was that tramp talking to you?" April suddenly resurfaced.

"That was Clarence, and he's not a tramp."

"Clarence? Well, I don't want you talking to these sorts of people, Alice. They're no good for you," April scolded.

"I am *these* sorts of people, Mum, don't you get it? These people are all fucked up in the head."

"You are NOT fucked up in the head!" the anger in April's voice rose fast. "You are a silly girl who thinks it's smart to play with knives, and we are getting you sorted out today!"

"Yeah, pop me a few pills and I'll be back to normal, won't I?" Alice scowled back at her. "If it all goes according to your plan; you won't have to tell anyone that you've got a nut job for a daughter. Then you can carry on pretending we've all got perfect lives, can't you?" she snapped.

"Alice, how dare you talk to me like that? I know what's best for you!" the last words crumbled out of April's mouth and she gave a small squeak, tears following while she tried to swallow them back. "I've always done my best for you, and this is how you repay me? How can you do this to me?"

That was the last drop in the bucket of rage that Alice had been accumulating over her lifetime. She got to her feet, stood over her mother and exploded.

"To you? How can I do this to YOU!? It's not about you, you stupid bitch! It's about me! ME... Alice! Not April; Alice! I'm the one going through this and for once in my life it isn't about YOU or DAD, it's about ME!" Alice spat her hate-filled words as hot tears escaped down her cheeks. April was silent – her face red and her lip trembling, but for once in her life, April kept her mouth shut.

Everyone had stopped to look and listen to the furore. One of the patients started clapping and Alice could hear them whispering. An assistant with a kind face and soft features came and took Alice by the arm, leading her into a private waiting area.

"Perhaps you'd better wait in here, okay? Do you want a tea or something?"

Alice just shook her head and looked down at her fingers.

"The doctor will be in to see you shortly," the nurse soothed. Through her steady tears, Alice looked around the dingy room and helped herself to the box of tissues on the table. She wanted to sleep, to escape the pain for just a while.

After a long wait by herself, a short, plump female doctor walked in with a clipboard and sat down on one of the salmon-pink chairs.

"I'm Dr. Minesh, and you are Alice Wilde, is that correct?" the doctor asked, not looking up from the clipboard.

"Yes," Alice confirmed.

"Okay, so my notes say that you've been harming yourself and you're suicidal?"

"Yes," she confirmed again.

"Why is that?" the doctor asked, without making eye contact.

"Dunno," came Alice's despondent reply.

"You must have a reason why you want to hurt your-self?" Dr. Minesh's tone was clipped and clinical.

"Someone left me," Alice answered in a small voice, her shoulders hunched and her face looking down.

"A boyfriend?"

"Someone I cared about."

"Alice, you're very young," the doctor responded. "I know it seems like the end of the world when someone leaves, but you will get over it. We can't go hurting ourselves every time someone leaves us, can we?"

Alice had no energy to converse with the patronising doctor,

"Are you going to help me or not?" she asked, flatly. The doctor raised an eyebrow and sighed.

"I've read your notes, and the questionnaire you filled out. The results indicate you're severely depressed. I am going to prescribe Venlafaxine for you, 75mg once a day, and we'll review you in six weeks."

Dr. Minesh scribbled on a prescription pad and tore it off. Alice took the prescription and left the salmon-coloured room, leaving Dr. Minesh writing something on her clipboard.

Alice shoved the green prescription in her bag. She didn't speak to her mother on the car journey home, nor did April speak to her daughter. Instead, Alice's mind wandered to what poor Clarence had said: "*It's too late for me now. But you still got a chance.*" Everyone promised that one day she'd forget about this pain, forget about Will and that the connection would fade away. One day she would wake up and he wouldn't be the first thing she thought about. She didn't believe it – how could so much pain ever go away?

———

As she woke on a rainy November morning, Alice reached for the packet of cigarettes on her bedside table. She lit one up and lay in bed, letting the smoke fill her lungs. April opened the bedroom door, from which she had removed the lock.

"Do you think you could knock?" Alice said sharply, "I could be naked in here."

April chose to ignore her daughter's question and ploughed on with her own line of enquiry: "Let me see your arms," she strode over and checked Alice's skin to see if there were any new marks. She did this religiously every morning, much to Alice's annoyance.

"Are you just going to mope around the house all day?" she enquired. "Because if you are, you can at least do the dishes. Right, I'm going to work, I'll see you later. And clean your face up, you look like shit," April flounced out of Alice's bedroom and slammed the front door on her way out of the house.

"FUCKING BITCCCHHHH!" screamed Alice, hurling the nearest thing she could find at the wall which happened to be a teddy bear. "Don't worry April, I'll do your fucking dishes!" Alice said to her absent mother.

She looked in the mirror, noting the make-up smudged underneath her eyes, and lit up another cigarette, sucking hard. The anger coursed through her rapidly. "I'll do your dishes alright," she mumbled, getting up and heading over to the kitchen where she took hold of the washing-up bowl filled with plates, glasses and cups, carried it through the back door into the garden and tipped the contents out on to the concrete. Glass and crockery smashed and shattered into shards and splinters. Alice suddenly experienced some small release. She looked at the shattered 'everything-must-be-white-and-matching' crockery and felt a pang of satisfaction. Then, she returned to the kitchen, scribbled a note that read *'I did the dishes'*, and left it on the drainer. She knew she would be in trouble, but what was new? She was yelled at every day for being depressed; she might as well do something to deserve her mother's anger.

A sudden chill came over Alice as McAvoy unexpectedly surfaced in her mind again, like a furious hit of a pick upon ice. Her pained heart beat faster. She went back into her bedroom and lit up another cigarette, trying to squash the emotion rising up in her. Despite her efforts, her face was hot and wet with tears again. She lay on the bed and closed her eyes, tears leaking through her lashes and dropping into her ears. She imagined him holding her, his deep voice, his big protective hands cradling her. The memory of his words felt like a knife twisting in an old wound, and the more time that lapsed, the more Alice questioned whether he was as genuine as she'd thought. Did he even think about her? she wondered. She cried harder and hugged her pillow close to her chest. Her unruly dark hair stuck to her face with the moisture. Alice prayed for sleep and eventually drifted off with a vision of McAvoy's brooding eyes staring into her own.

She dreamed that she was walking through a vast forest. She was trying to get somewhere, but she couldn't remember where she was heading, only that it was important that she got there. Tall trees veiled her path, and she caught glimpses of faceless white beings hiding behind them. Then, a hooded figure appeared, faceless, with amber eyes. It held out its hand, offering her red capsules. Before she took them, Alice heard ringing echoing around her brain. Alice woke up to the noise of the house phone and dragged herself to the hallway to answer it.

"Did you take your medication today?" April's hoarse voice asked.

"Yeah," Alice replied, somewhat dazed.

"Did you do the dishes?" April continued.

"Yeah."

"Well, that's something," her mother conceded. "I'll be home at six."

"Okay, bye," Alice hung up before April could say anything else.

Her parents had fucked up their job, and she was paying the price. They were still fucking up, the pair of them too wrapped up in their own dramas to see that their little girl was suffering under the weight of the pressure they'd always put on her. Alice realised that McAvoy was only the catalyst for her breakdown; the beautiful, unique catalyst that had been removed from her life and left a gaping hole that would not heal.

She filled a glass full of tap water and popped two of the red capsules from their blister pack, swallowing them together with a gulp of water. The dose had been increased from 75mg to 300mg Venlafaxine daily. Dr. Minesh had told her they would up the dose until she felt happy. Alice's visits to Green Haven were predictable; she saw the same faces around and occasionally had a conversation with one of the other sorry souls waiting for the psychiatrist, though she never saw Clarence again.

At her last visit, Alice had witnessed a thin-lipped woman with olive skin and long, wavy black and grey hair was insisting that she must go home as she'd forgotten to put her knickers on. The psychiatrist had tried to explain that she had to be admitted, and the woman became frantic, confessing that she hadn't been taking her Lithium.

Strangely, Alice felt safer there than she did at home. These people were like her and for the first time in a long while she felt that she belonged somewhere.

However, she had no respect for Dr. Minesh: it was clear that all she did was hand out drugs like sweets so she could tick things off on her clipboard and finish her day. She never asked Alice if she wanted to talk about any of her problems, and Alice didn't want to share anything with the unfeeling doctor.

She sometimes saw Gary, the cognitive behavioural psychotherapist. He was in his mid-twenties and slightly chubby, with a friendly face and thick eyebrows. He used to ask her about her cutting habits, and how she was feeling. Alice would confide in him and his brows would raise with genuine concern as he questioned her further. Sometimes she thought about fucking him. Her thoughts became more and more reckless as time went on, as did her actions.

Alice had taken to cutting her thighs instead of her arms as April's military-style checks didn't stretch to other areas of her body. She wondered what McAvoy would think if he could see her now. Would he hold her tight? Would he care that she bought packets of paracetamol and aspirin every time she went out, just in case it all got too much? Maybe he would think she was a loser. Alice's scalp prickled for a second at that thought. Sometimes, she would take a trip to his apartment and listen at the edge of the river to the flux of the water. She observed its wild nature; ebbing and flowing, swirling and still. It provided temporary relief for the toxicity that was engulfing her life.

That night, alone in her bedroom, Alice took three new packets of aspirin out of her bag and added them to her bedside drawer where she'd been collecting pills. She had five packets of aspirin altogether, each with twenty tablets in. She eyed the silver boxes next, each containing twelve paracetamols each, and there was one packet of sleeping pills. She looked at them lovingly, calmly, and decided that when the time came, a combination of the pills she'd collected should be enough to do the job.

Chapter Twelve

Will and his father sat together in the waiting area of the Springside Private Hospital. Jacoline had been admitted the previous night after she had started convulsing. The doctors were doing tests and had instructed Will and Scott to wait outside.

"She'll be okay, son," Scott said.

"Dad, she's dying," Will told him. "She's accepted it. You have to accept it, too."

"No, William, I am paying for the best treatment for her, they *will* save her," Scott replied in a raised voice.

Will turned to face his father. "Listen to me. All the money in the world can't save her. She wants to die, she told me. We've been arranging her funeral. Please, Dad," Will pleaded.

"No!" Scott snapped and started pacing up and down the corridor. Will sighed in frustration and ran his hands through his hair for want of something to do. He saw a doctor walk out of Jacoline's room and looked up in anticipation; Scott did the same.

"Well?" Scott asked urgently.

"I'm Dr. Hendrix, I'm the senior oncology specialist here," said the man in white. "We're running some blood tests on Mrs. McAvoy to find out what's causing the convulsions. Until we know more, I'm afraid it's just a waiting game. You can go in to see her now."

"Why don't you know what's wrong with her?" Scott asked, red faced, "This is your field, isn't it? You must have seen this sort of thing before?"

"I'm sorry Mr. McAvoy, I realise it's not much to go on but we are doing everything we can to stabilise your wife," Dr. Hendrix replied. "It's possible the cancer has spread to her brain, but we're not sure yet."

Scott tutted, made a dismissive hand gesture at the doctor and stalked off to his wife's room.

"Sorry, he's not handling this very well," Will informed Dr. Hendrix as he followed his father to Jacoline's bedside.

There, he found his mother writhing and twisting, her limbs flailing and her eyes flickering and rolling in her head. Will was barely holding it together, he could hardly stand to watch her. *Where was she?* Her consciousness certainly wasn't in the room. There were bars up at the sides of the bed to stop her falling out.

Scott took a seat in the chair at the side of the hospital bed, put his head in his hands and slowly rocked from side to side. Will took his mother's hand on the other side of the bed and suddenly Jacoline's back arched violently and her body lurched to the left. A nurse dashed in, closely followed by Dr. Hendrix. A second nurse ushered Will and Scott back out into the waiting area. Will could only see what was happening through the window, which was obscured by the slats of the privacy blind. He saw and heard the commotion around Jacoline and a loud beeping from one of the machines by her bed. Will knew this was it: they'd spent the last months doing everything she'd been too scared to do in the past. They'd done things that a mother and son should do, and found peace with one another. He watched, through the unforgiving slats of the blind, the last essence of life leaving his mother's frail body. Then, the doctors and nurses stopped their frantic behaviour. The room fell silent as they shook their heads solemnly at one another.

His mother's time on this earth was over; she would be at peace now. Scott banged on the glass, shouting, and Will watched him press his thumb and finger into his eyes. It was as if he was watching everything in slow motion – the noise around him was distant from his ears and he became an observer of fate.

That night, the wind blew strong in the darkness. Branches of the trees that lined the streets caned against themselves. Will and his father entered the family house in silence. Scott trod lightly up the stairs and sat on Jacoline's bed, Will followed and watched his father running his hand over the blankets. He picked up her bandana with the blue flowers and smelled it, squeezing it in his hand. Tears pushed through his closed eyes and he let out a roar. Will sat beside him and hugged him hard. He'd never seen such an emotional reaction from his father – ever.

"What am I going to do without her?" Scott's question was pleading. "We didn't have a perfect marriage, but we were always there, side by side, for thirty-four years. That's a long time."

Will didn't reply, but he felt a sudden surge of compassion for his softened father.

"She loved those Plumbagos," Scott gestured to a glass vase of wilting flowers by the bed. "She asked Sam to plant them all over." He opened the bedside drawer in search of tissues and saw a note in there wrapped around his and

Jacoline's wedding photo. He unwrapped the note, which was addressed to him.

*D*earest Scott,

Remember me like this. Remember how happy we were here. The world was ours. Do you remember where we met in London, just outside Trafalgar Square? You were so busy, you weren't looking where you were going and walked right into me! I remember it as if it were yesterday. You picked my bag up off the floor and handed it to me. I knew then that I was going to marry you.

I know you've been having a hard time trying to deal with my illness. I knew you were in here every night. We've got an amazing son; you have to help each other now. I'm sorry I wasn't a perfect wife. I tried my best.

All my love,

Jacoline xxx

*S*cott broke down again and sobbed on his son's shoulder. Will put his arm around him and rifled in the drawer, still looking for tissues. He discovered a small envelope addressed to him and slipped it into his jeans pocket.

After he'd put his devastated father to bed, Will went into his own room. The place was so silent and still. With exhaustion, and all emotions spent, he fished the envelope from his pocket and looked at it for a long moment. The writing on the front was childlike and sloped down towards the end. The envelope wasn't sealed, just tucked in, and for a moment Will wasn't sure he had the strength to read what was inside, but decided that he had to. The friction of the white paper as he opened it made a welcome familiar sound. Inside the envelope was a note folded into a small square, and something else. As he unfolded the square, a delicate clink sounded on his desk as his mother's diamond and emerald ring dropped out and landed on its edge, sparkling.

*T*o *my darling boy,*
You deserve all the happiness in the world. This ring is for you to give to someone special. Find happiness, that's all there ever is.
All my love,
Mum xxx

A ll the letters were different sizes, and the lines overlapped. Will could see that she had struggled to write the short note. He grasped the ring between his thumb and forefinger and scrutinised the diamond and emerald twist as if it was going to proffer him some sort of answer. He slipped the ring on to his little finger and climbed into bed, dog-tired. His eyelids drooped instantly and his heavy head fell into the pillow like a dead weight.

T he following morning, Will approached his dad, who was sitting on the terracotta-coloured leather couch in the living room surrounded by perfectly positioned and perpendicular furniture. He held the TV remote in his hand, although the machine wasn't switched on – he just sat and stared at the blank screen.

"Couldn't sleep?" Will asked.

"Not much, son. You?"

"Surprisingly, I slept well," Will replied. "I was drained."

Scott made a nondescript sound and continued to stare at the TV screen.

"Dad, we're going to have to talk about what happens now."

"The funeral, you mean?" Scott said numbly.

"No, that's organised already. I mean, after the funeral," Will clarified.

"After?"

"I need to go back to London, Dad. There's nothing for me here."

"Oh, thanks very much, Will. Your mother has only just died and you want to leave already! What am *I* supposed to do?" His father looked hurt.

"I didn't mean that, Dad – I just mean that my life isn't in South Africa anymore. I left someone important behind in London. I need to go and put it right." Scott had not detached his gaze from the blank TV screen and Will gently removed the remote from his father's hand, setting it down on the coffee table.

"Will, please stay," Scott asked, facing his son suddenly, his eyes wide. "At least for a while... I'm scared."

Will was taken aback, he'd never known his father to be scared of anything before. He was the impenetrable force – the face of iron.

"Scared?" Will shook his head, confused. "What are you scared of, Dad?"

"I don't want to be alone," Scott replied. Will saw that his dad was serious. "I don't know what I'll do in this house all alone. I don't think I can do it. You're all I've got left now, son. Maybe this is an opportunity – a blessing in disguise."

Internally, Will was fragmented. He could sense the pleading behind his father's words, desperation even. He knew Scott was trying to cling on to some sort of hope. *Could he really abandon him now?*

Scott spoke again: "You can join me in the business – you studied law anyway and I can train you up to work with me. Maybe we can make good on everything that's happened. Everything happens for a reason, you told me that. What do you say?"

Will didn't answer but looked at his father's hopeful face. He thought of Alice and how he'd left her; vulnerable to the world and her sorry circumstances. He felt the honesty and hope in Scott's words, like a veil had been lifted, revealing – finally – the man underneath the iron mask. Nervous energy jolted through every cell in his body as he pondered this crossroads. *Which decision was the right one?* No-one could give him the answer, and his life would work out completely differently depending on his choice.

He did not answer, but he knew he couldn't wait at the crossroads forever.

Chapter Thirteen

The glass of water was waiting on the side table, and next to it, two red capsules of Venlafaxine. Alice had been on the maximum dose for just under a year; it hadn't helped – not one bit. Every day she did not want to live. She was trapped in the nightmare scenario of the mechanical theatre piece she'd adored so much when she was young, except that there was no off switch. Her dull, ebony hair lay wild, recently cut bluntly by her own hand when she'd become angry at her reflection; the reality of her useless, limp existence.

The phone rang in its shrill, demanding tone and made Alice jump. She picked up the receiver, wishing she hadn't as soon as she heard the slurred greeting on the other end.

"Sweet pea! Darling girl! How art thou on this fine day?"

"Why do you have to be so theatrical?" she asked, annoyed.

"Oh, you're such a bore, O miserable one! Why art thou such a misery?"

"Did you have something to say, Dad?"

"Actually, I missed you. I haven't seen you in weeks," he garbled.

"It's months," Alice said flatly, her father's false enthusiasm prickling her.

"Oh…Well, what have you been doing, then?" he asked.

Alice could say that she'd been suffering, researching the best combination of pills that would take her life without the risk of the attempt failing. She could say that she'd been taking more and more sleeping pills to try and knock herself out at night just to have a few hours of not feeling empty. But she didn't say any of this to Christopher. He didn't even remember the night that he'd come over to April's – he had no idea that Alice had attempted suicide, he just carried on as he always did, destroying everything he touched.

"Applying for jobs, not much else," she lied.

"Can I meet you somewhere, to talk?" her dad asked.

"You were meant to meet me a few weeks ago, do you remember? I waited for you for an hour." There was silence on the other end of the phone. "Are you still there?" she asked. Her question was answered with muffled wailing and sniffing.

"I'm a terrible father! I know, Alice. I know I've let you down. Maybe I should just jump in the Thames and have done with it," through his exaggerated tones was a blunt hit of honesty, stained with Christopher's personal blend of emotional blackmail. Alice knew they both played their parts as comfortably as a hand fits a glove; Alice assumed the role of rescuer and Christopher played the victim. Even as she spoke, she was tiring of the cabaret they performed. This particular show was on its last curtain call.

"Dad, don't say that. Things aren't that bad. There's

still time to make things… better," she just about managed to squeeze the lie out of her mouth.

"No, it's too late," he groaned.

"I'll meet you, okay?" she surrendered, predictably. There was silence for a moment, followed by the sound of Christopher wiping his nose.

"Do you hate me, Alice?"

"No Dad, I don't hate you."

"You ought to hate me, darling girl. I wish you did. If you hated me, I could leave this place."

She knew what he meant; he wanted life about as much as she did. The emotion rose in her throat and she swallowed it back expertly.

"Meet me tomorrow outside the old cinema at noon, okay?" she said and ended the call.

She sat on the floor of her bedroom, observing the bloodstain that had never quite come out of the carpet. She wondered vaguely what Christopher wanted to talk to her about, but didn't pay the thought much attention. There was a time when he'd woken her up in the middle of the night to ask her what the difference was between a bee and a wasp – it could be something just as trivial tomorrow.

Alice cast her mind back to all the times she'd cleaned up Christopher's vomit, the first being when she was six years old. She'd held his hand and told him things would be okay as she watched him puke into a paper bag, his eyes bulging, bloodshot and watering with the pressure behind them. She'd had enough. Nineteen years was long enough to be the parent to her father.

Alice's thoughts turned to McAvoy then. She did not know what to do with the love within her when the recipient was not there to receive it. It seemed to have turned rancid, corroding her insides like acid. *Can love really do such a thing?* she pondered. Despite the knowledge of all her issues and everything that had accumulated to bring her to this moment in her life, the connection with Will had been real, the feelings were swirling and alive. It hadn't stopped hurting. She wondered when losing him would stop feeling like her heart was being tightened in a vice. Wasn't a year long enough for it to start feeling better – at least a little?

April had been wholly accommodating – at first. Alice could tell she was subconsciously trying to make up for the unspoken incident which Alice still had a reminder of in the form of a scar on the side of her head, where her hair no longer grew. Her mother had spent a few weeks buying Alice trinkets for her bedroom and having wine and movie nights with her; the sort of things mothers and daughters are supposed to do together. The smiles were false; like the painted lips on ventriloquist's dummies. Mother and daughter existed together – that was all.

As the time approached seven pm, Alice pulled on some jeans and leather boots. The jeans hung off her shrinking frame, her hip bones rubbing against the denim. She ruffed up her hair with her fingers and grabbed her black coat. She wore thick silver chains around her neck that were almost chokers and small silver rings all the way up to her left ear. Her mother hadn't approved of the one that appeared in her nose after a trip into town – she didn't approve of many things her daughter did lately.

"I'm going out, I'll be back later," Alice shouted to April, who was chain smoking in the living room. Before she could make it out of the doorway, her mother's shadow appeared behind her.

"Let me see your arms," April demanded.

"I'm meeting someone, I'll be late," Alice replied.

"Have you been cutting again, Alice?"

"No. I'll see you later," Alice exited through the front door before April could say another word.

She walked to the local pub where she went most nights, having made friends with a gang of misfits in their forties and fifties. They drank and smoked; Alice did, too. They spoke about this and that, escaping from their lives for a while. Alice liked the distraction, she didn't have to be a depressive self-harmer when she was there; she didn't have to think about McAvoy. She could be whatever she wanted.

Later that night, after too many vodka and cokes, Alice went home with Reggae Dave – a skinny, white man with dreadlocks and a fondness for playing Bob Marley songs on the jukebox. She got on with him well enough; she wanted him to make her forget her life for a while. His flat was just a short walk from the pub and on arrival, Alice let Reggae Dave lead her straight into the bedroom. The smell of weed and damp filled her nostrils, and she sat on the bed, which she noticed was covered in cat hair. Reggae Dave kissed her clumsily, groping her breasts; Alice went along with the motions. He pushed his tongue so far into her mouth she thought she might gag; he tasted like alcohol and cigarettes. He didn't smell like aftershave, or like anything really, except unwashed hair. He took off his ripped jeans, pants and 'Alice In Chains' band T-shirt, quickly flinging them on the floor, and climbed into the bed, still wearing his socks. Alice figured she should undress too and get into the cat hair covered bed. She lay there, noticing how messy his bedroom was as he searched blindly for a condom. There were rows upon rows of CDs stacked in no particular order. Alice noticed an old faded tattoo on Reggae Dave's upper arm, which she couldn't make out in the dim light.

"Got one!" he announced proudly and started

unrolling the rubber over his semi-hard erection, having lost the initial excitement with all the fumbling around. "Here, grab this," he told Alice, putting her hand on his penis. Alice did what was required, not that she really knew what was required, having never had a penis in her hand before now. "Put it in your mouth for a bit," he told her, and she obliged, her mouth full of the taste of the latex condom. She felt him get harder as she sucked, then he climbed on top of her, penetrating her forcefully, and Alice squeezed her eyes shut at the physical pain inside her; the pain of being fucked. Alice looked out of the window while Reggae Dave continued to pound her as he groaned and gained momentum. She suddenly felt very sober, she suddenly missed McAvoy more than she ever had and tears were pricking behind her eyes. After one last massive groan from Reggae Dave, his sweaty body went limp, and he rested his weight a little too hard on her small frame, squeezing her ribs under his dead weight. She was thankful when he rolled off her and discarded the filled condom, fumbled around for a spliff he'd made earlier, and lit up.

Alice lay there unmoving for a while, wondering why she had just done what she'd done. Her stomach was tight with a heavy feeling she couldn't place. She shared the spliff with Reggae Dave, then made her escape when he rolled over and started snoring.

It was cold as she walked home that night. She felt numb apart from the warm pain between her legs. He hadn't distracted her from her torturing thoughts. If anything, the encounter had only reminded her that her first time should have been with someone who cared about her, and not a meaningless fuck that lasted for seven minutes. Alice's virginity had gone to a loser, but what did it matter, anyway?

April was asleep when Alice got home, and she headed

straight for the shower. The bathroom soon filled up with steam from the too-hot water, and Alice scrubbed her body hard until it was pink and blotchy. She took a bar of soap and vigorously washed away any trace of Reggae Dave from between her thighs – she didn't want his smell on her, or the residue of his sweat.

Alice cried herself to sleep, squeezing her black plush stuffed dog against her face as she did most nights now. She had bought it for herself a few months ago – a small comfort to hold during the long nights when her darkest thoughts surfaced.

***

A lice lit up a cigarette and sucked hard while she waited outside the old cinema. She watched people walking by and cars driving past. The hair on her arms stood on end in the winter weather, and the rapidly reddening tip of her nose was the only colour to her pallid complexion. She was about to start walking away when she saw the familiar figure walking towards her. Alice greeted him emotionlessly and noticed that he looked older than the last time she'd seen him a few months ago.

"Hi, sweet pea," Christopher's alcoholic breath made her hold her own for a moment. She could gauge that although he'd only had a couple of drinks that morning, it merely added a fresh layer to weeks of accumulated alcohol odour.

"Hi," Alice replied flatly.

"Let's walk," Christopher said, and they soon found a nearby coffee shop to get warm in.

"So, how are things?" he asked.

"Okay," Alice said.

"I heard that you're on antidepressants," her father looked her in the eye.

"From who?" she enquired, suspiciously.

"Does it matter?" Christopher asked.

Alice sipped a coffee the waitress had just brought over, looking at her father blankly.

"What's wrong, Alice?"

"I really wouldn't know where to start, Dad," she said, the line in between her eyebrows deepening with the anger that was surfacing. "I've been struggling for most of the year, and you were nowhere to be found. I moved out of gran and grandad's because of you, because you make everything worse with your self-pitying alcoholic bullshit. So, forgive me if I don't suddenly want to have a heart-to-heart with you over cheap sugary coffee."

Christopher looked stung.

"I'm sorry," he whispered.

"Yeah, me too," Alice replied coolly and stared out of the window.

"I'm going to tell you something that not many people know about, Alice," her father spoke after a moment. "Only granny and grandad know, not even your mother knows. I'm very aware of how much I've fucked everything up and I'm still doing it, but I can't get their faces out of my head."

"Whose faces?" Alice asked, looking Christopher in the eye now.

"Years before I met your mother, I was with someone for seven years. Her name was Joanne. Joanne and I had two children together – a boy and a girl."

"What?!" Alice asked, taken aback, "I've got half-siblings?"

"You did," Christopher paused, rubbing his temples

with both hands, "They died in a house fire, along with their mother."

The sorrow was written all over his face. Alice couldn't believe what she was hearing. "Their names were Toby and Emily. They were two and four years old. Emily had blonde hair and Toby had dark hair like yours, both had blue eyes like me. I failed them. I was supposed to protect them and I let them die."

"What do you mean? What happened?" asked Alice, wide-eyed, eager for her dad to continue speaking.

"I'd gone for a stupid night out with some people from work. I didn't even want to go, but it was my first teaching job and Joanne said I should go and be sociable – you know, make an effort. While I was out and they were sleeping, a fire started in the house. It was reported to be faulty wiring. They had no chance of getting out... my poor babies..." Christopher broke down into sobs and people in the coffee shop started to look at him and Alice. She held her dad's hand and told him it was okay, though she knew that it wasn't.

"Joanne had managed to lock them all in the bedroom, but by the time the fire brigade were called, the smoke had got to them. I'll never forget seeing them lifeless and cold; my angels, all three of them. If I hadn't had gone out, maybe I could have saved them..."

"Or you could have died, too," said Alice, with sadness.

"I wish I had, Alice. Well, I can't say that, otherwise you wouldn't exist now, and you're the best thing in my life. But I've ruined that, too."

"It wasn't your fault, Dad. You can't blame yourself forever."

"But I do. I can't live with the guilt or the sadness. I thought I could have a family again, but I ruined it all. That's the truth of why I drink, Alice. It blocks out what

I've done, but it never lasts. Something needs to change – it's time for change."

"What do you mean 'it's time for a change'?" Alice asked, just as her phone rang on the table beside her. She looked at it, not recognising the number, and looked back at Christopher.

"Answer it," Christopher told her as he blew his nose on a serviette. Alice reluctantly took the call outside and she could see her father watching her through the glass pane. A little jolt of excitement ran through her as she ended the brief call, but she was more preoccupied with what her dad was getting at just before her phone rang. She re-entered the coffee shop, sat opposite her dad again and looked at him.

"Well?" he said, "Who was that?"

"It was the council – I've got an interview for a library assistant job. I applied a few weeks back."

"That's fabulous darling, well done you! I'm sure you'll get it."

"Yes, maybe," she replied, "but let's get back to what we were talking about. It's important."

"I'll tell you everything you want to know Alice, okay. I'll be honest. But what I wanted to tell you was…," he looked at his daughter, frown lines forming on his fore-head, Alice looked back at him with anticipation.

"I'm going to India," he declared.

"Oh, to see Auntie Jane?"

"Well, yes – Auntie Jane has invited me to stay. I need to sort myself out and I can't do it here. I'm not the father I want to be, or the person I am capable of being. All I'm doing is messing your life up. Maybe if I can get away from it all, I can change."

"Away from me?"

"No, not from you. I mean yes, I will be away from

you, but you are not the problem. Do you understand that? I'm doing this for you, to be better *for* you."

"How long are you going for?" Alice asked, with a sudden sadness that her dad would be so far away.

"As long as it takes," he replied, his eyes bloodshot with tears.

Alice paused to process this information and took her dad's hand in hers "Then go. Go and find out how to be a better person."

"I'll miss you so much, Alice," he said. "I don't know what the journey holds, but I'll be thinking about you every day, and I'll write. I don't know how you became such a good, wise, beautiful person. I know I can't take the credit for it. You have more strength in your little finger than I have in my entire body, and I'm so proud of you."

A tear fell from Alice's eye and her dad caught it on the tip of his finger. "Can I keep this?" he asked. Alice smiled, and for a while they just sat there, not speaking and not needing to, a perfect reflection of each other.

Chapter Fourteen

5 years later

Michael unpacked his delivery of flower essences and lined up the small brown bottles neatly in his drawer labelled *treatments*.

The cupboards and drawers of his office were full to the brim with herbs, homeopathic treatments and various oils and liquids. Everything had a label, and Michael knew just where to look if he needed something in particular. His office occupied the spare room of his house; it was just the right size for what he needed. The dominating Victorian medicine cabinet where he stored his items was made from white painted metal that had tarnished over the years – there were a few rusting dents here and there and the cabinet was uncharacteristic with the warmth and character of the other rooms in his home. Michael had fallen in love with the medicine cabinet one day at an antique's fair. Despite knowing it would not fit with his usual decor, he'd bought it there and then; a rare and beautiful find.

The cabinet seemed to carry energy of the past; he

visualised it in an old hospital, stacked with calligraphically labelled bottles and tinctures. It gave him comfort to think it had perhaps belonged to doctors who had tried to make a difference for the better. There was a twinge in the pit of Michael's stomach as memories came flooding in of doctors who hadn't done their best – doctors who had flouted the agreement they were supposed to abide by: 'Do no harm'. He swallowed his anger down as he remembered the interactions he'd had with them over the years; he wasn't going to let those memories ruin his day today.

Michael had seen one patient that morning: a regular he was working with to help alleviate depression, anxiety and weight issues. He used functional medicine to treat his patients holistically, rather than suppressing symptoms with traditional prescriptions, which was standard practice, Michael discovered, whilst earning his medical degree.

He'd thought of George during the session; the best friend he'd had for a few precious years and the catalyst for him to embark on the study of medicine. Michael's heart still squeezed when he thought of George and the dimming light he'd noticed in his eyes as he'd got increasingly unwell. The waning glow had reminded Michael of the batteries in his childhood toys when they'd started to run low; sometimes there was just a little life left until they gradually wound down to a complete stop. George had accepted his fate and Michael could only watch it unfold, powerlessly. He made a life decision right then that he would not fall prey to illness if there was anything he could do about it – especially given his circumstances.

Michael eyed the little private box he kept under his desk. This one was filled with his own personal treatments and remedies. He reached into the box and selected a flower essence bottle, placing the dropper under his tongue. Amongst the various sizes and shapes of blue and brown bottles were two white plastic containers with prescription labels stuck to them. Michael unscrewed one of the containers and tipped out two tablets, which he set aside on his desk next to a glass of water. He took these tablets at regular intervals, as he had done every day for so long now that it had become second nature. Michael took a deep breath, leaned back in his office chair, and closed his eyes.

He allowed himself a certain amount of time each day to think about the woman he cared about. He had liked her from the moment he had first encountered her at the library, where'd she started as the new manager. She'd smiled at him and told him to have a nice day. The more he saw her, the more he liked her. She had sleek black hair that seemed to swish when she moved. He liked her long limbs, her graceful and light movements; there was always a smile waiting for him. He looked forward to talking to her, and the little ritual they had begun together once a week at late night closing. It was Michael's weekly highlight, although he knew it couldn't go any further than that. If she knew the truth, she would never want him.

His racing thoughts turned then to a particularly stoic male consultant haematologist he'd seen as a teenager. The man's white hair was short and blunt, standing up like a stubbly haystack, he'd kept the appointment concise and to the point. He'd callously told Michael not to bother with relationships, telling him there was no point because no-one would want him once they knew. This truth from a stranger settled in Michael's belief system, and twenty-five years on, he was still living his life by the harsh words of a cruel man who was probably dead now. Michael reasoned that he was too old for this young woman in any case – *what would she see in him?* He hated the insecurities that crept up on him from a place hidden so deeply he forgot it was there.

Michael rarely dwelled on the hand he'd been dealt; he knew the importance of a positive mindset for his health's sake. He had bent and broken his psyche until it had moulded into what he needed it to be. He'd done the work on himself; he was an awakened man, and yet in the quiet moments within his day, he felt a pang of loneliness and a longing to give and receive the love he was capable of.

He'd made it his life's mission to help others through healing. He'd worked hard, got his qualifications, bought a nice home and still there was a hole within him that wasn't filled. He hadn't expected to become attracted to this unsuspecting woman who dominated his thoughts and gave him silent hope. He knew attraction is never a choice, only the action taken upon it is. He couldn't allow himself to venture into this delicate territory with her. What if it ruined the sort-of friendship they had built up together? Michael decided he could care about her from a distance and still enjoy feeling the fierce beating of his heart in anticipation of seeing her. He could enjoy the fluttering in his stomach and the slight dampness that presented on his palms in her presence. His heart had been cracked open by this attraction, even though she didn't know it. Perhaps that was the reason he'd met her – to allow his heart to open once more, and now that it was open, he reasoned with himself that this would just have to be enough – *wouldn't it?*

From the outside, no-one would ever know Michael's secret. He wondered if maybe it was possible for someone to love him for how he was once he had come clean. He had never exposed his depths before – the unspoken truths that lurked beneath the surface. Now he was toying with the idea that there could be possibilities previously unthinkable to him before.

'*Alice Wilde*' he'd read on her nametag six months ago. She'd pulled a lever somewhere within him that had started a ball rolling through a vast set of twists, turns and obstacles in Michael's mind. It reminded him of a game of Screwball Scramble he had once played at George's house. Sometimes he imagined telling this woman everything – the secret that had ruined his life – and fantasised that she would wrap her long arms around him and say that it didn't matter. He squeezed his eyes shut and thought about it so hard that maybe, if he kept on imagining, it would come true.

Michael's thoughts were interrupted by the shrill ring of the doorbell. He pottered over to the door and let the expected caller inside. She flicked her long red hair over her shoulder as she entered.

"Okay, Mister," said the redhead, setting down her bag of tricks on the floor and pulling her hair up into a high pony tail, which she secured with a black band. "Are you ready for me?"

Michael nodded and started unbuttoning his shirt.

"Be gentle with me today, Elise," he said.

"Aren't I always, sweetheart?" She winked at him as he led her into the bedroom and closed the door behind them.

Chapter Fifteen

Alice walked back to her rented flat, close to where she worked. It wasn't fancy, but it was home. Her little kitchen was her haven; it had a small window that overlooked communal gardens and trees from the second storey. Somehow, having that little window made all the difference. She would look out as she cooked, blended, chopped and whisked. Alice was not a microwave meal kind of girl; there were fresh herbs on the windowsill – basil, rosemary and coriander. Their smell gave her hope and focus. When Alice had been battling depression, she'd started cooking, reading about natural cures for depression and all the ingredients necessary for a healthy brain. She'd quit smoking and started running; each furious thud on the concrete was a step towards recovery. The ground swallowed her sorrows as she ran and ran until her heart was ready to burst. She started writing down recipes and making herbal tonics. Little by little, she became less sad. The gap in her heart began to heal over – at least on the surface.

C ooking was how she filled her time now that she had a lot of it. She was alone but not lonely, and she'd finally found a balance that didn't depend on anyone else. Alice didn't have a television, just a bookshelf brimming with non-fiction, self-improvement reading material. She went for walks that took hours, passing the allotments and enjoying views of the sun setting on the little sheds and growing plots; they were pieces of people's salvation, too, and the thought of this made her smile. Sometimes, though, she wanted to share these thoughts with someone else, or send someone a text message about what had happened in her day. Alice was beginning to notice that even though she was okay as she was, she was missing that connection that most people crave: someone to share things with, laugh with, love. Perhaps she wasn't so unusual after all.

Alice took out her yoga mat and changed into some leggings and a grey sweatshirt, scraped her hair into a messy ponytail and started moving into her regular poses. She stayed in downward dog for a while, feeling fresh energy flowing through her brain. The pull on her calves felt good, like it was wringing out her day. Alice had kept her heart sealed up after Will McAvoy, packing it away safely like a box of Christmas decorations kept up in the loft. The thought of him didn't make her want to cry anymore, except on occasions when she was feeling extra sensitive or he had invaded one of her dreams. She had put him away somewhere in the attic of her mind to gather dust; an unanswered question, an experience unfulfilled.

In her darkest days, Alice had let men touch her, do what they wanted to her, and she'd switched off, unemotional, like a ragdoll. They got close to her body but not to her heart – never her heart. In those desperate times, when she couldn't fuck her misery away, she would try to release it with a scalpel. After four years of trying to cure her pain with more pain, she realised it would never serve her purpose.

As she moved into corpse pose, Alice stared at the light fitting above her. It was fashioned from frosted white glass to look like a lotus flower. Alice counted the glass petals and took deep breaths in and out. In an hour she would go to visit Hetty and Bill, as she did once or twice a week. She had a routine, a good life, but there was something lacking – an echo of longing within her.

T hursday came – the day of late closing time at the library, where Alice had worked her way up to become the manager. There was one hour to go and Alice went into the staffroom to make a drink. Before she got to the kettle, she stopped in front of the mirror and moved her finger across her bottom lip to smudge in a bit of inconsistent lipstick. She smoothed down her long, straightened hair and short fringe. She was pleased enough that she looked presentable, apart from the white raised tracks along her left arm. She never bothered to hide her scars; they were part of her past. In fact, she only remembered she had them when someone commented from time to time.

Alice looked forward to Thursdays, to her visits from Michael. He'd been coming every week like clockwork for the past six months, and she had observed that he usually checked out books on nutrition and health. She liked that about him. Her stomach flipped with anticipation as she waited for him to walk through the door at any minute. She filled the kettle and flicked on the switch, listening intently to the hiss and bubble of the boiling water. The steam rose steadily from the spout; it seemed to take forever. Alice put two teabags into the waiting cups, and as expected, heard the door click open a moment later.

In walked Michael Enver at 6 pm on the dot, wearing dark blue jeans and a long-sleeved shirt with cufflinks. Alice always assumed he'd come straight from work, although she never asked if he had.

"Hello, Dear One," he greeted as he saw her head pop out briefly from behind the staffroom door. There was no-one else in the small, quiet building besides the pair.

"Just a minute," Alice called, her cheeks suddenly feeling hot. She fanned herself with a copy of the council's free newspaper that she'd spotted on the table in the staffroom, thinking how ridiculous she would feel if Michael could see what she was doing. At that moment, she was grateful for the thin wall that separated them. When she had composed herself, Alice walked out of the staffroom carrying the two cups of tea and set them down on the table where Michael had seated himself.

"You are an angel, do you know that?" he said with a smile, picking up the steaming brew, blowing over its surface and putting it down again without taking a sip.

Alice smiled in reply, feeling butterflies in her belly – the way she always felt around Michael. She sat opposite him and noticed how well his shirt fitted over his chest; tight, but not too tight. His aftershave was a grounding scent with deep notes that aroused something inside her.

"So, Michael Enver, what's new?"

"Ah, not much, Alice Wilde. I'm working on a book at the moment, did I tell you?"

"No," she replied, "That's exciting! What's it about?"

"I won't bore you, dearest, but the gist of it is natural therapies as treatments for viruses. You know, nerdy stuff."

"That's amazing – and it's not nerdy," Alice said. "You're really smart."

"I'm not that smart," he said, a coy smile on his lips.

"Yeah, okay, *Dr. Michael!*" she replied, laughing.

"Well, I guess I am a bit smart then," he conceded. Alice nudged his arm playfully and surveyed him while he picked up his tea and took a small sip.

"No biscuits today? You've lured me here under false pretences," he said with mock indignity.

"Sorry," she said, "trying to eat healthily."

"Don't tell me you're on a diet, because seriously…" he scanned her body without finishing his sentence and Alice could see the embarrassment on his face, she knew he hadn't meant to 'check her out' so obviously, it didn't fit with the gentlemanly way he had about him. Still, she was pleased that he had looked at her in that way.

"Anyway, Michael, your book thing is amazing," she attempted to save his blushes by changing the subject. "If only you knew a library manager that could get your book on our shelves," she teased.

"Hmmm, but what would I have to do to earn such favour?" He raised an eyebrow at Alice and her cheeks flushed at the playful exchange between them.

"We'll have to see, won't we?" she replied. She noticed that his blue eyes lit up when he spoke about something that excited him. He became animated and Alice soaked up his positive energy.

Michael's hair was mostly grey, hanging in soft-looking curls, and when he smiled, dimples formed in his cheeks. Alice liked his angular jawline and the little line that traced the shape of his top lip, more prominently when he smiled. She looked at his hands fiddling with the cup of half drank tea. She wanted those hands on her, imagining them sliding from her neck, down her naked back, to her waist.

She was biting her lip as Michael spoke, as though she had lost track of what he was saying.

"Alice, are you okay? You look miles away. I'm not boring you, am I?" Michael asked.

"No, gosh Michael, I don't think you could ever bore me. Sorry, I was just having a thought. What were you saying?"

"Well, I was just saying that I enjoy these Thursdays, dearest. Gives an old man something to look forward to," he told her.

"You're only forty-six – that's not old," she replied. Michael smiled then.

"And how do you know I'm forty-six? I've never told you that."

"Erm…intuition," Alice fibbed, pulling a face at having been caught out. She had discovered previously that he was exactly forty-six and a half, having worked it out from the date of birth on his library record.

"Intuition, eh? Well, your senses are not to be argued with." He winked at Alice. "That's old though, isn't it?" he asked. She could tell that he was looking for some approval on the question of age.

"You're not old, Michael. You're… distinguished," she laughed, wondering if she'd said the right thing.

"Distinguished, eh? I'll take that," he replied, and he seemed to relax a little more. "Anyway, dearest, last time we talked, you told me your father lived in India, how did that come about?"

"It's a bit complicated," Alice began, then paused and rubbed her earlobe; a subconscious self-comfort action she'd developed in the last few years.

"That's okay, I've got time."

"I mentioned that he had problems with alcohol, didn't I?" Alice said.

"You did," he replied.

"Well, he went to stay with his sister – my auntie Jane. She's lived over there for years, teaching English as a foreign language. My dad and I were really in a bad place. He was wasting his life on drink and he decided to cut his losses and start afresh. He writes to me every week, he said he would, and he kept his promise."

"So, how do you feel about him being over there?" Michael enquired, his head slightly to one side as he scrutinised her face.

"Good, I think. I miss him, but at least I have some sort of functioning relationship with him now. He's been travelling around Asia. I can tell he's changed by the way he talks and writes. He's my dad again. He does all this healing stuff now. Last time he wrote, he was teaching reiki and yoga in Goa. So, even though he's over there, I'd rather him be there and happy than here and not happy."

Michael nodded in acknowledgement.

"I understand. It's difficult when insecurities and issues engulf a person. It's very difficult to break free." He looked a little sad as he spoke, then picked up his teacup and took a sip.

"So, what's your secret?" Alice asked, causing Michael to splutter his tea slightly. He wiped his mouth with his hand and looked embarrassed for the second time during their meeting that day.

"What do you mean, 'secret'?" he asked her, his face serious.

"Well, you know some of mine. Tell me some of yours," she said. Michael looked at her nervously for a long moment before answering.

"I'm quite boring, really. You know I'm into the herbs and all that jazz. My parents are pretty normal, apart from my dad's weird fascination with garden gnomes. No brothers or sisters, and my guilty pleasure is Fleetwood Mac songs. That's about it."

"Well, you're a nice man – you've never mentioned a relationship. I'm surprised, I thought you'd be married." Alice flushed slightly at what had just popped out of her mouth, seemingly by its own volition.

"Erm... I guess it's hard to find the right person. That's so cliché, isn't it?" Alice noted him rub the back of his neck self-consciously.

"A little. But that doesn't mean it isn't true," Alice replied softly to ease Michael's nervous smile.

"I always wanted the whole nine yards; lots of kids running about, a loving partner, a house with a rainbow over the top, y'know, all that stuff. I even thought about adopting before now."

"Awww, that's really sweet, Michael. It's never too late, I'm sure you'd make a great dad," Alice smiled at him, feeling secretly glad that they were on the same wavelength.

"And you?" he asked with interest. "I can't believe a beautiful and interesting young woman like yourself hasn't got a queue of men waiting." Alice laughed a little louder than anticipated, feeling her cheeks flame again. "Well, I'm a bit weird, you know – and also I've been through quite a lot of emotional stuff. Someone really hurt me once, and quite honestly, it put me off opening my heart up again. I don't want to get into the details though, if you don't mind. I'll need to start locking up in a minute. Time flies, eh?"

Michael looked at his watch.

"I didn't realise that was the time already. There's literally not been a single customer in the last forty-five minutes. I'll just wait with you until you lock up, can't be too careful."

"That's kind, but I'm a big girl. I don't need protecting." The words seemed to come from a deep defensive trigger and Alice didn't know why she said them. She wanted Michael to stay for as long as possible.

"I'm sure you can hold your own. Just humour me. I'd feel much better if you let me wait with you," he said.

"Okay," Alice replied, feeling butterflies in her stomach again. Michael was ticking boxes without even realising it. She started switching off the computers while he busied himself washing up the teacups.

"You're after a job aren't you?" Alice asked, digging him in the ribs playfully as he walked past her. Michael raised his eyebrows and shot her a look that was so unintentionally sexy that Alice almost forgot what she was doing. She switched off the lights and they left the building together, Michael opening the door for Alice on the way out.

"Such a gentleman. See you next week then I guess?" Alice said, with more than a hint of hope in her voice.

"Maybe," Michael replied, winking at her as he turned and walked the opposite way.

Alice walked home in five minutes and immediately started her yoga routine on her return. She played Michael's voice through her head as she went through her poses; his kind words, the tone of his laugh. She imagined kissing him and her body was immediately aroused at the thought. In her mind he was passionate and she imagined him pushing her hard against the wall, gripping her hair and pinning his body against hers. She imagined what he would feel like inside her, exchanging energy with a person who cared about her, maybe even making love for the first time in her life at the age of twenty-four instead of the mechanical sex of her dark days. She breathed out hard and let her head fall to the side on the hard, wooden floor. On her bookshelf, right at the bottom left-hand corner was a sight that she hadn't set eyes on for a while. The tattered spine of *Jane Eyre* in white typeface on a black background, bold as brass. She had almost forgotten about the book Will had given her so many years ago – almost. That book had witnessed the depths of her sorrows, and there was a little tug of emotion deep in her belly. Alice ignored it and turned away from the book, looking back up at the glass petals on the ceiling before moving into her next position.

W hen Michael arrived home, he was still buzzing from Alice's energy. He headed straight for the fridge to heat up some pumpkin soup he'd made the day before, and as usual, he spoke to the photo of George stuck to the refrigerator door with magnets.

"Just maybe," he told the inanimate image of his late friend. And George, as always, looked back at him with his lanky frame and mousy brown scruff of hair.

When Michael and George were both twenty-five they were playing football as they usually did every Tuesday afternoon on the common near to where they both lived. George had fallen over for no reason at all and hadn't been able to regain his balance from light-headedness. Michael had taken him back home to his mother's house.

Following the strange event, the days and weeks passed by, with Michael noticing that George wasn't at the support groups they usually attended together to deal with what had happened to them both. He hadn't been to visit Michael as he always did a few times a week, either. Michael had knocked on for his friend a couple of times but was told by George's mum that he wasn't well enough to see anyone, and that she would pass a message on. One particular day Michael visited, George – ever the rebel –

had heard his friend's voice and sneaked out of the back door to see him.

"Oi," he said, in a weaker voice than Michael had remembered. Michael spun round and was shocked to see the transformation that had taken place over just a few short weeks. George had always been tall and stringy – like a beanpole – but he was so thin now he seemed to struggle to hold himself upright.

"Jesus Christ. What's wrong?" Michael blurted out.

"It's my time. I can't shift this chest infection, and apparently I've got a kidney infection, too. Everything hurts, man." George mustered a smile, but he already looked like he was tiring of standing outside in the cold.

Michael noticed that George's tongue was coated with thick white mucous when he spoke.

"They can treat you, George, they can give you antibiotics, you need the hospital," Michael almost choked on the words. He knew they were empty. He could see in George's sallow eyes that the light was dimming. It almost didn't look like his face anymore. His once enthusiastic movements were frail and his cheekiness didn't quite mask the solemnity it hid, as if he was trying to recapture something that had gone. George's body was being ravaged by infections that he couldn't fight off, and Michael could not only see that he was losing his friend, but was faced with a mirror for his own mortality.

"I discharged myself from the hospital. My body is failing, they more or less said it's too late for me now," George spoke weakly. "I don't want to die in hospital with tubes in my veins." He glanced over his shoulder, "I've got to go now mate, my mum will do her nut if she finds me out here. You're my best friend, you know that?"

"You're mine, too," Michael replied, trying to suppress the tears he could feel forming in the back of his eyes.

"Why didn't you tell me?" he said, his voice breaking with emotion.

"I didn't want you to be upset. I'm scared, mate," George said, suddenly bursting into tears and falling to the floor. Michael joined him, and the pair sat embracing each other for the first and last time, on the cold stone floor beneath them. Neither uttered another word.

Three days later, George's mother paid a visit to Michael to tell him the inevitable news – George was gone. Michael smashed a hole in the wall with his fist that day. He was angry for George; his life was only just beginning, and it had been taken away unfairly and much too soon. It was on that day that Michael had decided he was going to study medicine. His life had been shaped by George's experience, and he'd be damned if he was going to watch anyone else needlessly die. If he could do anything to stop that, he would.

He took two tablets from the familiar white bottle and swallowed them dry. *Alice wouldn't want him*. The harsh thought surfaced in his brain and brought all the pleasantness of his evening with her crashing down. Why would a young woman waste her time on someone old and sick? Stupid fool, he punished himself. Stupid fool.

Chapter Sixteen

C hristopher sipped his morning chai in the Indian sunshine, listening as the waves gently rolled over the sand towards him. The air was warm and Anjuna market was already busy with a hubbub of sellers. They let him be nowadays, now that he was as good as a local. With his bare feet in the sand, Christopher petted a cow that had plonked itself down just within reach of his fingertips. He practised Pranayama every morning, which he'd learnt in his yoga study; he felt glad to be alive.

Christopher had beaten the odds and thrown off his demons after being dragged down by them for so many years. What were the chances that he could have clawed himself out of the mess he was in? He couldn't explain where the inner strength had come from, nor the series of synchronicities that had led him to start finding himself and learning about various healing techniques that had originated in Eastern medicine. He could only conclude that the universe had given him a massive leg-up in an effort to help him save himself.

He was grateful to his parents for loaning him the

money to get a plane ticket in the first place, and for the unwavering patience of his sister, Jane. After staying with Jane initially in Bangalore, Christopher had travelled to an ashram in Kerala as he began his spiritual journey. Since then, he'd followed the will of the universe, visiting various ashrams, volunteering at retreats in exchange for meals and a room, and started learning skills he could teach. He now held regular yoga and ayurvedic healing classes, mostly for English and American seekers of enlightenment. He guided people on various journeys, including those in the throes of mid-life crises, recovering addicts, and others who had simply become lost in life. Christopher celebrated his sobriety each morning with a ritual of tea and gratitude.

Something had awakened in him that day at the grave-yard in London, where he seemingly spoke with the spirit of Father Oakley. He knew this was some sort of communication from spirit. He missed Alice and wrote to her without fail once a fortnight. Initially, Christopher felt guilty that he'd left her behind, but reasoned that he wasn't bringing any good to her life. He was dragging her into his toxic thought patterns and victimhood. He came to find peace with his decision through the process of reconditioning his thoughts, his feelings, his practices – his whole being. Eventually, Christopher learned to forgive himself, and was able to release all the guilt that had weighed him down like a ball and chain. He realised that forgiveness comes in its own sweet time; it cannot be forced or enticed along.

Forgiveness, he thought, was like a lotus flower that blooms when it's ready and not on anyone else's schedule. He found joy in this notion and noticed now how human nature is to try and force things along instead of letting them unfold. He watched people try to force happiness, force forgiveness, force healing – force connections instead of observing themselves and honouring where they are right now. He used to be one of those people too; he was glad not to be that way anymore. Christopher had carved out a meaningful existence for himself here in India, but there was a nagging pull right at the back of his mind: his daughter was nearly five thousand miles away.

C hristopher had recently returned from Vietnam. The trip had sealed his faith that he was on the right pathway. He had spent some time in a magnificent stone temple, cool and comforting under his bare feet. Smoke from the incense stick he lit inside the grand arch had risen in a straight line before dispersing into curls that danced through the air. He'd sat and faced the vast golden Buddha before him, adorned with flower necklaces at its gigantic feet, smoking incense sticks and notes containing prayers scattered everywhere.

Christopher had taken a deep breath in and prayed – and this time, he believed it. He prayed every day, practised gratitude and renewed his sense of purpose. He had eventually come to realise through his travels that happiness is a practice, not a destination to be reached. Happiness seemed to be a misconception among most, which is why everyone was so desperately *unhappy* all the time, he thought. He had lived among some of the poorest yet happiest souls and observing them had taught him how to live.

Christopher walked towards the flood of light cascading in from the stone doorway of the temple, immediately feeling the pleasant heat of the sun hitting him on the back of his shoulders as he ventured outside. Here, there was chanting, singing and the buzz of high energy and joy. He stopped in wonderment at the sight before him – a pair of stone lions with a vast array of offerings. Meat had been placed inside their open mouths, and a carpet of food lay before them: whole loaves of bread, eggs and fruits, as well as lit candles. An abundance of flowers and money decorated the statues. Vietnamese currency was of such low value that the people had adopted the American dollar as their own, and dollar bills are what Christopher could see in any available space near the lions where it could be tucked. Suddenly, he found himself completely overwhelmed with the aromatic smells of incense, the sounds of chanting and laughing – it was joy. Joy coursed through his body like an enormous energetic beam, and in that moment, he knew that everything was finally mending, healing and transforming. In that moment, the heaviness he'd always placed upon himself lifted finally as he granted himself forgiveness.

Christopher had left the temple as if he were floating and headed for the bustle of Hanoi, observing the old women, their leathery faces full of wrinkled wisdom, working as hard as packhorses. They carried heavy baskets tied on to a single long stick, which was balanced across their shoulders. The baskets were often full of fruits, but sometimes it was bread loaves or small, sweet donuts. He admired the generations of strength and grit that ran through the ancestry of the weathered street sellers and always bought a fruit or a loaf from them when the chance arose. He bought six sweet donuts for a dollar and sat at a tiny table with an equally tiny chair outside one of the coffee shops. There he sat for a good length of time, sipping warm coffee sweetened with condensed milk. He watched life through the lens of those who put all their energy into working to survive – but they seemed happier for it. They were doing; they were being. Not wallowing in the past; not blocking out life. Christopher had stayed in a hostel run by a pleasant Vietnamese chap. He said his name was Henry, to make it easier for the Western tourists to remember him. A lad of eighteen with lightened brown fluffy hair and a pointy chin. He slept where he worked, on the floor at his desk in a sleeping bag. Henry did not seem to mind it much and always had an accommodating smile. Christopher saw, at his time in that hostel, the daily offerings made at the Buddhist shrines, which could be found in most homes and shops. This one was placed by the door, and the offerings would range from sweets to money – Christopher even saw a packet of *Choco pies* there once.

Since his initial visit to the hostel where he'd since taken up residence, Christopher had bought a small brass Buddha that he kept in his pocket. He held it in his hand multiple times a day and listed his reasons to be grateful. His life had begun to change; he was no longer the man he'd left back in England, though there was the smallest nagging feeling in the back of his mind. He identified it as fear of the unknown. What if he went back to England, came face to face with his demons, and crumbled? As Christopher sipped the last of his coffee, he knew he had to return to his hometown of London soon. He loved Asia; it had been his most valuable teacher and friend, but he knew deep in the pit of his belly that it was only meant to be part of the journey. He had left behind the most precious part of his life – his daughter.

Christopher made his way back to the hostel and handed Henry a dollar to use the internet. He sat down at the desk, put on his headphones and clicked Alice's name on the Skype call. The familiar noise sounded in his ears and he waited for her to answer.

"Hello?" came her familiar voice.

"Can you hear me?" Christopher said loudly and moved his eye right up to the lens of the webcam.

"Dad, moving your face closer to the screen doesn't make you sound any clearer," Alice said, laughing. "You look well, or at least, your eye does. Back up a bit, old man."

"Less of the old, thanks!" Christopher's trouser leg was suddenly dominating the webcam now. "Look at these," he instructed, shoving the stripy material closer to the camera.

"What?" his daughter asked.

"New trousers! Snazzy or what?"

"Erm…*what?*" Alice remarked in regard to the baggy rainbow pants that her dad was still trying to get close to the camera.

"Oh my God, Dad, sit down, people are probably staring at you!"

Christopher obeyed and the picture now focused on his tanned face.

"How are you, and granny and grandad?" he asked.

"All fine," she responded. "I saw gran and grandad last week. Grandad got a new *Bose* CD player and told gran it cost forty pounds, but really it was one hundred and twenty."

Christopher's laugh boomed down the call and Alice smiled at the sound of it.

"Excellent!" he said. "Listen, Alice – I'm coming back soon."

"Oh, okay. Let me know when and we can plan some stuff," Alice suggested.

"I mean for good," he replied tentatively, feeling nervous and excited at his declaration.

"For good?"

"I think it's time for me to come back, sweet pea," he

said. "Five years is long enough and I'm missing my baby girl. It feels like the right time."

"Okay, Dad. If you feel like it's right, then it probably is."

"It's time for us to start again, too," he added. "A new chapter, don't you think?"

"Sounds like a brilliant plan, Dad!" Alice beamed.

"It's nice to see you smile, Alice," he told her, grinning back.

"Yes, things are looking up and that's great news that you're coming back. I've got to go now, but keep me posted, okay?"

"Okay, sweet pea. Love you, bye," Christopher signed off.

"Love you too," she replied.

Christopher felt exhilarated at the prospect of seeing Alice. It was time to go back to England, to the home he had not been to for several years. It was time to return to the former location of his hardest times to see whether he had indeed truly healed from those experiences, or whether they would uncover something within him that was hiding in the shadows of his heart.

Chapter Seventeen

Michael paced up and down his hallway, looking at his watch like it was going to give him some sort of answer. It was 6.45 pm, and he had been debating whether to go and see Alice for their usual meeting. His head was telling him to nip the connection he shared with her in the bud. His heart was pulling him to go and see her. His stomach felt knotted with his indecision, and the thought of Alice sitting there waiting for him.

Michael eventually grabbed his coat and the pile of library books, heading out of his front door.

When Michael reached the familiar door of the library, wet from the rain that had started to fall in the dull summer dusk. He saw Alice jump at the sight of him on the other side of the glass. All the lights were off and Alice was wearing her coat, ready to go home. As she opened the door tentatively, Michael noticed that she looked a bit sad, not seeing the usual big smile he was used to.

"Hi, Dear One," Michael said, feeling instantly lifted at the sight of Alice. "Are you okay?"

"I'm okay." Alice smiled lightly.

"I know it's Thursday, and you were expecting me sooner. Sorry, I messed up," Michael told her, feeling genuinely awful that he'd nearly decided not to come. How could he not? Now he was here with Alice. It felt so right to be in her company. Was he really going to cut that off because of his insecurities?

"Don't worry about it, Michael, you're getting wet! I was just closing up but come in for a minute," Alice ushered him in and locked the door.

"You are one in a million. I'm sorry it's so late," Michael replied, still feeling guilty. He stood there with steamed-up glasses dotted with rain and an armful of books. He could feel the water dripping from his hair onto his face and down the back of his neck, which made him shiver slightly.

"Give me those," Alice ordered, taking the pile of wet books out of his arms and setting them on the side.

"I'm glad I didn't miss you altogether," Michael told her, watching her light movements. "You're beautiful," he blurted out, immediately feeling unsure of whether he should have said it. Alice smiled, showing her straight, white teeth, and began dabbing his forehead with her black cardigan, which she'd left on the side of the counter. She gently removed the glasses from his face. She didn't replace them, but put them down on the desk next to the switched off computer.

"I can't see now," Michael whispered in the soft darkness. Her face was so close to his that he could smell her skin – a hint of argan oil if he wasn't mistaken; a sensual scent that was more than pleasant. The tip of her nose rested on his cheek for a moment and he placed his hand on the back of her head, stroking her soft, dark hair.

"Then close your eyes," Alice instructed gently. He did what she'd asked, and the next thing Michael felt was Alice's warm lips on his. His mind was telling him he should pull away, but he didn't – he couldn't. He was lost in her energy; her sensual smell. He was truly enwrapped in the attraction he felt for her, and in this moment he found it impossible to turn away. He had imagined often how she would taste if he ever dared to kiss her, and here he was kissing her now. Her warm tongue was in his mouth and he dared to touch her. He allowed his hands to grip her hips and pull her body towards him. He kissed her harder and Alice's hands slicked back his wet curls with both hands, pulling his face closer to hers.

"I want you, Michael," she spoke, in between the sounds of kissing and the breathing that was getting heavier between them.

"I want you too – like you wouldn't believe," he whispered. He ran his hand down the side of her face, her skin soft under his fingertips, then allowed them to find her delicate fingers, wrists and arms. His thumb found the old scar patterns of her left arm. He had noticed them before now but never asked her about them. He felt a sudden surge of compassion for her.

"I want to discover all the pieces of you, Alice Wilde," he whispered as he began kissing her neck slowly, sensually putting his fingers into her mouth. She sucked them while she ran her hands down his back and squeezed his firm buttocks through his jeans. He breathed harder and bit her neck gently as his penis hardened and pushed against her thigh. Michael paused for a moment and looked at her, suddenly feeling a sense of duty towards her, that he needed to tell her his secret.

"Alice, I…" he began, but she put one finger to his lips

to shush him and guided his hand down to her jeans and inside her knickers. He submitted and felt the lace material wet with her anticipation as she pulled him closer, his fingers pushing inside her. Michael couldn't remember the last time something felt so good.

"Oh God," she murmured, breathing hard. She unbuttoned his jeans quickly and let her hands find his erection, gripping it firmly and feeling his hot skin against her cold hand. She pulled him to the farthest corner of the library, in-between the bookshelves in the gathering dusk, and pushed him down on to the floor. Michael couldn't quite believe what was happening, he'd fantasised about this, about Alice, about making love to her, but he never thought it would come to pass.

The rain was coming down harder and the low echo of summer thunder filled the sky. Michael's blue eyes were full of yearning and anticipation as he pulled Alice's T-shirt off furiously. She discarded her bra and Michael surveyed Alice straddling him, the streetlamps shining through the window semi-illuminating the curves of her body while he cupped her small breasts in his hands. His head and his heart were battling; he needed to stop this before it was too late. But his body, his instincts, were far too strong to listen to his reasoning brain.

"There are things you need to know," he got the words out quickly just before Alice's lips came down on him again. He reciprocated; he couldn't help himself.

"I know all I need to," she whispered as she let his hardness penetrate her. Michael grabbed her hair in wild handfuls and pulled her down to his chest, the tension in his body building as she moved her hips sensually on top of him. Her body moved – lithe and catlike – while his searching hands found her slight curves. The glare through the window highlighted her breasts and hipbones and he was transfixed.

"Put your hand around my throat," she demanded, and guided his gentle hand.

"This is reckless," Michael whispered, in awe of what was happening.

"Yes," she agreed and placed her long fingers over his hand on her throat. "Tighter," she commanded, and Michael firmed his grip. He could feel the pulse of her carotid artery on the tip of his thumb; it seemed to excite her. Her movements became more frantic and Michael felt her body tense up as she cried out and grabbed a fistful of his still-wet grey curls. He pulled her down hard on top of him, her eyes locked with his as he clenched his teeth, gripping hard on to her thighs. He was going to come inside her. He couldn't stop himself and with one final movement of Alice on top of him, he'd filled her up with his warm fluid, his body jerking with the release of tension. He pulled Alice down close to him. She was breathing hard and closed her eyes, forehead against his chest.

"Fuck." Michael said, confused with lust and realisation. "Alice, I'm sorry, I didn't mean to. I mean, I couldn't stop myself."

"It's okay," Alice comforted, "I can get a morning-after pill. I didn't plan for this to happen either, I just saw you and I don't know what came over me. I don't make a habit of this. It's been a long time since I've been attracted to someone like this. Please don't think less of me."

"God, Alice. I'd never think less of you. You're an amazing woman," Michael told her. "I just have so many fears. You don't really know me."

"Let's not talk now. I just want to lie with you for a while. Is that okay?" she asked, softly.

"Okay," he agreed. Alice lay on Michael's chest as he

stroked her hair and stared up at the ceiling, the feeling of guilt tightening in his stomach. He should have been happy and relaxed lying here with this beautiful, unusual creature who had just made love to him, but he wasn't. He squeezed his eyes shut and tried not to think about what he'd done, or what he was going to tell Alice.

Chapter Eighteen

A few weeks later, Alice found herself sitting in a local restaurant with her mother. It was bustling – and the last place Alice wanted to be. Lunch with April was always a bit of a chore, but their relationship had improved significantly, especially since April had started volunteering at a care home; something Alice never visualised her mother doing.

April was perusing the lunchtime menu at Carluccio's; their preferred Italian. They met up about once a month to have an obligatory mother-daughter 'catch up' whereby Alice did a lot of nodding and agreeing to get through the experience.

"Did I tell you Dad was coming home?" Alice said, causing April to look up sharply from the menu.

"What? When?" she replied.

"I don't know, details are to follow. He seems happier."

"I should think so," April retorted. "He went off galli-vanting around Asia on a five-year holiday. He should be over the bloody moon and nothing less!"

Alice decided to abandon this line of conversation and change the subject from her now-irritated mother.

"What's new then, Mum, are you still seeing Keith?"

"Ugh, No," April wrinkled her nose. "He wasn't very proactive, you know."

"Oh, I liked Keith, that's a shame," Alice sympathised.

April flicked her hand as if swatting a fly away. "Yeah, I'm better off without men, I think. What about you anyway, when are you going to get a boyfriend – or a girlfriend?"

"Oh, well, I don't have either," Alice looked down at her napkin.

"What's the matter?" April asked her daughter, "You look miserable."

"Nothing," Alice replied.

"Yeah, right. I've known you for twenty-four years, Alice Wilde."

Alice rubbed her forehead, trying to find the words to construct a sentence.

"Erm... I sort of met someone. Well, I've been getting to know him and I haven't heard from him."

April took a drink from her wine glass and Alice did the same.

"Maybe he's busy. How long haven't you heard from him?" her mum asked.

"Three weeks," Alice replied quietly, feeling awkward and wishing they'd never got on to the subject in the first place.

"Did you sleep with him?" April enquired casually.

"Mum! You can't ask me that!"

"I'll take that as a 'yes', then," April surveyed Alice, who looked down at the menu without replying. "Men get what they want and leave. It's a sad thing, Alice. It's just in their nature."

"Not every man is the same, Mum," Alice responded, feeling like she was about to cry. "I'm going to the bathroom."

As she excused herself, a tear rolled down her cheek. She looked at herself in the bathroom mirror: dyed black hair, pale skin and red-rimmed eyes. Maybe that's why he hadn't come to visit her. Thursdays passed painfully with a negative space where Michael usually was. Deep down Alice doubted herself, and Michael's absence brought all her insecurities to the surface. She analysed every moment that had made up that evening at the library, her mind circling. She'd come on too strong and asked him to grab her around the throat, he'd felt her scars – no wonder he hadn't been to see her.

"Fucking idiot," Alice reprimanded her reflection and banged her fist on the mirror. Her collarbones protruded and goosebumps appeared on her skin as she shivered. She'd felt wretched for the last three weeks; she missed Michael and didn't have any answers. She was sick to her stomach and tired of mentally punishing herself.

Alice splashed her face with cold water and let it drip down her skin, reminding her of the now-cruel memory of Michael coming in from the rain that night. She thought about his blue eyes that had never judged her – not until now, at least. She couldn't help but think that he was judging her now, silently, from a distance. Alice became aware of her mobile phone vibrating in her pocket. It proved a welcome distraction.

"Hello?"

"Hi," came the familiar voice of Louise, her only remaining friend from college. The floodgate of tears opened at the sound of someone who loved her unconditionally.

"Alice…are you there, babe?" Louise asked.

Alice tried to respond through her breaking voice, her face wet with tears.

"Sorry," she squeaked.

"You still haven't heard from him, then?"

"No. I'm such an idiot, Lou. I scared him away by being my stupid weird self. I was too full on. Not to mention he probably thinks I'm some sort of slut for having sex with him just like that."

Just at that moment, a woman exited one of the toilet cubicles and glanced at Alice disapprovingly. Alice frowned, although she didn't really care for the judgements of strangers at that moment.

"You had been getting to know him for like six months, wasn't it? It isn't like you only just met him. He's in the wrong for not getting in touch. He obviously isn't the right sort of man if he's willing to sleep with you and disappear."

"I checked his library record the other day," Alice said. "He returned books to a different branch, so he wouldn't have to see me, I assume."

"Ugh, what a spineless twat," Louise remarked, the sound of disgust evident in her voice. "And he's definitely not in a relationship?"

"In a relationship? He can't be. He kept saying there was something he needed to tell me, but I didn't listen. I don't know what to think."

"I know, but you haven't had the best of luck at picking men, honey," said Louise. "Sorry to remind you of McAvoy, but look how that turned out when you thought he was all genuine and stuff. You want to see the good in everyone, but maybe not everyone is good. I'm sorry, I feel like I'm making it worse. I don't want you to go through that again. It took years for you to get right again after he left."

"It's fine. I know you're about as subtle as a poke in the eye, that's why I love you," Alice smiled weakly. "You're right, I don't make good choices."

She didn't want to think about McAvoy again. She was curious from time to time to know whether he was okay, and that was all. She wanted him to be okay, even if she was never part of it. She pushed the thoughts out of her head; thoughts of him would not bring any good to her life. "Would it make me a stalker if I looked up Michael's address?"

"Babe, let's not pretend you haven't already looked it up," Louise said.

"Okay, I have. He only lives fifteen minutes away from me. I just want to know Lou, I want to know why he's just gone without a word, I want to know why men think it's okay to just leave me. If I can find out why, then I can start forgetting him. I didn't want to go through this again."

"I know," Louise replied, a touch of sadness in her words. "The McAvoy thing nearly finished you off, I don't want to see you go through it again – I nearly lost my best friend."

"Nothing could be as bad as that, don't worry, Louise. I promise you won't lose me."

It felt familiar and forbidden to bring up McAvoy again; like it was giving him fresh energy in her life. An unexpected squeeze in Alice's chest made her inhale sharply. "It's nowhere near on that scale. But yes, he's hurt me. Michael is the first person since Will who gave me hope of a real connection." Her eyes started to fill up again.

"No more tears, babe. We'll go tonight. I finish work at five thirty. Meet me by the clock tower at six and we'll go to his house."

"I've got to go, I'm at lunch with my mum," Alice said. "Love you."

"Good luck," Louise replied. "Love you too. Bye."

Alice got through the remainder of her lunch date with her mother, though she hardly touched her food. As five forty-five pm approached, she was nervous at the prospect of going to Michael's home. She didn't know if she might lose her nerve. She tried to put it out of her mind and pressed the button on her coffee machine, twisted her hair up in a chignon and threw on her all-purpose black dress that was draped over the sofa. She burnt her mouth on the espresso and almost dropped the blue Moroccan patterned cup. The smell of coffee turned her stomach and made her retch. She didn't realise she was so nervous. The mention of Will had also set her on edge. She'd buried him deep down at the back of her mind again. He was another question that did not have an answer, much like Michael. She wondered sadly why she was so disposable to men she thought cared about her.

At six pm Alice found herself waiting at the clock tower for Louise, who was late as usual. She didn't remember how she got there, but now she was waiting, she was churned up with adrenalin. Her friend pulled up in her purple Nissan Micra and signalled for Alice to get in.

"I don't know if I can do this," Alice told her friend as she put her seatbelt on.

"Just breathe. We'll just go and see where he lives and take it from there," Louise said. Alice exhaled a long breath and looked on as the masses made their way home from work. She imagined whether they would be going home to a family, a partner or children. Some of them looked as though they'd go home to an empty house; some of them might go out for a drink. How many of them were having affairs, she thought, how many of them slept with someone else and never called them?

"Left or right here?" Louise interrupted her thoughts.

"Right."

Louise pulled into a tree-lined avenue and slowed her speed. The wind blew the green leaves on the trees, which were vibrant against the blue sky. Alice felt nauseous as they drove nearer to Michael's place.

"What door number?"

"Sixty-six."

Louise parked the car and looked at her friend. Alice scanned the buildings. The house that was numbered sixty-six was red brick with a grey roof. Most of the bottom half of the house was obscured by vast bushes and plants, and Alice could see only the top windows, and the sliver of a red front door.

"Nice place," Louise piped up.

"Yes," Alice said absentmindedly. "Lou, we're right outside, what if he sees us?"

"What if he does? That's the point isn't it?"

"I don't know what the point is. I can't think," Alice looked at the upstairs windows of the charming house and saw Michael walk over to it for a moment, put his hand up against the glass and then go back in. "He's in there," Alice informed Louise, who turned to try and get a look. They both stared at Michael's window for a long moment. "What do I do now?" Alice asked.

"Do you want to knock?" Louise replied.

"God, no. Are you crazy?"

"We *are* stalking this guy," Louise said. "I'd say we're pretty firmly in the crazy category."

Just then, the pair saw a red-haired woman walk across the room and pass the same window where Michael had just been standing. Alice felt a fresh pang of pain in her chest.

"Did you see that? Did you see her?!" Alice asked.

Louise put her hand on her friend's knee and squeezed it.

"Yes," she replied.

"He's with someone! I can't believe it. How could I have been so wrong about him?!" Alice was dumbfounded.

"Maybe it isn't what it looks like?" Louise offered half-heartedly.

"It's six twenty, past working hours, and I haven't heard from him since we had sex. He kept saying he had to tell me something, and I didn't listen. I didn't think he was going to tell me he had a fucking girlfriend! I'm failing to see other possibilities here. That's why he's been avoiding me. I'm a fucking idiot, Louise! I want to go home."

Alice didn't cry. She felt anger building up inside of her. Anger at herself, at Michael – at her naïve belief that she had found something real in a world where there are so many illusions. She had only found another man who had let her down. It pulled on old wounds that she'd ignored because she didn't want to deal with the pain. Another hollow promise, but he never promised her anything – it was all in her head.

Louise drove Alice home in silence. She pulled over and looked at her stony-faced friend. "Let me stay with you", she offered.

"No, thank you. You know what I'm like when I feel like this; I need to be on my own," Alice replied.

"You shut the world out and suffer alone," Louise told her, putting her hand on Alice's shoulder.

"It's just my way. I just need to process it. I'll call you tomorrow. Thanks for taking me," Alice spoke robotically without looking at Louise and got out of the car before she could say another word.

As she turned the key in the lock of her blue front door, Alice reverted to autopilot. Her stomach felt empty, but it was too tightly knotted to eat. She poured a glass of wine from an open bottle in the fridge, crumpled on the sofa and took a slug from the glass, spilling some wine on to the hardwood floor with a splash. She stared into the glass.

"Fucking fucking fucking loser," she chastised herself and drained her glass, getting up to pour another one. Alice misjudged the space on the kitchen counter and sent her glass tumbling to the floor where it splintered into pieces. "Fuck!" she yelled, frantically gathering the shards. One of them nicked her on the wrist and a small blood spot appeared, bright and vibrant. Alice watched the bloodspot.

Sometimes she toyed with the idea of cutting again, but that was as far as it went. Some sort of invisible force always stopped her from doing it. She didn't really want to; it was merely an old coping mechanism that registered in her brain.

"Fuck you," she said aloud, thinking of Michael. Her phone lit up at the same moment with a Skype call from Christopher. She watched it ring and ring until the sound stopped – she couldn't put on a brave face right now and pretend she was okay. She didn't want her dad to see that she wasn't. Alice fetched the dustpan and brush, sweeping the rest of the shattered glass up and dumping it in the dustbin. She sank down on her sofa in the wretched silence, squeezed her eyes shut as tight as she could and refused to think of Michael.

Chapter Nineteen

The summer evenings were light and vibrant; defiant against Alice's stormy heart. A weeping willow swayed in the light breeze just past the windows of the library where Alice was preparing to lock up. She began switching off the computers, setting the answer phone and encouraging the remaining borrowers to check out their items. She was planning on going running after work – she kept herself occupied so she didn't dwell on why Michael hadn't been to see her for nearly a month. Still, at every closing time, Alice hoped he would show up and have a perfectly rational explanation as to why he hadn't been in touch. But he never did. Some days at work were quiet, giving Alice's brain ample opportunity to enter overdrive. Was that woman she'd seen really his girlfriend? It didn't make sense to her – he was so genuine, wasn't he? Alice wasn't naïve, she knew how the world worked by now; she knew men sometimes talked the talk in order to get a fuck, but it didn't ring true when she thought about Michael – of all his words and the energy between them. She'd done her crying and was not prepared to be hurt again – not after the agonising process of getting over Will, not after fighting to want to live, not after everything her parents had put her through.

Alice muttered to herself as she checked out Mrs. Avalon's books on cassette. She briefly wondered if the kindly old woman had ever had her heart broken. By the age of eighty-something she must have, and yet she was still here, still going. The thought gave Alice some small comfort. She assisted Mrs. Avalon in exiting the front door and locked it behind her. Alice took a minute to brush her freshly dyed black hair; dramatic against her skin, which was a shade paler than usual. The collar of her black, short-sleeved ribbed top came right up to her neck – it was snug against her breasts, and her trousers clung midway down her hips. Alice picked up her bag and started unlocking the front door when she stopped dead in her tracks, mouth parted in shock. She was frozen to the spot as she looked through the glass panel of the door and saw Will McAvoy staring back at her.

Slowly, Alice turned the key and opened the door, not taking her eyes off him for a moment.

"Alice," he said, eventually, with an expression that could not be defined as either a smile nor a frown. Alice did not speak, she just stared at him, wide-eyed. His face was more lined than ever – more than it should have been after a period of just five years. His hair was greyer but the same style she remembered; the sandy, greying curls tamed with hair product. She noticed that he was clean shaven and smelled of aftershave – the same scent she had inhaled so readily five years ago. The smell brought her right back to everything that had happened, the way smells do sometimes. She hadn't encountered that particular scent since she'd last smelled it on him. All of a sudden, her eyes felt hot behind their sockets and the constant knot in her stomach just got tighter.

"Say something, please," Will urged, rubbing the back of his neck, seeming unsure what to do.

"Hello, Will," Alice uttered. She had still not taken her eyes from his. The liquid gold she once knew was now dull; brassy. She took in every detail of his form, registering the changes and similarities in the way he'd looked last time she'd seen him. His stature did not seem as dominating as it has when she was his student – perhaps it was because she was older, or maybe the world and its experiences had broken him down. She noted that he looked troubled, but still with the stoic handsomeness that was so very *him*.

"What are you doing here?" she asked faintly. She could barely believe that he was standing in front of her.

"It's good to see you," he told her, but was met with no response. "Would you walk with me, so we can talk? I need to explain."

"Explain?"

"Why I left," he answered.

"Why have you come here now? Is it to ease your conscience?" Alice didn't recognise the words coming out of her mouth. She sounded angry – she was angry. She had replayed this scenario over and over again. In her visions, she threw her arms around him and held him tight so that he couldn't disappear again. Now that he was here, she didn't feel that way. He was a stranger coming to stick a plaster on a wound from the past, and Alice wasn't sure she wanted to enter into that territory.

They walked to the park nearby; it was brimming with life. Children playing and dog walkers dotted everywhere – it was a scene that Georges Seurat could have painted himself. Everyone looked so carefree, going about their business in the warm breeze. Alice wondered if, to an onlooker, she and Will looked like friends, partners, or maybe a brother and sister going for an evening stroll in the park. It was surreal to be walking with him again, echoing the first time she had walked with him in the bustling school corridor all those years before.

Will stopped and turned to face Alice. He looked at the white raised marks on her inner forearm, perfectly parallel, ten of them in a row. He grabbed her arm firmly, running his fingers over the deeper scar on her wrist, which was wide and jagged at the edges. Alice let him, part of her wanted him to see how much he had hurt her.

"I'm so sorry, Alice," Will told her. His brassy eyes seemed to melt as the emotion fell from them.

"Why are you crying?" she responded. "What's done is done. You never owed me anything, but I won't lie about the fact that my world fell apart when you left. You *were* my world. I got through it – only just. I'm fine now. I don't want to open a can of worms that's only going to hurt me again."

Will pulled her hand to his mouth and kissed it delicately, as if it were a powdery butterfly wing. He held her hand to his face for a time, and Alice fought back the feeling that his touch was like home.

"I would like to know why you left, if that's what you've come to explain," she asked, gently.

The two began to stroll slowly, Will speaking, Alice listening. The pair walked and talked for hours, first in the park, then going on to the coffee shop and then to another park. When Alice learned of Will's mother's fate, she softened towards him. She realised that she was not the only one who had been through hard times, and yet what had happened could never be changed. There was pain between them, and what could ever come from that except more pain?

The sky started to turn dull with impending dusk as the reunited pair continued their walk.

"I care for you, Alice. I have love for you," Will spoke softly. "You feel like a part of me and for the last five years I've felt like something was missing. It was you."

"What do you want from me?" Alice asked. "You have love for me? Does that mean you are in love with me? I don't know what to do with that information. I can't be the plaster that heals your wounds from Victoria. Is that what this is?"

"I know. You aren't a plaster, I promise. I've come to terms with a lot of things over these last years. I know you aren't a substitute for my sister, and I don't want you to be. I just want you to be in my life somehow, even if it is at a distance," he told her.

"Listen, I'm staying in the UK, my dad is following soon. We've been working together in his law firm and we're setting up business here. I guess we were too caught up talking about everything else that I neglected to mention the details. I wanted to be as close as I could to my mother's roots in London, and to be close to you, but that's your choice and I'll respect whatever you say on the matter."

Alice considered Will's words but did not let him see past the wall she had placed in front of her emotions. "After my mother died, I didn't know which direction my life was going in. I chose to follow my father and at least try to salvage a relationship with him. He's been training me up – although my side of the business will be providing free legal assistance for underprivileged families, much to his distaste. He's all about the money; the type of clients he deals with are stinking rich, it makes me sick. All money and no morals. He's relocating with me because I'm all he's got left now, and he has the guilt of being a shit parent."

"I see. Well, I'm glad you've found your direction, but I'm not here to give you comfort, Will. I can't be picked up and put down at a whim. I'm a person with feelings and you fucking hurt me once. You can't just casually breeze into my life and be wishy washy about what you actually want."

"Of course," Will said. "I understand why you're angry with me, I don't blame you. My mother told me that happiness is all there is, and it stuck with me. You are part of that happiness. I could have stayed in South Africa, but I was compelled to come back to England. A big part of that was because of you. I know you may not want me in your life, that's a chance I was willing to take. I'm just hoping, that's all."

"I'm feeling a bit lightheaded, Will," Alice responded. She couldn't think straight with the confusing declaration he'd made towards her. She felt sick. "It's probably the shock of seeing you and all these emotions. I need to go home and think about all the things you've said, okay?"

"Of course. Could I at least make sure you get home safely? I promise I'll leave straight away." Alice could see a familiar spark return to Will's eyes, and she felt drawn in once more with those invisible hooks. She looked away; she didn't want to risk him reading the fine print of her soul while she felt so vulnerable.

"Okay," she agreed. "It's just a fifteen-minute walk from here."

Will smiled and guided her by placing his hand on the

small of her back. She shivered at his touch, even though the weather was still reasonably warm. His hands had made her feel protected once, and they still did now.

When they arrived at Alice's flat, she unlocked the door and stood facing Will in the doorway. She was deliberately blocking it so that he wouldn't invite himself in. She couldn't handle him at this moment and just wanted to lie down on her bed until her head felt less fuzzy.

"Thank you for walking me," she said.

"How are you feeling now? Still lightheaded?"

"A little. I'll be fine once I've had a lie down."

"When can I see you again?" he asked.

"I don't know. Don't push me, I just need time to think."

"I know. I'm sorry," he said. "Let me give you my phone number, and you can call or text me anytime, okay? Anytime, really. Even three am."

Alice smiled in acknowledgement and handed him her mobile phone so that he could tap his number in. As she returned the phone to her pocket, Will suddenly grabbed her and hugged her tightly, stroking the back of her head as he had done once before when her mother had injured her. Alice felt small and vulnerable in his arms, trying to defy the feeling again that he felt like home. She buried her face into his shoulder and experienced a flood of emotions and memories as she smelled his familiarity again.

After a minute, he released his tight hold and placed his hands on each of her wrists while looking her directly in the eyes. "You have been so missed," he said, kissing her gently on the crown of her head. "Please, will you let me know how you're feeling later?"

Alice nodded. She closed the door behind him and went to her bedroom, falling with tiredness on to her bed.

She was exhausted all of a sudden and felt like she could sleep for an eternity. She was almost about to drift off when there was a knock at the door. She felt a sudden pang of anxiety that Will would be standing there, expecting her to do something, or say something.

She pulled herself up and opened the door, surprised to see Michael's face looking back at her.

"Michael! What are you doing here? How did you know where I live?!"

"Don't judge me, but I sort of followed you after you'd finished work the other day to see where you lived," he confessed. "I promise I'm not a weirdo, but I had to speak to you and I didn't think coming to the library would be the best place to do that."

Alice would have thought it was an odd thing to do, too, had she not done it herself a couple of weeks before.

"It's not a good time, Michael. I'm not feeling very well. You've been avoiding me since we had sex and quite frankly, I haven't got the mental capacity to deal with anything else today."

"What's wrong, are you okay?" he asked, worry clouding his expression.

"Just light-headed and tired. I might be coming down with something. I just need a rest," she said.

Michael's face was serious as he surveyed her with doctor's eyes.

"Any fever or sickness?" he asked.

"No, I'm okay, Michael. Don't fuss," she said, as she removed the fingers from her wrist that were checking her pulse.

"Please, Alice, let me come in, it's really important," he urged.

"What's wrong?" she asked, grudgingly moving aside

so he could come in. He stood there for a while, just staring. He looked gaunt and wrung his hands together.

"Sit down, Michael," she said. "You're making me nervous."

"Alice, I've been too scared to come and see you since that evening we…" he trailed off.

"Had sex?" Alice finished the sentence he didn't want to say, raising her eyebrows at him as they stood in the living room, face to face.

"Yes," Michael replied. "You're probably thinking all sorts about me being just like other men, and that I just wanted to get into your knickers, but I promise it wasn't all about that. I wasn't even expecting that, and then when it happened, I couldn't stop myself."

"It's okay, Michael, you don't have to be sorry that we fucked. I'm just sorry that I thought it was more than it was."

"No, Alice, it was more. It meant something to me, but the thing is, I haven't been honest with you."

"You're with someone," Alice stated, rather than asked.

"What? No!"

"I saw a red-haired woman through your window – your bedroom window, I assume," Alice replied, her face set. "Don't lie to me now," she warned.

"How did you know where I lived?" Michael looked momentarily surprised, his brow furrowing again a moment later. "Never mind. You've got it all wrong. Oh God. That woman is called Elise Montague, I studied with her – she does acupuncture and other treatments on me, she's been working with me for years because of my illness. We do treatment exchanges."

Alice surveyed him, confused. "What illness?"

"This is hard for me to say. Please don't judge me and don't panic."

"What?" she repeated.

There was a silence for what seemed like an age as Michael flapped and paced around looking at his fingers, which were knotted together.

"I've got HIV. I should have told you, but I was too scared that you wouldn't be interested in me anymore if I did. Then the whole sex thing happened, and I was completely irresponsible. I'm so sorry."

Alice's brow furrowed. She let the words sink in.

Then she looked up at him, fearfully. "Could I have HIV? Is that why you looked like you'd seen a ghost when I said I didn't feel well?" A jolt of shock went through her with the sudden realisation.

"No, you won't have it. I just get scared when people I care about are unwell. Listen to me, I got infected with HIV thirty years ago, through no fault of my own. It's a long story. I've been on medication to control it and keep me well ever since. I have an undetectable viral load, which is tested every six months. It means I can't pass it on to anyone else. I wouldn't have put you at risk if I wasn't sure about that."

"When was your last test?" she asked, still alarmed.

"Four months ago. It's always been consistent, Alice. I know I've fucked up, and you'll probably never trust me again, but I'm willing to do anything to make it up to you. If you want peace of mind, I'll come with you to get a blood test, just so you're not worried. But I know you're okay."

Alice felt hot all of a sudden and rushed over to the sink to vomit. Her mind was swirling, and all she wanted to do was lie down. Michael rubbed her back and guided her to her bedroom.

"It's okay, I'll look after you, dearest," he told her. Michael fetched a glass of water and put it by the side of

Alice's bed. She was too weak to protest when he undressed her and put an oversized T- shirt over her limp body so she could sleep. She noticed that he looked the other way to preserve her dignity. "You're okay," he whispered as she lay down and he stroked her head until she fell asleep.

The next morning, the smell of eggs and coffee woke Alice from her death-like sleep. She was in exactly the same position as she'd fallen asleep in, and it took her a few moments to recall what had happened the night before.

"Good morning, Alice," Michael chimed, appearing in the doorway with a tray bearing poached eggs, toast and coffee. There was even a little purple flower, which Alice recognised from a patch of wildflowers that grew down the road. She suddenly felt self-conscious. She was pretty sure she didn't look great first thing in the morning and she probably didn't smell great, either.

"Michael," Alice said, her speech sounding cracked through her dry throat.

"Who else?" Michael replied with a smile, handing her the tea tray.

Alice sat up and surveyed the breakfast items, the ghost of a smile on her lips.

"Gosh, I don't think I've ever been brought breakfast in bed before."

"Well, you deserve it. Don't worry, I slept on the sofa," Michael said, filling in Alice's unasked question. He perched on the side of the bed; his kind face was soothing. "How are you feeling today?" he asked.

Suddenly, everything came pouring back into Alice's consciousness. She was sick, Michael had told her he had

HIV. A chill ran down her spine and she looked at Michael with realisation.

"You lied to me," she said.

Michael's face drained and his smile disappeared.

"I'm sorry I wasn't upfront. I got scared," he admitted. "But I stand by what I said – you are fine. I can't pass it on to you. You feeling ill now is just a coincidence."

"You said your last test was four months ago, how do you know something hasn't changed?" she enquired, feeling anxious.

"Because I know. I am a doctor, remember?"

Alice poked the poached egg with a fork and watched the orangey yolk ooze out on to the plate. A wave of nausea came over her again, but she managed not to vomit this time.

"I'm still feeling quite queasy; it might be better if you left," she suggested. "Thank you for the breakfast, but I don't think I could eat a thing, and I need a shower."

"Listen, I'm taking you to the clinic today so that you can have a test. You need reassurance and I'm afraid I won't take no for an answer. This is all my fault so please let me try and fix it as much as I can," Michael looked her in the eyes, his face serious. "I know I broke your trust and I'm deeply sorry. I've been alone for a long time. The illness makes me feel like I'm some sort of freak of nature – it's certainly not something women want to hear, so I tend to steer clear. Obviously, things have happened between us, and you may well never want to see me again, but before that happens, I'm taking you to get checked out."

"You know what, Michael, if you had just told me in the first place, I wouldn't have thought any less of you. It wouldn't have made me not fancy you, I would have accepted it. Maybe you shouldn't judge people by how others have reacted in the past."

"I'm sorry," he replied, emotion threatening to break his voice.

"I need a shower, then we'll go," Alice said, pushing the uneaten breakfast aside and heading for the bathroom.

An hour later, Alice and Michael were seated at the walk-in clinic. Alice filled out some forms about why she was there and what she wanted testing for. She decided to tick all the boxes – she thought she might as well get tested for everything while she was there. When it came to answering how many sexual partners she'd had and when, Alice felt like everyone was looking at her. In her hand, Alice held a urine sample pot, which the reception desk had given to her.

"I'm just going to the toilet," she informed Michael and managed to fill the pot without getting urine everywhere. She concealed the filled container in her bag so that she didn't have to hold a jar of her own wee while sitting with Michael. After all, she didn't really know him as well as all that yet.

There weren't many people in the waiting room, thankfully. To her right was a plump girl wearing leggings and flip-flops, who was arguing with 'Troy' on her mobile phone – her boyfriend, Alice assumed. On her left was Michael, and to his left was a small-framed Asian girl glued to her mobile phone. Alice wondered what she was getting tested for.

"Do you want me to come in the room with you?" Michael asked.

"No," Alice replied automatically. Then: "Yes – maybe. I don't know."

"I'll come in," he said to her, giving her hand a squeeze.

The wait was short, but it felt like an age to Alice. Having read the posters on the walls about ten times apiece, she then pretended to read a magazine from the waiting area table to distract herself from thinking.

"Alice Wilde, please," came a Nigerian accent as a nurse shouted from a doorway. Alice looked at Michael and they both rose and entered the treatment room.

The nurse looked through the forms and nodded, saying: "So we are testing for everything, darling, yes?"

"Yes," Alice replied in a quiet voice.

"Don't look so worried, darling, most results come back negative."

"She's here because of me," announced Michael. "I have HIV, but my viral load is undetectable."

"I see, and you had unprotected sex?"

"Yes."

"I see. Okay darling, we are going to dip your urine, take some blood and some vaginal swabs. Are you okay with your boyfriend sitting in?"

Alice looked at Michael.

"It's up to you, Alice," Michael said. "I'll stay with you if you want me to."

"I'll be behind a curtain, right?" Alice asked, hesitantly.

"Yes, darling," the nurse replied.

"Okay, fine. Let's get on with it," Alice said, and the nurse gestured for Michael to take a seat by the door before pulling the curtain around the hospital bed. The nurse dipped some paper in the urine pot and set it aside while she performed the other procedures.

Alice focused on her breathing during the invasive process: being naked from the waist down and probed with swabs by a stranger wasn't her idea of fun. The nurse made short work of the swab samples and told Alice she could get dressed. The subsequent blood test was a welcome relief; Alice watched the dark crimson filling the little tube. She'd always had prominent veins – good for drawing blood.

"Are you okay, Alice?" Michael asked, as the nurse taped a cotton wool ball to Alice's arm.

"Yes, I'm fine," she said. "Thanks for staying."

"We'll send the samples to the lab, the results will be back in a couple of days," the nurse informed Alice.

"Oh, I thought it would be the same day," Alice replied.

"No, darling. We'll call you if anything abnormal comes up on the results." The nurse analysed one of the urine strips and held it up, double checking it.

"We've got a positive here for pregnancy. Did you know you were pregnant?" the nurse asked Alice.

Alice didn't say anything, she looked at Michael, wide-eyed. He had a look of shock on his face.

"I took a morning-after pill," Alice stated, shocked.

"Did you vomit at all after taking it?" the nurse asked.

"I did, I remember now. I felt unwell after a few hours and was sick."

"You would have needed another tablet if you vomited the pill back up. Your GP should have told you this."

"She didn't," Alice replied, blankly.

"Well, there are options available if you don't want this pregnancy," the nurse said. "Let me get you some leaflets."

She bustled out of the room and Michael came over to Alice.

"A baby," he stated, shocked. "That must be why you've been feeling poorly. Oh lord."

"I think I need to let it sink in," Alice said. "How do you feel about it?"

"I know it's unexpected, and we aren't even sure about us yet – if there is an us. But I can't help feeling like this could be a good thing." Alice could see that he was beaming at the thought; he was positively glowing. "I won't pressure you, I know there's a lot to talk about. Maybe fate brought us together for this reason. I'm sorry, I'm talking too much."

"You're not, I'm interested in how you feel about this," Alice responded, surprised at such a positive reaction. "I'm not angry Michael, I probably should be pissed off that you weren't truthful, but I understand why you weren't. You're a doctor and I trust what you're telling me about being okay, but I'll still breathe a sigh of relief when I get the results through. Obviously, this baby changes everything."

"It does. I thought I'd missed my chance of being a dad. I promise I'll be the best father you've ever seen – if you want this. No pressure, again. Sorry," Michael looked down sheepishly.

Alice was dumbfounded: her life finally seemed like it made sense. She suddenly had a purpose, and she knew with every fibre of her being that her purpose was to have this baby.

"I'm making no promises about me and you, Michael, but I think I really do want this baby." Alice covered her face with her hands, shaking her head at the revelation. The nurse walked in with a pile of leaflets and handed them to Alice.

"You will need to make an appointment with your GP, whatever you decide. To put your mind at rest, I have never encountered someone contracting HIV from a person with an undetectable viral load. This also means that if you are clear, your baby will be clear. It will be confirmed in a few days for you."

"Thank you," said Alice, feeling surreal. Michael touched the edge of her hand with his little finger. Alice was in disbelief that there was a little life growing inside her. Michael held the door open for her and they left the building, their lives completely different from when they had entered it a short while ago.

Chapter Twenty

Will applied the final stroke of pastel green paint in his new office. Scott had insisted on black and white as the colour scheme for McAvoy and Son, but Will protested that it was too clinical. In the end, they settled on their own styles for their own offices. Will wanted his to be low-key and relaxed, creating an air of approachability, in contrast with the typically intimidating grand and expensive lawyers' offices – the type that Scott was used to. Will had picked out large plants to place strategically in the office to make it comforting and decided on a light wooden desk in contrast with Scott's chic black glass one.

"I suppose it looks quite good," Scott conceded as he entered via the double doors.

"It does, doesn't it?" Will replied, pleased with his handiwork.

Scott surveyed a photograph that Will had placed on his desk: it was an image of Jacoline. Will had chosen a picture of one of the scattered happy times he remembered growing up: a trip to Table Mountain. His mother was pictured with one arm across Will's chest and her other arm around Victoria. In that photo, Will remembered the exact feeling of being loved.

"She'd like this," Scott said, surveying the image. Will gave his father a nod and continued finalising the touches to his office.

"So, this girl you told me about – What's going on there?" Scott ventured.

"I don't know," Will said uncomfortably.

"She was a big reason you wanted to come back, Will, you need to get some clarity on the situation."

"She was shocked and upset to see me, understandably. We talked – I told her why I'd left. I gave her my number, and she hasn't called yet. Maybe she won't. It's only been a week."

"You said you had some sort of unbreakable bond with this girl Alice, so now you have to win her back," Scott responded.

"It's not like a court case, Dad. I can't just put forward my case and expect her to forget how much I hurt her."

"Sometimes, you have to be persistent to get what you want is all I'm saying," his father continued.

"So, Richardsons are staying with you, I assume?" Will said, diverting the subject from Alice.

"Of course. I can fly back if there's a case on and anything paperwork-wise I can do from here. They've been with me too long to use anyone else – I know too much," Scott smiled wryly.

"Hmmm," came Will's disapproving response.

"'Hmmm' nothing, Will. You might not like what they stand for, but we wouldn't be where we are if it weren't for their custom."

"And where is that?" Will asked, with more than a hint of scorn.

"Rich, Will. All the best intentions in the world are not

going to buy a nice house or a nice car – or family holidays all over the world. Only money does that."

"What about all the families they've hurt pushing vaccines that have been tampered with? Using people as human experiments and disguising it as pharmaceuticals?" Will probed. "What about the scandals about infection experiments, and all the people who are maimed, brain-damaged or even dead because they're pushing chemicals into God knows what? Don't you care that you're helping them do damage?"

"I'm not helping them do damage, I'm helping them not get caught for doing damage," Scott replied. "We've spoken about this, Will, and we are never going to agree on this point. You are a do-gooder, and I'm a greedy man. I like the rand, the pounds and the Bitcoin. I don't pretend to be something I'm not. This is me."

"I wish that one day you would see the light, and choose compassion over money – just once," Will told his father. It really was a wish he hoped would come true. He had to hope that Scott could find meaning in something that didn't cost anything; something that was driven by his heart and not his head.

"I love you, son, even if I'm not as you'd wish me to be. I've got to go on some errands now, I'll see you later. Dinner at seven at this new steakhouse I found, I'll text you the address."

Scott left and Will looked at the walls, admiring what he'd created. He sometimes wondered how he could have been born having half his father's genetics when they were so opposite. The double door clicked again.

"Sorry, we're not open yet," Will called, and turned to see Alice standing there.

"Hi, Will," she greeted, "should I come back another time?"

"No, no, no. Come and sit down," he pulled her gently by the wrist over to a pastel green sofa in the waiting area – it matched the paint on the walls.

"It's so good to see you," he said, smiling, feeling fizzy with anticipation. "I thought you weren't going to contact me."

"Yes, I've had a lot going on since I saw you last. The place is looking good," Alice remarked, looking around at the office.

"Here, let me make you some coffee," he volunteered, bounding over to the machine and flicking on the switch.

"You remembered the address; I didn't think you would," he continued.

"I did recall you telling me you were opening up in Greenwich. Then I drove past a sign that said: McAvoy and Son, and here I am," Alice replied.

"I'm so glad – I've been going a bit crazy wondering whether I'd hear from you," he looked down, colour creeping into his cheeks. "I didn't want to push it. I almost came to see you a few times but decided against it. You needed the space to think and I respect that."

Will clumsily yanked down two cups from the cupboard and waited for what seemed like an age for the coffee to start pouring from the automatic machine. Finally, the fluid flowed. "Do you want sugar?" he asked.

"No, thanks," Alice replied, "relax, Will – I'm not going to bite."

He brought the cups over, hands shaking a little with the adrenalin hit of seeing Alice, and set them on the small table by the side of the sofa.

"You know, I watched you walking away from my apartment all those years ago, when you'd come to see me," Will recalled remorsefully. "If I could go back in time, I wouldn't have pushed you away. It broke my heart, watching you walk away and knowing that I had to go. I was trying to protect you by keeping you at arm's length, if you can understand that."

Alice put her hand lightly on top of Will's.

"I remember it, too," she said. "It's one of many memories I wish I didn't have. I never got over you. In my mind I always called you my salvation." Her eyes glazed over slightly as she spoke about old feelings. "When you left, it was so hard to live, the emotional pain was too much. I literally couldn't bear breathing without you, yet somehow I'm still here. But I cannot forget that pain. I understand why you did what you did, if that helps."

"I know," Will said, sadly, looking down. "I'll never forgive myself for that. But I have all the time and the determination in the world to make up for my mistakes."

"I don't know what you want from me, Will. The conversation we had last week made that less than clear. We have a bond, that much is obvious, and it's too strong to have only a friendship. It kills me to say it, but maybe our connection was only meant to be active for that short time all those years ago – maybe there are other reasons for it that we will never know. My circumstances have changed quite suddenly, and that's where I need to focus my energy – not on a conundrum that seems to have no solution."

"Everything has an answer," Will replied, clutching at hope that she wasn't going to walk away from him.

"I dream about you all the time, Will," Alice confessed. "I've dreamed about you for five years, and now I don't want to dream about you anymore. I've dedicated this heart space to you in the time you were gone," Alice told him, placing her hand on her chest. "I wanted you back so badly, Will, and you didn't come back. I felt like part of my soul had been ripped out, and no-one was there to make it better for me. I had to do it on my own. Now, I have a chance to walk away from that pain and the idea of you and me that I'd clung on to. We both had fucked-up childhoods, we're connected by pain and a longing for happiness, but that doesn't mean we ought to be in each other's lives." Alice's green eyes looked all the more vibrant with the tears now falling from them. "I wanted you to be the one, but maybe I was looking for a saviour. When you left, I realised no-one was going to save me apart from myself, and that's what I did. Maybe that's what you have to do, too."

Will leaned over and kissed her on the cheek, catching her off guard. The salty taste of her tears moistened his lips. "It's more than that, Alice, you know it is. We are connected by more than just pain. I love you, Alice, and you love me. Tell me you don't."

Alice looked at Will, shaking her head.

"I'm pregnant, Will. My baby is more important than anything else, more important than you or me. I won't let you mess my head up again; it's too much to bear."

"Pregnant?" There was a long pause. Will looked down at his hands, and then back to Alice, his eyes full of pain. "Are you with the baby's father?"

"It's complicated," she replied. "But I think I owe it to him to give things a go, at least for the baby's sake. It's not just about me anymore."

"I can look after you – you and the baby," Will added hastily. In his mind now were the words of his father: *win her back*.

"Will. Please don't."

"What is this man even like? How do you know he's right for you?"

"I don't know, Will. That's what I need to find out. But I know that he's kind and considerate. He wants to look after me and the baby, I can't rob him of that chance because the person I loved five years ago has suddenly come back."

"You still love me, Alice. I can feel it."

"Yes, you're right," she admitted, "but that doesn't change things. Besides, Will, you're talking like you want me as a partner. You said before you care about me like you cared about Victoria. I don't think you even know what you want."

Will looked desperately at her, trying to process her words – and failing.

"Do you love this other man?" he ventured.

"That's none of your concern. I've made a decision and you have to accept it."

Will's face was contorted with frustration.

"Yes, I do have to accept it. I'm losing you all over again."

Alice looked at him with bloodshot eyes,

"You never really had me, and I never really had you. There is a baby growing inside me, and that baby has to come first. I'm sorry." Alice turned and left through the double doors of McAvoy and Son without looking back, leaving Will devastated, staring at her untouched cup of coffee still steaming on the table.

Chapter Twenty-One

Alice's six-month baby bump was subtle, but unmistakable. She brushed her hair for the sixth time that morning as Michael looked at her adoringly.

"You look beautiful, but I don't think you'll have much hair left if you brush it anymore!" he told her. He was excited that he was soon going to be introducing Alice to his parents. It still made him tingle all over that she was his girlfriend.

Alice laughed and assessed her reflection. Michael came up behind her and placed his hands on the small swell of her tummy. "You'd hardly know there had been a bun cooking in there for six months, although these are getting bigger," he slid his hands up to her breasts and kissed the side of her neck.

"You know I like that, but we'll be late for your parents if you continue," Alice quelled. Then her expression changed, "What if they don't like me?"

"What's not to like?" Michael said, kissing her gently on the lips. He looked at the small swell of her tummy that could still fit into her jeans; his baby was in there; he could still hardly believe it.

Alice had received the confirmation phone call a few days after their initial clinic visit that she and the baby were HIV negative; just as Michael had reassured her. Things had gotten better and better from there. The more he got to know her, the more he felt like this was the person he'd been waiting for his whole life. She would have macabre days sometimes, and on those days Michael had learnt that all she needed was for him to hold her close and make her feel safe – and that's what he did. When he had days where his insecurities rose to the surface, Alice would put her hand lovingly on his cheek and tell him that she felt fortunate to have him, and lucky to have gotten pregnant with his child.

"Taxi is here, Love," Michael called, and Alice picked up her coat on her way out.

"I'm nervous," Alice whispered in the back of the taxi.

"Why?" Michael asked, squeezing her hand.

"I don't know," she frowned. "I obviously got pregnant really quickly and they might think I'm young and irresponsible or something."

"Well, you are," Michael laughed, and Alice elbowed him in the ribs. "I'm kidding," he soothed. "They are so thrilled at the prospect of being grandparents, I doubt you could do anything to make them not like you!"

"Don't jinx it!" Alice replied and slid her hand up Michael's leg.

"Steady on – I can't arrive at my parents' house with a huge erection," he winked.

"Huge?" Alice teased.

"Well, moderate at least," he whispered wryly.

They both laughed. It was always this way between

them; it was an easy relationship, despite the uneasy beginnings.

It was only a short distance to his parents' and the couple decided Alice would actually have to meet Michael's mum and dad before the baby was born. They arrived at a modest little house with a quirky faux well in the garden, Michael saw Alice catch sight of the infamous garden gnomes and laugh. She grabbed his arm tight, feigned shock on her face.

"Gnomes… thousands of them!" she joked, and Michael shushed her jovially. The door opened, and the couple were greeted with enthusiasm before being led in by Michael's mother. She was a short, stocky lady who was practically through and through. She wore a well-used apron and her short, naturally whitish blonde hair was tucked behind her ears. She wore no make-up and swayed from side to side when she walked, like she might topple over.

"Alice!" she trilled in a heavy cockney accent, "I'm Margaret and this is Bert," she gestured to her husband, who was sitting in his armchair watching TV. "Bert, come and meet Alice!" she ordered, and he immediately rose from his armchair and came over to greet them. Bert was taller and thinner than his wife; he had Michael's smiling eyes and seemed just as enthusiastic as Mrs. Enver.

"So, this is the one who's finally captured our Mikey!" he said, animated.

"Hi, Dad," Michael chimed in, and Bert ruffled his hair as one might a ten-year-old boy's. Michael chuckled and smoothed his hair down.

. . .

"Sit down in here then, Mum is bringing some tea and cake," Bert gestured to them to take a seat on the sofa. "Do you like tea and cake, Alice?"

"Oh, yes. Of course," she answered politely, "I like your gnomes," Alice remarked. Michael rolled his eyes at her and hit his own face in a mock despair.

"Oh yes," Bert beamed, looking flattered by the attention his gnomes were receiving. "I've got fifty-seven now. I'm quite a keen gardener. The gnomes keep me company!"

Alice smiled as Margaret came in carrying a tray bearing a teapot, cups and cake.

"Here we go, lovelies. Tea's up." Margaret started pouring and dishing out cake with her earthy hands that were wrinkled through domestic work. Margaret was the kind of woman who would muck in with anything that needed attention.

"We're so glad our Michael has found a nice girl at last. We thought we might never have any grandbabies, and of course his illness complicates things, but you'll know all about that by now," Bert said.

"Yes – well, I know a bit," Alice replied.

"She knows enough, and Alice and the baby are healthy, which is what matters. Don't bore her with the details, Dad," Michael responded, not wanting his HIV status to become the main point of focus.

"It was a life-changing event, Michael. If you and Alice are spending your lives together, she should know about your past as well as your present," Mr. Enver turned to his wife: "Don't you agree, Margaret?"

"Absolutely," Margaret nodded, and Michael mouthed the word 'sorry' to Alice, who continued to smile and nod appropriately.

"You see; it never should have happened. Michael should never have got HIV in the first place. It was a pure medical mess up," Margaret continued. Bert and Margaret then took turns in sewing the pieces of the story together for Alice. It was comforting, in a way, that they'd been together so long they knew how to be so in tune with each other.

"Michael is a haemophiliac, as I'm sure you know. He needs regular injections to make his blood clot so that if he gets a cut or something, it won't just bleed and bleed," Margaret began.

"He was only sixteen when it happened," Bert went on. "He was climbing over a wall to take a shortcut to college, and he fell. He broke his wrist, didn't you Mikey?" Michael nodded at his dad and allowed the conversation to continue, figuring that they might as well get the full story out the way so it didn't have to be dragged up again.

"He had a splinter of bone sticking through the skin. It would be a bad thing for a person with no health issues, but for a haemophiliac, a wound like that could be fatal."

Alice listened intently, Michael had never told her the full story behind how he had contracted HIV, and she hadn't pushed him to.

"A neighbour had seen him and called an ambulance – they got him in pretty sharpish. I was at work at the time. Margaret followed on once she'd been informed, didn't you, Love?"

"Yes – I was worried sick. I've always been worried about this boy," Margaret said, nodding at Michael.

"Oh Mum, I'm a big boy now. You don't need to worry about me," Michael replied, mildly embarrassed.

"Mums never stop worrying about their children. You'll find this out soon enough, Alice," Margaret turned to address her directly. "It's the curse that goes along with the blessings of motherhood. But it's worth it, when you're the one they come to when they're upset and you can make it better – *if* you can make it better." A slight melancholy came over Margaret, and Michael gave his mother a little smile of encouragement.

"So anyway, the hospital had given him the blood clotting injection first and foremost before treating the wound. This is when Michael's life changed forever – we just didn't know it yet," she added.

"The clotting factor in this particular batch was infected with HIV. It wasn't until years later that we discovered that Michael was HIV positive. We were dumbfounded as to how it could have happened. We got a letter though the post from the hospital, it informed us that Michael had been infected by bad blood – a letter, that's all. Not a phone call, not a meeting – a piece of paper with his fate stamped upon it," Bert said, a note of righteous anger in his voice.

Michael felt Alice squeeze his hand, and she lifted it to her lips, kissing the tips of his fingers. He was trying to read what she might be thinking – perhaps she didn't want to know the details of how his body and blood were infected forever. Maybe she would think him less of a man: a frail, diseased specimen that she was stuck with now he'd unintentionally impregnated her.

The insecurities of his illness hadn't reared their ugly heads for a long time. Michael was mostly positive and lived his moments well. He filled his life with books and learning about herbs, diseases, natural treatments and energy healing, amongst other things. Helping other people attain better health somehow filled the hole that had been left within him by of the unfairness of his illness. It was with him every day, living with him and breathing with him. The constant threat was there that he might become sick; like friends of his had over the years. A lot of them hadn't made it.

He'd met George at a group specifically for people who had become infected by contaminated blood batches. George had been a plucky young thing who didn't let things get him down. Michael found him a breath of fresh air; not only did he understand what it was like living with HIV through no fault of his own, but he just lived life exactly on his terms. The pair became inseparable.

George and Michael would often play football together, and George would always be round at Margaret and Bill's having dinner or cake. *"You're here for a good time, not a long time,"* was something George used to say a lot, and it never really registered with Michael until George wasn't there anymore. When the time came for silence to fall in place of George's brashness, it nearly broke Michael. His tears soaked his pillow every night for at least a year. He would hear Margaret sob sometimes too, through his bedroom wall.

Michael hadn't engaged in risky sex or been sharing needles; neither had George. It was the common perception amongst people when they thought of HIV, he'd discovered. He'd fallen off a wall, one stupid day when he'd woken up late and taken a shortcut because he didn't want to be late for college. His parents had both been carriers for haemophilia, and he just happened to be one of the unlucky thousands to receive an injection from an infected batch of blood. Over the years he'd played scenarios in his head again and again: what if he'd taken a different route? What if he'd gone to a different hospital? What if he'd got up fifteen minutes earlier instead of snoozing through his alarm? These circling thoughts had tormented Michael over the years, but he'd mostly come to terms with them now. The 'what if' game is always a dangerous one, because it's a game that can never be won. Michael chose to live, instead of being consumed by the unfairness, bad luck, karma – or whatever people chose to call it.

He took walks out in nature, come rain or shine, and bought and prepared healthy organic food. His fridge was often all the colours of the rainbow, filled with bright bell peppers, chillis, broccoli, aubergines and carrots. He made juices with turmeric, ginger and cayenne pepper and did not relent in his quest for health. Michael realised how fragile human existence could be and was familiar with the idea that moments can be cut short at any time. He didn't want to waste his.

Now, he had the biggest opportunity of all: to become a father and have a loving relationship. He had to keep fighting the lurking insecurities – their only desire being to ruin everything he was trying to build up, and he would not let that happen.

"Are you okay, sweetheart? You look spaced out," Alice asked, tenderly.

Michael smiled and whispered: "I'm okay. I've got all I need right here."

Alice turned to Margaret and Bert.

"So… how did this even happen?" she asked, "I mean, how did the clotting factor become contaminated in the first place? They must test it all, surely?"

"A good question," Bert piped in. "One that thousands of people affected have been asking for years. There are all sorts of court cases that have been ongoing for God knows how long. Some of them lead nowhere; some of them seem like they've got a hook into a lead for those who are responsible, but then paperwork goes astray, records go missing. It's being covered up by the people responsible. Imagine the compensation they'd have to pay out if they were pinned down for being found guilty, not to mention the other repercussions for them in their drug-making industry – no-one would want to touch their products. But, there will be justice, one day – I know it. Good wins out, that is my firm belief, and I'm sticking by it."

"That's my belief too," Alice told him, taking a sip of her tea.

"But, all that aside, we are so proud of our Michael, and we're going to be grandparents!" Margaret interjected with a broad smile. "Do you know what you're having, love?"

"Erm… we wanted it to be a surprise, didn't we?" Alice turned to Michael.

"Yes, a surprise – but it will either be a boy or a girl," Michael replied wryly as Bert chuckled.

"In other news," Michael continued, "We're moving in together next week, so we have everything ready and settled for when the baby comes."

The conversation got going and Bert and Margaret cooed over the pair. Together, they chatted away about how wonderful it would be, all the things they would need to prepare and how they would both still need to give each a little of their own space. They insisted on buying a cot for the new arrival and all in all, the visit went as smoothly as a first meeting could be expected to go.

The couple left, covered in hugs and kisses from Michael's parents, and made their way back to Alice's place.

Alice asked Michael to stay over with her that night, and she contemplated how her flat would soon no longer be her home – she felt excited by this, and a little nervous. She looked over at Michael, in bed next to her in the darkened room, his face only lit by the streetlamps outside. The light cascaded on to the top of his nose and highlighted the edge of his cheekbone and a few of the curls that lay softly framing his face. He looked like a Greek statue; just perfect in that moment.

"I love you," she whispered, and Michael moved from his perfect position to turn and face her. She could see he was smiling.

"You've never said that before," he replied.

"I know."

"I love you too, Alice, and I love that baby," he said, patting her tummy.

"I'm really happy, Michael. I don't think I've ever been this happy, in all honesty. Everything has always been so hard – like trudging through mud. Now, things seem easy. Can things just be easy?"

"Well, yes. I guess they can," he replied, "We can make them easy."

"Okay," Alice smiled as she turned over to find a comfortable position. Michael automatically snuggled up to her from behind and she felt comforted and content with him. Her eyes fell onto her pink notebook on her bedside table: her dream diary. She felt a moment of unsettlement as she mentally evaluated her latest dreams. Every one of them had centred around Will McAvoy. Alice closed her eyes and prayed for dreamless sleep.

As Christopher disembarked his flight and made his way to the taxi rank at Heathrow airport, the cold air made the hair on his arms bristle. He hadn't thought to dress for an English winter, instead wearing the sandals and baggy pants of his everyday life in India; a chapter he'd chosen to close. He got into the taxi with his luggage; his life over the past five years or so packed up into three large cases.

As the taxi pulled away, destined for his childhood home, Christopher contemplated this and that as he watched the busy world through the car window. He took a breath in and exhaled deeply, feeling a little tingle of excitement in his belly. Alice had informed him of her pregnancy a few months back and he'd collapsed into tears of joy in the middle of the internet café he was using at the time. It reminded him of the cycles of life that keep progressing, no matter what. Things happen whether you choose to be a part of them or not, and he knew whole-heartedly that he wanted to be the best grandad he could be to this new little soul.

The taxi ride passed quickly, and before he knew it, Christopher was standing on the doorstep of Hetty and Bill's with his bags in a pile next to him. A little knot of anxiety formed in his tummy; he hadn't seen his parents for years. The familiar road was quiet and still, it was midnight and Christopher took a moment just to pause and enjoy the silent darkness.

His fingertip hovered over the bell, and he mentally prepared himself before he pushed it. It didn't take long for the door to click open, and he saw his father standing there. Neither of them spoke, but surveyed each other for a minute. To Christopher, Bill looked much the same as he always had. Suddenly, Bill lunged forwards and gave his son a tight hug, much to Christopher's surprise. He could not remember the last time his father had hugged him, he was sure it was when he was a young boy, after that it had been handshakes or nothing. Christopher could feel a little sting of tears behind his eyes at this newfound affection from his father.

"Welcome home son." Bill said, discreetly wiping his eye with the back of his hand. "Come on in then, I'll get the bags," he invited, ushering Christopher into the warm house. Christopher smiled at the familiar smell of his childhood home, and sat, feeling renewed and content on the old chintz sofa while his dad made him a cup of tea.

Chapter Twenty-Two

Twelve months later, the blue-eyed toddler giggled with glee at his parents' applause. He balanced on his immature feet for a few moments before toppling over and landing on his bottom. Raphael's nine months on this earth seemed to have passed in a heartbeat. It was perfect – almost.

Michael excused himself to go to the bathroom, closed the door behind himself and doubled up in pain before sinking to the floor. His face contorted, his teeth clenched in an attempt to silence the pain. These episodes had become common over the last couple of months, and Michael was finding it harder to hide them from Alice. The cool, tiled floor where he now lay his head was familiar; soothing – he didn't have to pretend he was okay when he was lying there. Those tiles had seen more sweat, pain and inconsolability than he could ever let on to the world – to Alice. Michael lay there for a long while, letting his thoughts blur, like a camera losing focus.

A knock on the door broke through his clouded mind,

and Michael quickly mopped his forehead with a hand towel.

"Are you okay in there, sweetheart?" Alice's voice was muffled through the door as she repeated the question she'd asked him frequently of late, and Michael found himself lying to her every time.

"I'm fine, I'll be out in a minute," he replied, in as normal a voice as he could muster.

"Okay, hurry up because Raphael is trying to pull down the Christmas tree again!"

Michael heard her chuckle become more distant as she directed her attention back to their toddler. The guilt started welling up inside him again. He put on a brave face and went to re-join his family, sweeping up his baby boy up in his arms, albeit weakly. With aching muscles, he flew his son around the room like an aeroplane.

Christmas was fast approaching and flakes of snow fell softly past the window. Michael knew he needed to talk to Alice, but every time he thought about speaking up, a knot formed in his throat and the words dried up on his tongue. He gazed blankly out of the window, stuck in his own thoughts while Alice made them hot chocolate in the kitchen. He heard the milk boil over the pan and sizzle on the metal hob.

"Are you okay, Alice?"

"Yes, just got distracted. I won't be a minute," she called. The sentences exchanged between them these days were short. Michael knew the distance was growing between them with all the things he wasn't telling her. The day continued as it always did; it was pleasant enough until night began to creep in.

Alice rocked Raphael until his eyelids started to droop. They had been lucky with him being a content baby. Once in his cot, Raphael always rolled over to sleep with his bum up in the air and slept through the night – a parent's dream.

"I'm just going to put him to bed," Alice informed Michael. Michael already felt a sense of dread spreading within him at not having the baby as a distraction from the awkward space between them – the growing distance that had become like a common and unwelcome intruder in their home.

Alice closed the door to Raphael's bedroom and crept quietly into the living room. She'd made Michael's place warm and inviting, created the perfect family home. Michael had been pleased with the energy she'd injected into the place. At the time, he'd told Alice that he hadn't realised how cold it had been until she'd brought the warmth in.

She sat down next to him on the big L-shaped sofa, where they'd made love so many times, but not for the past few months. Michael didn't look up from the book he was reading until Alice physically took it from his hands.

"What are you doing?" he asked.

Alice looked at him with eyes that were pleading for something.

"What's wrong?" she asked.

Michael looked her in the eye now; he hadn't looked at her directly for weeks. He'd forgotten how beautiful she actually was, and in that moment, he felt like a fool for how he'd been acting.

"I haven't been very well, Alice," he admitted. "I didn't want to worry you. I realise I've been acting like a thoughtless idiot. I'm sorry," Michael looked at her, his eyes suddenly sad.

"I can't bear this space between us," Alice responded. "I feel like I'm living with a stranger, like you don't want to be around me. You're always disappearing to the bathroom or out for a walk or off to bed early – anywhere that's away from me." Tears began to spill from her eyes and drop on to her flushed cheeks. "When you say you're not well, what do you mean exactly? What's wrong?"

Michael pulled her close and squeezed her, which only made her cry harder. He kissed her on the forehead and held her face in his hands.

"I'm sorry," he said. "I know I've been distant, and I was stupid enough to think we could just carry on like that. I should have talked to you. I've been burying my head in the sand."

He saw her looking at him, her brow furrowed with worry. Adrenalin pumped like crazy through his body, and Michael knew he had to face up to what was happening. He took a deep breath. "I had some tests done because I've been feeling unwell for a while, I'm waiting for the results to come back. Best-case scenario could be hepatotoxicity – that's just a fancy word for liver damage. My symptoms seem to fit, but they could also fit with the worst-case scenario. I was trying to pretend things were okay."

"We're meant to share everything with each other, aren't we? I'm not going anywhere," Alice reassured.

Michael put his head in his hands and released his pent-up emotions in a huge, uncontrollable sob. Alice held him in her arms as he shook; suddenly he felt so small and vulnerable.

"But, what if I am?" Michael blurted, his deepest fears coming to the fore. "I'm really fucking scared. I do everything to make sure I stay healthy, and now I'm sick. This is the first time in my life that I've been happy. I've got a beautiful girlfriend and a healthy son. It could all be taken away just like that. It's not fair." Michael broke down once more at the thought of losing everything he'd ever wanted. He punched the sofa with his fist, his palm marked with nail indentations from anxiety, his nails bitten down to the skin.

"You're not going anywhere; do you hear me?" Alice replied. "I'm not losing you, and Raphael is not losing his daddy. If it is your liver, then what?"

"I'd have to go for further tests to find out the extent of the damage, and I'd have to change my drugs, seeing as though that's the only thing that could have caused the damage in the first place."

"Okay, that sounds like a feasible solution," Alice said. "What about…the worst-case scenario?" she asked.

"I'm hot one minute and shivering the next, I'm losing weight – I've seen it before, Alice. I watched George die. I watched his body deteriorate, unable to fight, waiting for that one infection to finish him off. He was diagnosed around the same time I was. We were friends for four years. I can't help thinking of the similarities."

"Look at me, Michael," Alice instructed. "You're not going to die." She tilted his chin towards her, his tears dripping down over her fingertips, "when did you have the tests?"

"Only today. I was hoping I would just start feeling well again. Putting off finding out if something is really wrong, I suppose. I'm just a flawed human like everyone else. I don't want to die, I don't want to leave you and Raph," Michael cried desperately. "I'm supposed to protect you and look after you, Alice – I can't fail at that."

"Listen to me, I don't want to hear any more talk about dying," she told him firmly. "You're thinking of all the worst things that could happen, but they haven't happened, and they might never happen. I'm sorry about George, I know that affected you so deeply, but you are not him."

"I don't know, Alice. This has shaken me and I'm finding it really hard to be optimistic."

"I know it's hard, Michael, but let's focus on getting the results and taking it from there, okay?" Alice squeezed his cold hand. He was deteriorating; he'd lost his spark.

"I'm tainted, Alice, I'm always going to be tainted," he went on. "I'm a walking fucking disease, whether I find a new combination of drugs or not. You deserve better than this."

Alice drew herself up and spoke calmly: "Michael, you listen to me. You are not your virus, okay? You are a wonderful, loving person who I count myself lucky to be with. You have given me our beautiful son who was meant to walk this earth, and you were meant to walk this earth as his father. You are all of these things, and you happen to have a virus. That doesn't change who you are or how much I love you. I love everything that you are – and that includes your blood, infected or not."

Michael couldn't speak. He wondered how he could have found someone so accepting – someone who actually loved him unconditionally. It really didn't matter to her; he could feel her honesty. In the back of his mind, though, there was dread – the fear of illness that had always hung over him.

The evening turned into night and Michael warmed his cold, trembling hand inside Alice's warm one while they sat in silence. He tried to push the thoughts out of his head that he might leave them both behind; he didn't want Alice to deal with his loss. He didn't want Raphael to forget him. His eyes focused on the ticking clock on the wall in front of him, knowing that he could not slow it down.

Chapter Twenty-Three

Scott sat at his polished desk at McAvoy and Son, staring at the screen on his Apple Mac. He wasn't really in the present moment; he was reflecting on his life – something he'd rarely done in his sixty-two years on this planet. He could hear Will tapping at his computer through the half-frosted glass partition. That's all he did: work. Scott had attempted to get Will to open up about Alice – something that was alien to him. Jacoline had always addressed the kids in talks about feelings and emotions. His efforts were counterproductive in any case – Will had only clammed up even more. All he had told his father, some time ago, was that Alice was pregnant and had chosen to distance herself from him, and that he had to accept it.

Will was helping the community, just as he'd wanted. He gave free legal aid to poor families who had found themselves in strife with no means to pay, yet Scott could see that Will was more miserable than ever. Scott advised his son that it was time to leave thoughts of Alice behind and move on, and noticed that over a year later, Will seemed increasingly stoic, throwing himself into work to avoid thinking about Alice. This attitude reminded Scott of himself, and it bothered him. As much as he wanted his son to forget about this girl, he didn't want Will to live an unhappy life – as he had done.

Scott was a success at making money, he'd worked his fingers to the bone for it. He hadn't come from a privileged family – on the contrary, his home life had been cold and strict. There was little money and little love to go around, yet he uncovered a fierce determination at his core and would not let his upbringing define him as a man. As soon as he was able, Scott had taken his first job delivering pizzas and saved up for his own education, putting himself through law school and working the entire duration to support himself. His parents were not interested; it was as if they had expected to leave their children to their own devices as soon as they were out of the womb – like abandoned harp seals. Scott didn't care for his parents, as they hadn't cared for him, but he loved his own son. Sometimes he wished he could show Will that everything he had done for him and Jacoline had been in their best interests. He made sure they never went without food or clothing; he went above and beyond so that they would not want for anything. But now, sitting here in his office, Scott reflected on all the times Jacoline had needed his support and he'd put work first. He remembered all the times he hadn't read with Will or taken him out on his bike. He hadn't really been there all those years.

Scott felt an uncomfortable feeling spread through him, a heavy knotted feeling – it was guilt. What did all those years mean if Will wasn't happy now? Scott sprang up from his chair and went through the double doors to the cold air outside. For the first time, he looked at people. He looked at their faces – some smiling, others frowning or indifferent. All these people had lives and feelings and stuff going on that wasn't apparent to an onlooker. He breathed in deeply, feeling grateful for the first time in his life for a lungful of air. He felt like someone had flicked on a switch at the back of his head, and suddenly he could see.

The doors clicked behind him and Scott moved aside for Will's clients to leave. A middle-aged black woman with greying hair and her teenage son walked past him, the mother turning to Scott with a smile and saying:

"He's really saved us! He's a good egg. Thank you."

She moved on before Scott could reply. He felt an inner sense of pride for his son, though he knew he was nowhere near being able to take the credit for Will having turned out to be a 'good egg'.

After a few minutes, Scott went back inside the building, rubbing his hands together to regain some warmth. He went over to Will, his face thoughtful.

"Hey, son, let's take a lunch hour, we'll go to that Chinese buffet place down the street."

Will looked up at him, eyebrows raised. "A lunch hour? You always work through lunch, what's going on?"

"Nothing's going on, I just want to have lunch with you. Is that a crime?"

"Erm, no, I suppose not," Will replied, "okay, let me finish up here."

Scott handwrote a sign and stuck it in the front window, saying they'd be back in one hour. He felt a little buzz of excitement doing it. He'd never in his life stuck a 'gone for lunch' sign in the window before. The energy of this new venture with his son seemed to agree with Scott, and he felt alive for the first time in a long while.

Will and his father walked in silence to the Chinese buffet at the end of the street. They chose a table in the corner of the bustling place, sat down, and were immediately served with prawn crackers.

Scott glanced at Will, venturing the question – although he already knew the answer: "What's wrong, son?"

"Nothing," Will replied, not looking up at him.

"Alice?" said Scott, which provoked Will to meet his gaze.

"Yes, Alice. You're going to tell me to forget her. It's been a year and a half since I last saw her," Will told him. "Time ticks by, but it's just not that simple to forget."

"I'm not going to tell you to forget her – I realise that it would have happened by now if you were going to do that," his father responded. "So, instead, tell me something about her and I promise I won't judge you."

Will looked at his father for a long moment before he spoke.

"We just connected, all those years ago. I never forgot her, and I just can't believe how much I missed my chance to be in her life. Twice – twice we've been pulled away from each other by fate, or whatever you want to call it."

Scott watched Will turn over a prawn cracker in his hand, "I'm pissed off, Dad. I'm pissed off that the universe has dangled this carrot for so long and there was never any hope for her and me. It's fucking cruel, and now some other man is living the life I wanted to have with her. When I met her, she was vulnerable, I wanted to look after her the way I failed to look after Victoria. I thought the attraction was some subconscious desire to try and fix my guilt about my sister, but now, all these years later, I realise that there's more to it. I want to make her happy. I want to be the person she calls when she's upset, or the person she tells when something happens in her day. I want *her*."

There was a moment of silence as Scott considered his son's words.

"Victoria wasn't your fault," he said. "I don't know if I ever really told you that, but I should have. Your mother and I messed up, and I'm sorry that you had so much burden placed upon you. You did more for her than most brothers would have done. I'm proud of you for that." There was another brief silence; Will looked blankly at the menu.

"I'm sorry about Alice and how things have worked out. Do you want me to have her partner killed?" Scott said with a smirk.

The atmosphere melted to something much nicer, and even Will's stony expression broke into the ghost of a smile.

"She told me that she always thought of me as her saviour. That's all I ever wanted to be, and not only did I not achieve that, I did the opposite. I hurt her and left her to deal with it by herself, without a word."

"You did what you needed to do, Will, and you never had any intention to hurt her," Scott soothed. "You've got a good heart, and that makes you a better man than I have ever been."

"I've seen changes in you, Dad. I don't think you're as heartless as you'd have people believe," Will replied.

Scott flicked his head back in acknowledgement and started eating the prawn crackers. "Maybe you're right," he said. "I know I've made mistakes that I can't make up for. I can only make better decisions from this day forward. I've even become disinterested in taking on Richardsons' cases – I don't know if I want to play that part anymore, but I fear I'm too deep to get out."

Will put down his menu and looked Scott square in the face. "That's major, Dad. Getting out of Richardsons' clutches would be the best thing you could ever do. Do you really think you can cut them loose?"

"I'm pondering it, Will, and that's as far as it will go for now," Scott replied. "Like I said, I know too much. I've had to make a lot of evidence disappear over the years; they trust me."

Over the next half hour or so, they ate and talked pleasantly, just like a normal father and son, before heading back to the office. Scott felt a surge of positivity from their conversation – he was bonding with his son, and it was a long time overdue.

A s they approached McAvoy and Son, Will stopped dead in his tracks. There was Alice, standing outside the double doors, looking serious.

"Hi, Will," she greeted him timidly and half waved with her hand. Scott sensed the awkwardness and let himself into the office, leaving Will and Alice outside alone.

"Alice, what are you doing here?" Will asked. "Come inside," he beckoned before she could answer his question.

They entered Will's organic green office space and Alice perched herself on the edge of the sofa, clutching her bag to her lap. Will sat at the opposite end, twisting his fingers together nervously.

"I'm sorry," Alice said, bluntly.

"For what?" he replied.

"I'm sorry for the way things happened, and I'm sorry for being here now and probably making you feel awkward."

"You've got nothing to be sorry for, okay?" he turned to look at her. "You look well, but you look worried – is something the matter?"

Alice burst into tears and Will's instinct was to hold her, but he didn't feel it was his place, or whether she would want him to. He handed her a tissue from the box on the table, moving just a touch closer to her. He waited patiently for her to speak, trying to quell the dormant emotions now rising up within him.

After a few moments, Alice began: "I came here for some legal advice, and if I'm really honest with myself, I wanted to see you."

"Okay, well here I am, much the same as when I last saw you," he smiled weakly. "I work a lot. But never mind me. How are you and your baby? Tell me about him – or her?" Will's words were peppered with sadness; she was living his dream without him.

Alice smiled as she spoke.

"He's amazing. We called him Raphael, and he's just a ball of giggles and love. He's nine months old now."

"I'm happy for you – really," replied Will earnestly. He *was* happy for her, despite his other mixed emotions.

Rubbing his face nervously, he ventured:

"Why are you so upset?"

Alice paused and her eyebrows knitted together

"It's Raphael's dad, Michael," she began. "He's sick and I'm really scared. He's trying to hide it, and he thinks I haven't noticed. That is partly why I'm here. I'll get straight to the point; he was given HIV contaminated blood products years ago by the hospital – I'm talking thirty-odd years ago. It's ruled his life ever since, and all the cases brought forward to investigate it have met dead ends. I want your opinion on whether you think this is something you could take on as a case." Alice stopped to blow her nose on the pocket tissue. "Someone has to answer for this; thousands of people have been affected and they've just been forgotten about. Now, it appears that his drugs aren't working like they were before and I'm worried for us. I'm angry for all the families that have been ripped apart – unsuspecting victims being infected through no fault of their own. I just needed to do something, and here I am. I'm sorry, Will, I probably shouldn't have brought this to you." Alice was exasperated and confused; the tears renewed themselves and Will handed her another tissue.

"Alice, I'm sorry you're going through this. Are you and the baby…well?" he almost tripped over the last word, not knowing whether he was being insensitive.

"We're clear of HIV if that's what you mean," she replied, "It's Michael who is suffering."

"I am familiar with some infection scandals," Will responded. "I'll have to do some research on the blood products, although this isn't my area of expertise – but I may be able to help. I'd need to discuss it with my father and maybe set up a consultation with you and Michael to get all the details. My father would be the best person to take on this case, he has far more knowledge in this area, and under the circumstances of our personal relationship, it would be best if I didn't get too involved. How does that sound?"

"That sounds good," she replied, seeming relieved.

Will didn't look at her, he couldn't connect with her in this moment and then watch her walk away again.

"Okay," he said. "Give me your phone number and I'll be in touch."

As Alice jotted down her details on the piece of paper, Will looked at her small, delicate hands shaping each number with the McAvoy and Son branded biro. She handed him the small square of paper and had a flashback of when they were stuck in the school cupboard together, making origami bugs.

"Sorry," she apologised automatically as she accidentally brushed his hand. "You will always be my soulmate, Will, and I will always love you," she confessed. "Please never doubt that, never forget it, I've kept away from you to protect you, and to protect myself. I can't afford to be around you too much; the pull is too strong. I never wanted you to think I didn't care, but I reasoned with myself that it might be better if you did think that. I had to find the strength of a lion to do the right thing."

Will met her gaze.

"But you're here now. You could have gone to any solicitors at any place. You've chosen to come here, to me."

She half-smiled. "I'm an imperfect human, Will. We all are. I think about you every day, and I dream about you still. I let down my guard and found myself coming here. Sometimes, even lions have had enough of being strong." She squeezed his two hands desperately in hers, turned, and left before he could say another word.

Will sat there, trying to assimilate the information Alice had just given him. He felt sorry for her predicament, but the overriding feeling after his short conversation with Alice was one of hope. She still loved him, she thought about him every day, the same as he thought about her. His father's words versed through his brain '*win her back*'. He decided in that moment that he wouldn't rest until he made her see that he was the one she should be with. He was determined – he wouldn't fail.

Chapter Twenty-Four

M ichael waited for the text message reply from the client whose appointment he'd just rescheduled. It was the third one he'd postponed this week. Letting people down wasn't his way; he was disappointed in himself but didn't feel up to seeing his clients – neither physically nor emotionally. He had a session booked later in the day with Elise, who had started some energy treatments on him, but Michael felt worse, if anything. He was contemplating the very real prospect that he could die; it was the most afraid he'd been since he'd watched George slip away.

"Hi, sweetheart! Someone wants to give their daddy a big cuddle," Alice trilled as she plonked Raphael on Michael's chest.

"Hi, buddy," Michael pushed his dark emotions away on sight of his baby boy's beaming face. He squeezed him tightly and tickled his ribs, sending Raphael into cascades of uncontrollable giggles. Alice smiled at the exchange between father and son as she rubbed her tired eyes.

"How are you feeling, love?" she asked delicately.

"A bit better today I think," Michael lied, pausing for a

moment and looking at his girlfriend. "I love you, you know?"

"I know. I love you too," Alice replied.

"I know we haven't been intimate for a while," he continued, rubbing the back of his neck apprehensively. "I don't want you to think it's because I don't want you, because I do. I just can't at the moment."

"Don't be daft, I understand completely," Alice reassured, brushing a few stray hairs away from her face. "Look, I wanted to talk about something," she knelt on the floor in front of Michael, their eyes level. "I hope you don't mind, but I went to seek some legal advice a few weeks ago about the contaminated blood products and whether you could have a case."

"People have been fighting it for years, Alice," he replied knowingly. "People who have lots of money to put into getting to the bottom of it have failed. I don't want to sound negative, but I'm not willing to gamble the little amount of savings that we have for something that probably won't pay off." He softened his tone and touched her little finger with his. "I appreciate you going, I know your heart is in the right place, but I don't see the use in pursuing it."

"I know, but I had to do something useful," Alice replied. "I'm not saying that we're going to take it forward, but the person I saw used to be a good friend of mine and he has agreed to set up a free consultation at his practice. I think it's worth doing that at least – what do you think?"

Raphael squirmed on his father's lap, reaching over in Alice's direction. She picked him up, stroking his back as he lay his head on her shoulder the way he always did.

"Since when did you have friends who are lawyers?" Michael questioned, looking thoughtful.

"It's an old friend, his name is Will. I hadn't seen him

for years, then found out he and his father opened a solicitors over in Greenwich." Alice's face flushed. "Will you come to the consultation at least?"

"Okay," he submitted with a sigh. "I'll come to a consultation. When is it?"

"He's asked if Thursday at two pm is okay," said Alice, surveying the text from Will on her phone.

"I've got to go and meet mum," Alice said suddenly. "She wants to plan how she's going to make Raph's birthday cake and wants to know whether to do a dinosaur or a robot. I did tell her that he's not going to know the difference, and that his birthday is two-and-a-half months away, but you know what she's like. She glanced at him over her shoulder: "Do you need anything before I go?"

"No, I'm fine. Have a good time with your mum," Michael answered. Alice rolled her eyes in reply and went to get herself and the baby ready to leave.

Something in Michael's brain was trying to get his attention but he couldn't place it; something about the name Will. He was sure Alice had mentioned him some time ago, or he was familiar with the name somehow. Michael's brow furrowed as he tried to locate the thought in his mind. As he heard the front door close behind Alice, he had an image in his brain of a pink diary. It was Alice's dream diary. He recalled seeing the name Will written on its pages one time when he'd knocked it off the side table. He didn't read the diary, but had noticed this name when picking it up to set it back in its place.

Michael spent the next hour distracting himself from the knowledge that he'd read this man's name in his girlfriend's dream diary. He went for a long walk, and kept telling himself that it didn't matter, that there was probably nothing to it, but still, he was curious. He couldn't shake the feeling that there was something unbeknownst to him that he should perhaps be aware of, but at the same time, he didn't want to betray Alice's trust. He resolved to ask her when she returned home.

Another hour passed, and Michael couldn't bear it any longer. He went over to the bedroom side drawer and took out the pink diary. His heart raced as he held it, knowing he was about to do something morally wrong. Nonetheless, he opened the book and started leafing through the pages of detailed dreams recorded in blue biro. He skimmed the pages, smiling when he saw his name or Raphael's involved in some sort of weird dream sequence. It didn't take him long to find the name he was looking for: two yellowed origami bugs nestled on this particular page, and his heart froze as he read the words:

'I saw Will through a pane of glass. There were people all around, but no-one would help me. I stood at the glass crying with my hand pressed up against it and he did the same. I just wanted to get to him.'

He continued to read the next pages, Will's name appearing almost daily in the entries.

'I was at a party outside with tents and lots of people. Will was there, and he was trying to catch my attention. I wanted to talk to him, but I pretended not to see him. He managed to come face to face with me, kissed me and told me that he loved me. I told him I loved him too, and then we went our separate ways. I felt sad when I woke up.'

Michael closed the diary; he didn't want to read anymore. He started coughing uncontrollably for a few minutes; there was an uncomfortable heaviness in his heart. Michael went back to bed, his chest sore from the coughing attack, and tried to block out the world with sleep for a time.

———

Will picked up the phone, his father watching him through the unfrosted half of the glass partition between them. Will glanced over and caught his dad's eye – he was shaking his head to indicate that he wasn't available to take calls. Will frowned in answer and ended the call quickly.

"That was Richardsons again, Dad," Will informed Scott as he walked into his office, uninvited. Scott didn't look up from his paperwork.

"You're going to have to answer their calls at some point, Dad – that's the fifth time this week."

"I know, I'm just trying to figure out the best way to address the situation," Scott replied. "They're desperate for me to take on their latest shitstorm. People are coming forward, claiming side effects from one of their apparently safe painkillers. Bleeds in the brain that have led to fatalities are the result, to be exact. I just don't want to be involved anymore."

His son looked at him wearily. "Well, I respect that decision, Dad, but I can't keep telling them you're not here."

Scott raised his eyebrows in acknowledgement and Will stood there for a long moment without saying anything else.

"Is there something else, son?"

"Erm, well I've set you up a consultation tomorrow at two pm," Will rubbed his forehead. "What do you know about infected blood products back in the 1980s and 90s?"

Scott looked over the top of his glasses at Will. "Infected with what?"

"HIV and hepatitis."

"Ah jeeez Will, I'm trying to get away from Richardsons!"

"So, Richardsons have involvement with this?" Will interjected with interest. "I suspected if anyone would know about this type of thing, you would. I didn't realise it was right on our doorstep, though."

"I can't say for sure, Will, until I know all the details, but there was foul play from them in that period," Scott replied. "I've been with them a long time, remember? I know all their secrets. They were shipping cheap blood products all over the world that hadn't been tested, from South African prisoners no less." He looked Will in the eye. "This stays between these four walls. It would be a hell of a coincidence if someone came to me to go against Richardsons of all companies – don't you think?"

"Coincidence, fate – call it what you like. Things happen for a reason, people and circumstances cross over all the time in an intricate web of synchronicities," Will told his father. "I truly believe this is one such circumstance. This is important, Dad, this is for Alice. Well, it's for Alice's boyfriend – he's the one who became wrongly infected. Please help her. You know how I feel about her and if we're in a position to help, then we should."

"And what do you get out of this Will, a broken heart again?"

"I get to redeem some of the shit I caused for her all those years ago, I get to be her saviour, like I always should have been – or at least play a role in it. Maybe she will even see me in a different light. Please, Dad – do it for me."

His father sighed. "I'll help if I can, Will, but I'm doing this solely for you. I can't promise anything, but I'll try."

───────

Later that evening, Michael lay on Elise's cream reiki couch, eyes closed, feeling tense. He inhaled the smell of burning sage, but it did not soothe him.

"Would you relax?" Elise asked him, "you're like a coiled spring. Let go of the tension in your shoulders."

"I can't, I'm too wound up," he said. His head was swimming with all kinds of thoughts; none of them good.

"I know you're scared, but it's going to be okay," Elise reassured.

"It's not that. I read Alice's diary," he confessed. "I know I shouldn't have. I'm pretty sure that this solicitor we are going to see is an old flame of hers. She didn't tell me, but from what she wrote there are obviously feelings there."

"Everyone has a past, Michael, even you and I," Elise reminded him. "We were good together."

"That was a long time ago, Elise. We were irresponsible uni students."

"You've always been responsible, Mister Enver. I never really got over you dumping me, you know."

"It wasn't like that – you knew the fears I had. I didn't want you to be subjected to a life with me and my baggage. Besides, you're married now – you're happy, aren't you?"

"Happy, what's that again?" Elise scoffed. "Okay, reiki done. You're in balance again."

Michael took a moment to regain his senses after sitting up from a lying down position.

"Aren't you happy?" he repeated.

"Not for years, sweetheart," she responded, "are you?"

"I'm not sure what I am at the moment; confused, worried, scared. Happy – not so much."

Elise put her hands around his waist then and moved her face closer so that the tip of her nose was almost touching his. He smelled her familiar perfume, the one she'd worn as long as he'd known her. He observed the grainy texture of foundation on her forehead and her chocolate brown eyes staring into his. He didn't move away, but sat motionless as the last tea light extinguished itself.

Chapter Twenty-Five

By the time the appointment at McAvoy and Son came around that Thursday, Alice was a nervous wreck – not because of the possible outcome of their meeting, but because Will and Michael were going to be in the same place at the same time, which was causing her some notable anxiety.

"Alice, would you please stop picking your nails – I'm the one who's supposed to be nervous, I think," Michael said, softly.

"Yes, sorry," she replied, giving his knee a squeeze. They were seated on a black leather sofa in the waiting area, from where Alice could see into Scott's office; Will and his father were discussing something that seemed important. She glanced over to the other side of the room where Will's office was, acknowledging the green sofa where she'd previously sat, and cried. She had wanted him to hold her, the way he had when she was eighteen. She shook the guilt out of her head and watched Michael unfold a leaflet that had been lying on the desk. She witnessed the white glossy paper tremble slightly in his hand; his overall presence was weaker than it had been, and his skin had a greyish tinge. Michael began coughing uncontrollably at that moment, and Alice rubbed his back.

"It's okay, sweetheart," she soothed, although she didn't believe it herself. The coughing fits had become regular, and once this latest episode was over, Michael took some deep breaths and wiped the spit from his chapped lips with a tissue. His eyes were bloodshot; he clutched his chest, which was rapidly expanding and contracting with each breath.

Alice touched his arm sympathetically "We'll get this over with and then get you home. I'm sorry I interfered and dragged you out here when you ought to be resting."

"I'm an adult, Alice – I agreed to come of my own free will," he responded. "Though I must admit, I do just want to get this over with."

They heard the glass door click open then and Scott invited them into his office, shaking hands with both of them as they entered. Will left his dad's office, giving both Alice and Michael a nod of acknowledgement, briefly shaking Michael's hand and introducing himself. Michael froze internally at the name *Will*: this was the man who had some sort of history with his girlfriend – though he didn't know what. Alice and Michael sat down at Scott's sprawling glossy black desk as he clicked the door shut behind them.

M eanwhile, in his own office, Will slumped into his green chair, more harassed than he'd imagined being upon meeting Alice's boyfriend. He decided to have as little involvement as possible in the case if Scott decided to take it on. He would be there for Alice, when she needed him for support and he'd try to protect his raw and delicate heart at least a little. He busied himself, making a few banal courtesy calls, while the clock ticked by painfully slowly. The woman he loved was just on the other side of that glass pane, and he couldn't do anything about it.

After exactly thirty-one minutes, Will heard the chair legs in Scott's office screech across the floor. He glanced up inconspicuously to see Alice and Michael getting to their feet. A second later there was a sudden crash and a thump – Will jumped up to see Michael's slight figure collapsing to the floor of the office. He rushed in and crouched by Michael's side – Alice was trying to revive him by slapping his cheeks, while Scott dialled the emergency services.

"He's breathing," Will stated urgently, holding the back of his hand to Michael's mouth. Alice's tears fell on to Michael's face and she squeezed his hand.

"It's okay, love," she repeated, over and over – more times than Will cared to hear. Alice looked at Will, her eyes pleading for reassurance.

"We'll get him to the hospital, it'll be okay," Will put his hand on hers, surprising himself. She didn't move it away, but stayed in a kneeling position on the floor, gazing at her boyfriend's clammy pale face, her hand in the protection of Will's.

Two paramedics arrived ten minutes later and strode in purposefully with a bag of equipment. Alice and Will automatically moved aside to let them work, answering questions as the pair assessed the situation.

"What's his name, love?" asked the paramedic with short, thick blonde hair. She was tall and big-boned, with an air of comfort and responsibility around her; the kind of person who immediately made others feel at ease and reassured. The other paramedic was older – a thin, balding man with dark hair and a cheerful demeanour.

"Michael – his name is Michael, he's forty-seven,"

Alice responded. "He's got haemophilia and HIV. He's been suffering for a while with a cough, tiredness, muscle cramps and aches. He just collapsed all of a sudden."

"Okay, love. That's helpful. What is your name and relationship to Michael?"

"I'm Alice. He's my...partner" She looked briefly at Will as she said the word 'partner' and he caught her eye. That word felt like a little arrow in Will's heart. He knew that Alice had realised that when she said it.

"Michael just recently started a different combination of antiretrovirals. We found out the old ones had caused some damage to his liver; he's waiting for further tests. He's been really worried. So have I," Alice informed the paramedics.

"Okay, let's take him in," said the balding paramedic.

The ambulance journey seemed like a blur. Alice felt like she was in an underwater bubble, only vaguely aware of the paramedic speaking into his radio. Will, beside her, held her hand, but she was numb to the situation. Her stress response had put her on autopilot; she was answering questions without knowing what she was saying and going through the motions without consciously thinking about anything. She looked at Michael on the bed in the back of the ambulance, his only movements caused by the turns and bumps in the roads as the ambulance rushed to the hospital. He had an oxygen mask fastened to his face and the blonde paramedic had inserted an IV drip into his arm.

They arrived at Southwood Hospital quickly and then ensued a flurry of activity: voices and people all around. The next thing Alice knew, she was sitting in a private waiting room, clutching a cup of coffee, the cheap plastic burning the skin of her fingers.

"Alice?" she looked to her side to see Will seated next to her, also clutching a plastic cup from the vending machine. "Alice, you haven't spoken for a while – are you okay?"

"Yes, I'm fine," she replied, still on autopilot. "I don't remember coming into this room. Where have they taken Michael?"

"They're still treating him. He's in the best place. I'll stay with you," Will's deep South African voice echoed around Alice's brain. In her current fog of thinking, his voice brought her back to when she was eighteen, and she hung on every word he said.

"You are the love of my life, Will," she muttered blankly. "No matter what I do, I can never change that."

Will looked at her, seeing her gaze transfixed on the wall in front, which bore an acrylic painting of ochre-coloured flowers.

"And you are mine," he replied. "I'm here now because you're hurting, because something terrible has happened, and I have to be here, just near you – just enough to watch over you."

"I'm sorry," Alice said, her eyes unmoving. "I don't want to let go of everything that happened between us. I'm scared of letting go. I couldn't bear to think of you with someone else, and that's unfair of me. I've made you face my relationship with Michael and I know if it was the other way around I would be devastated. I'm so sorry for whatever I've done to hurt you, Will. I just don't under-stand my feelings; I never thought I could love two people at the same time, but I do. I love you and I love Michael. It isn't the same love; each love is different, like each finger-print is different."

Will didn't speak for a moment, and Alice looked at

him in the eye for the first time since they'd left the McAvoy and Son offices. His irises were almost golden; almond-shaped eyes that she'd fallen in love with. Within those eyes she could read a thousand feelings that had been put to rest, and a few that were still being questioned.

"I believe that you do love both of us, I used to think love would conquer all – just like in *Jane Eyre*," he spoke softly, "the truth is in your choices. I saw how you reacted to Michael collapsing, how you spoke to him even though he couldn't respond. I wanted to try and win you back, but it isn't the right action to take. Every day you go home to Michael, you are choosing him. You chose your family, and I cannot argue with that. In South Africa I had a pair of onyx bookends on my shelf that were made from a single piece split into two; it was like me and you. It always used to make me feel close to you when you were thousands of kilometres away from me. As long as you're okay, wherever you are in the world, even If I am not with you, then I can be okay, too. I just need to let go of the idea of us, I think I am finally ready to try."

"Please don't let go of me," Alice pleaded. "I understand you needing to move on, but please don't forget me and put me down as an experience that gets filed away, like two dated origami bugs stuck in a book somewhere. Don't let that connection break altogether. Our souls are tied up with each other somehow. I'm scared to let go."

"I believe our souls are tied up together, you're right," he agreed. "But if that is true, then we can't ever really lose each other. Don't be scared."

"You're the only thing that makes sense to me, Will. I have my life, Michael, and my baby, and I'm fulfilled by all those things. But somehow, if you're not there, I don't know who I am. I know how selfish I'm being by hanging on. I promise I'll let you go, but don't let it be just yet. Please?"

"Okay, Alice. A lot has happened today; let's not think about this right now."

Alice leaned on his shoulder, and Will squeezed her arm. "It's okay," he lulled her and let her close her eyes for a while. They were both startled by the entrance of Michael's parents, looking worried. Alice immediately got up, she could see Michael's mother had been crying. They looked at Alice and then at Will as if to ask who he was and why he was there. Alice answered the unasked question: "This is Will. He helped when Michael collapsed."

Bert lunged over to him and shook his hand warmly and emotionally in both of his own.

"Thank you," Bert gushed, his forehead lined with worry – the crease in between his eyebrows was deepest of all.

Will nodded in acknowledgement and turned to Alice, saying: "I'll give you some space. You know where I am if you want me. Let me know how Michael is, will you?"

"Yes. Thank you," Alice said as Will left, then turned to fill in Bert and Margaret on what had happened. The three then waited for what seemed like an age, with nothing to do except drink more cups of coffee.

"Has your mum got Raph?" Margaret enquired.

"Yes, I called her earlier. She's going to keep him tonight until we know what's going on."

"Okay, dear," she said, putting her hand on top of Alice's. "I'm so glad Michael has got you. You're a good match for him, you know."

Alice smiled weakly, and Margaret continued. "There are a lot of people out there who wouldn't take a chance on our Michael, given the circumstances, but you saw through all that and saw the person he was inside. You've given him what he's always wanted. I'm grateful to you for that."

Alice burst into tears of guilt, confusion, worry for Michael. Her brain was overheating from racing thoughts. The sudden realisation hit her that Michael might die. She'd been pondering what she wanted not half an hour ago, caught up in the dormant feelings she had for Will. All the while Michael was fighting for consciousness. She felt sick at herself and cried harder still. Her tears were only broken by the sudden appearance of a nurse at the waiting room door with an unreadable expression on her face.

Chapter Twenty-Six

W ill flicked his pen across his desk, brought it back to his hand and flicked it again. He had been doing this for twenty-two minutes so far, his mind awash with Alice's confused words. It had been seven days since Michael had collapsed and Will hadn't heard anything from her. Whatever the outcome, he told himself that he couldn't be involved with the situation anymore. It was killing him.

Scott walked in wearing a black trench coat, carrying a briefcase full of paperwork. "Hi, son," he greeted. "Get some coffee on, would you?" Will obeyed absent-mindedly, flicking the switch on the coffee machine, Scott's eyes on him.

"No news from Alice then, judging by your face?"

"No," Will replied.

Scott's brow furrowed. "I'm finding it hard to want to help her case when I can see what it's doing to you."

Will turned to face his father.

"Please, Dad, if you know something that could help her and Michael, please do it, for me. Remember how upset Victoria and I were when Gregor died because of AIDS? Do it for *his* memory, for how much he meant to us – even if he didn't mean anything to you. This is your chance to put things right," he said, seriously.

Scott muttered something inaudible as he hung up his coat and lay his briefcase carefully on the table. He was quiet for a moment before speaking again.

"I do know something," he said. "I know a hell of a lot, in fact," he opened the briefcase and took out a number of old-looking files in yellowing jackets, briefly turning to the door to make sure no-one was watching. "This is just some of the wrongdoing that Richardsons have taken part in over the years, and this particular file pretty much gives enough evidence to pin at least some of the HIV infected blood products on them," Scott said, leafing through the pages of the foremost file.

"There are the names here of the prisoners who got sent to Van Rooyen prison – you know, the one on the south side of Sandton in Joberg?" Will nodded in acknowledgement and waited for his dad to continue. "These dates are between 1984-1990 and record the inmates who gave blood in exchange for phonecards," he added, handing the relevant pages to Will, who surveyed the list of names, date of births, blood types and signatures of the blood donors beside each column.

Scott then passed Will another thick file with the names of the prisoner intake at Van Rooyen in the 20 years prior to 1984. "These records show the health status of the inmate upon arrival, including HIV status," Scott explained. "If you cross-reference the intake records with the prison hospital records, you'll find a large proportion of them were already infected upon arrival to the prison. It doesn't account for anyone who became infected whilst serving their time inside jail, so the numbers are likely to be higher."

Will listened intently to this new information, eyes wide with realisation, as Scott continued. "The whole thing was a mess. That prison was so corrupt they even had inmates working as fucking pharmacy assistants – no knowledge about pharmacies, medication or anything. Richardsons made a deal with the head honcho of Van Rooyen – a worm of a man named Louw, only five feet five inches, always with a tight-lipped expression on his face and tiny dot-like brown eyes. Richardsons deliberately mis-labelled the blood as tested, when in fact it wasn't. Louw got paid off, and the blood was shipped to a number of different places to be made into clotting factors. Hospitals in different countries used various batches; they started importing the cheaper blood to meet demand. Sometimes people didn't find out for years that they were infected with HIV or hepatitis – in this way, it was very hard to pinpoint exactly which batches were at fault. Richardsons knew it was a profitable game to play."

"How did you even get your hands on these files?" Will asked incredulously.

"They've been locked up in my safe for years," Scott replied. "The one good thing my father taught me is to always think one step ahead of the game. You don't think I'd be covering up Richardsons' dirty work without having some sort of collateral, do you? You never know when someone can betray you – even a loyal dog can suddenly turn around and bite your hand.

I worked on a separate case with Louw in the 1980s, he was laundering money in a different business venture, he needed me to make some things appear above board, which I assisted him with. Not only did he set up the blood banks in the prison, but he also allowed Richardsons to do off-the-record drug trials, using the inmates as guinea pigs. Some of them died; some became brain-damaged. I saw one whose whole body swelled up, like a huge purple-tinged balloon. He couldn't even open his eyes – they were swollen shut and sunken into the folds of his face. Who's going to make a fuss over a few poor black prisoners?" Scott opened his arms wide in mock indifference.

He continued: "So, Richardsons paid Louw off, and he gave me all the files no questions asked – I was their trusted solicitor after all. I was supposed to make these files disappear. Back then, it was easier to hide information – not everything was computerised. Paper files could go missing at any time, or get destroyed in a fire, or water damaged, doctored, and so on...anyway, I kept a few select files from over the years locked away as a bargaining tool, in case Richardsons ever turned on me. But I guess I'm the one who turned."

Will stared at his father, processing the information for a moment. "So, what happens next?" he asked.

"Well, I guess you need to get in touch with Alice and see how she and Michael want to proceed – assuming he's still alive, that is," Scott responded. "Hasn't she even let you know?"

"Lay off dad, she's just been through a massive shock," Will scowled. "I'll call her now."

Scott shrugged and carefully put the files into his office safe. Will went back to his seat and picked up the phone. He held it off the receiver for a moment, hesitated, then put it down again. Scott was right: Alice hadn't called to let him know anything. Why wouldn't she call out of courtesy to let him know if Michael was okay? Will thought better of it and took up some paperwork, deciding to wait until she called – *if* she called. He had a busy day of client meetings ahead and was glad of this small mercy – anything to divert his mind from the thrum of repeating thoughts.

The hours went by quickly, but still there was no call from Alice. Scott's voice drifted through the open door into Will's office:

"Okay, Will, I'm going – could you close up?"

Will checked his watch and glanced up at his father as he appeared in the doorway. "It's only five minutes past four, where are you going?"

"Well, the last I was aware, I was co-owner here. I think that means I can leave anytime I want," Scott told him and laughed.

"Yeah, I suppose it does," Will conceded. "I won't be too much longer myself."

"Tonight is steak and beer night, remember?" his father said.

In truth, Will had completely forgotten about the little ritual they'd developed over the last few months, but he was glad of the reminder. Scott would cook fillet steaks with peppercorn sauce, which the pair would wash down with a beer or two before playing a game of chess. Their current game had been going on for four weeks. Will enjoyed this time; it was something to fill the void he felt inside.

"Can't wait, see you at seven," Will said with a smile. "I believe I'm ahead in the chess game?" he teased.

"I'm playing the long game," Scott replied, grinning back. "I never lose, remember? Bye, son," Scott said, before turning and leaving through the double doors.

Will went outside for a breath of fresh air. He took a big lungful; it gave him some clarity. He thought about when he'd last spoken to Alice at the hospital. He'd told her it was time to let him move on, but as he replayed himself saying it, it seemed like a line from a movie. Will's head might have told him it was the right thing to say, but his heart was saying something else entirely. It was urging him to connect – to explore and to love her. His soul was never going to stop wanting hers; they were each other's energetic counterbalance on this earth.

His thoughts were interrupted by a man with a wiry, whitish yellow beard, who appeared in front of him and spoke in a husky, semi-toothless tone:

"Excuse me, you couldn't lend me a pound, could you?"

Will dug around in his pocket and gave the man a pound, holding his breath to avoid the stench of old alcohol on his breath. The man's nose was red and bulbous, he wore a navy blue cap that had the word 'Valhalla' sewn on in white thread. It registered in Will's brain as an odd word to have written on a cap – he wondered if it was a team, or a clothing brand he hadn't heard of. He disregarded the superfluous thoughts and looked at the man – clearly homeless. He wondered if the money he begged for would be spent on booze, but who was Will to judge? If this man wanted to block out his reality, wasn't he entitled to do so? Will recognised him from the local area, his memory bank played over some of the times he'd noticed him before.

"Thanks. You're a good 'un," the man flashed him a gappy smile and went on his way.

Will looked up and saw Alice standing across the road, waiting for the green man to appear at the crossing and the busy rush hour build-up to stop so she could cross. She must be on her way to see him with an update, Will realised, smoothing his shirt down and running his fingers through his hair, forgetting his glasses were on top of his head. He quickly dived back into McAvoy and Son and took his seat before Alice approached.

A minute later, she entered the building and half-smiled at Will. He was suddenly nervous of the words yet to be exchanged between them.

"Hi," Will greeted, pulling out the chair out opposite his wooden desk for Alice to sit down. He decided the desk between them would be a wise choice — just as he had all those years ago. Alice sat down and put her bag on the floor.

"Thank you," she said. "I'm sorry I wasn't in touch sooner."

"It's okay, you've had a lot on your plate, I imagine. Is Michael okay?"

"It's still touch and go, he's very poorly at the moment," Alice told him. Will looked at her red eyes. She had no-make up on, she looked so vulnerable.

A pregnant pause filled the room as Alice spaced out, staring at the pot of pens on Will's desk.

"I'm sorry, I'm sure he will be okay," Will soothed. "Listen, my dad has been doing some digging. By some sort of improbable coincidence, the pharmaceutical company that was responsible for some of the HIV-infected blood products is one of his clients."

"What?" Alice gasped. "How can that be?"

"I don't know," Will admitted. "But I know you're a believer in energy attracting circumstances — so am I. Everything is a series of energetic exchanges. So, when you look at it like that, maybe it's not so improbable. I was pulled to come back to be near you; maybe this is the real reason why."

"It certainly seems that there's more to our choices than meets the eye," Alice said thoughtfully. "But, if they are your dad's clients, he's surely not going to act against them?"

"Actually, he's done with them," Will met her eyes.

"He's been toying with the idea of breaking away from them for a while now, and this situation has given him an extra push."

"So, he'll take the case on?"

"Yes, he's just waiting to hear from you to confirm whether you want to go ahead. He's got enough evidence to screw them over. He doesn't lose." Will lowered his eyes. "Like I said before, I don't want to have involvement in the case. It's better if I stay away from you as much as possible. I don't want it to be that way, but I'm never going to be able to switch off my feelings for you."

Alice placed her hand on top of his.

"I know, me too. I don't want to let you go, but that doesn't mean it's fair of me to keep you near. I love you enough to set you free."

Will looked solemn. He didn't want her to say those words. He didn't want her to let go of him; he wished the conversation was entirely different. His foolish heart wanted her and he felt emotion rise up inside him unexpectedly.

"Can I have a hug?" he blurted out, his sudden urge for comfort and compassion unfathomable.

"Of course," Alice said as she got up and they melted into each other as harmoniously as any two souls could. They were pieces from the same blueprint; the same source.

They didn't break the lingering hug, and a while later were curled up quietly with each other on the pastel green sofa, listening to the drops of rain beating heavily upon the windows. Will noticed the time on the clock – seven forty-five pm – and heard his mobile phone vibrating on the desk for the fifth time – his father wondering where we was, no doubt. He ignored it again, closed his eyes and let the fragrant smell of Alice's hair fill his nostrils.

He knew this was the end, and he wanted to hang on to the moment for just as long as he could, while he could still taste her on his lips, while their breathing was still in unison, before Alice's guilt kicked in. Somehow, it was a perfect closure. He kissed her on the crown of her head, her face resting delicately on his chest. Will felt Alice squeeze his hand tightly.

"I've loved you for a long time," she whispered

"I've loved you too, Alice-Bug," he replied, smiling at the name he hadn't used for so long.

When the salty sweat began to cool on their bodies, reality surfaced once more. Will felt Alice's tears drop on to his chest, and he held her just a little tighter.

"I want you to have something," he told her, and reached over to the drawer in his desk. He brought out a little box, opened it, and took out the emerald twist ring that had been his mother's. Silently, Will placed the ring on her finger, looking up at her with wide eyes, "My mother wanted me to give this to someone special, please don't object – it was one of the last wishes she had for me. Please keep it safe."

Alice cried harder, nodded and looked at the ring on her finger.

"I will," she replied, and kissed Will gently on the cheek.

The pair dressed in silence. There was nothing left to say. Alice touched Will on the cheek with her long, delicate fingers, and left the McAvoy and Son offices.

Will switched on the light so that he could close the computer down and lock up. He was in a bittersweet daze about what had just happened between him and the woman he loved. As he closed up the office, he noticed Alice's black leather bag on the floor. He picked it up and quickly ran out to see if he could catch her. She'd already reached the other side of the road and Will called her name. Alice spun round and saw Will holding up her bag. They'd left the situation perfectly, if it was a movie that would have been it, but this wasn't a movie – this was real life. Alice began to trace her path back to where Will was standing, waiting there with his messy hair fast becoming wet strips in the rain – like a lost little boy.

As she walked across the road, Will suddenly dropped the bag and started running towards her, shouting. His words couldn't be heard over the sound of the rain – and the rain couldn't be heard over the sound of screeching tyres.

T he streetlamps cascaded light at regular intervals on the wet tarmac. Alice blinked, disorientated. She was eye level with the road, her pale hand resting just short of the yellow painted line against the black of the road. Her head felt heavy, like a lead weight stuck to the hard surface. When she tried to move, pain shot down the length of her neck and spine. In contrast with her cold, wet surroundings, Alice was aware of the warmth still within her from her encounter with Will.

"Don't move," his voice sounded. She could see his face, just about, but she couldn't move her head to turn to him any further.

"Will," her voice came out much weaker than she anticipated.

"Don't speak," he urged. "Someone will come with help. Just hang on."

Alice saw Will's body shivering in the darkness, his leg

bent into an unnatural position. Alice felt dizzy and tired, but above all else, she felt cold. She could see blood on the road, mixing with the rain. She didn't know whose blood it was.

"I…was your…saviour," Will told Alice in a broken struggle to get the words out. Her tears were warm on her cold face as she tried to move again before stopping with the jolt of pain that followed.

"Will," she repeated, as loudly as she could manage. All she could hear was the patter of raindrops on the ground; no cars had passed; no other sound could be heard.

"Will?" she called again, but received no answer, and the two of them lay side by side on the road like fallen angels.

Chapter Twenty-Seven

Three months had passed since the night of the accident, and Alice now sat on the grass where she'd been reflecting for the past half hour. She'd broken her arm in three places that night and fractured one of her ribs; her wrist was stiff as she tried to move it now to place a yellow rose on the grave before her.

She'd visited every day since the funeral. The yellow roses were from her and Michael's garden; they always smelled the sweetest. Today, she'd placed an origami dove on top of the grave, white and crisply folded. The head-stone was fashioned from terracotta-coloured marble with letters etched in gold; Scott had spared no expense on burying the only child he had left. Alice traced the letters with the tip of her fingernail and looked at the ring on her finger – the last thing Will had given her. She squeezed her eyes shut; she had no tears left for the loss she felt on a level she couldn't describe.

A passing car had stopped to help on that fateful night; Alice could still hear the frantic voices in her head as she was pinned to the cold ground, unable to move. There was only silence in response to the paramedics trying to rouse Will. She found out later that the driver of the stolen blue Polo had died instantly – a local man, seventy years old with a white beard, no known family. He was familiar to the police as a homeless drunk – they'd dealt with him before. No-one knew why he would take it upon himself to steal a car; no-one would ever know now.

Alice had learned of Will's fate the following day, of the brain haemorrhage that had claimed his life. She kept playing out his last words: *'I was your saviour'*.

Not a word passed her lips for forty-eight hours after one of the nurses told her Will had died. She just lay in her hospital bed, staring at the ceiling; the grief too much to bear.

Her Will, the beautiful stoic love of her life who had given his life to save her, was gone – really gone.

The only thing that shook Alice out of her depression was one of the nurses coming to her with better news than the first one had – Michael was responding well to the treatment he was receiving. A porter took Alice in a wheelchair up to Michael's room in the same hospital and she looked into his loving eyes. She stroked his unshaven face and unruly hair. She felt compassion for his hurt body that was trying to heal and she held his hand, vowing that she would choose him every day for the rest of her life.

At that moment, the sun appeared and warmed the cold air in the graveyard for a burst of time. Alice shivered. Their story began with a seed planted when she was fifteen, a seed that grew through twists and turns, and lay dormant for years, flourishing and dying all at the same time. Their story was now only memories; bittersweet and irreplaceable – except for the fusion of life that was now growing in Alice's womb.

She felt a presence behind her, and a shadow suddenly cast over Will's headstone. Alice turned around to see Scott standing about a foot behind her and immediately got up; the feeling of guilt thick like sludge, heavy in her stomach.

"Will died for you," Scott said, his lined face sorrowful.

"I'm sorry," Alice told him, looking down at the soft earth beneath them.

"All he wanted was for me to be a better man," he continued. "In the past, I would have hated you, but Will wouldn't want that. He loved you more than I thought it possible to love someone. There was never going to be anyone else for him except you. I just have to trust his judgement and do what I think would have made him happy."

Alice looked at him briefly, the guilt compelling her to break off eye contact almost immediately. Scott went on: "He wanted me to win this case for you. I didn't agree with his sentiment, but he felt he owed it to you for hurting you all those years ago. I will win this case but I'm doing it for his memory, not for you – just to be clear."

Alice digested this and spoke softly:

"Will would be proud of you; I know he loved you very much, despite your differences. I know it might take you some time to see me in a better light than you do at the moment. I'll try to make you see that I was worthy of his love."

"Why would you bother doing that? We're not intrinsically linked."

"Actually, we are," Alice told him, gently taking his hand and placing it on her tummy. "Your grandchild is in here."

Scott looked at her, his lips pressing into a hard line, a tear forming in his eye.

"My grandchild... How long?"

"Three months," she said. "Against all odds, this baby still came to be, despite the accident. I'm grateful to have a part of Will to bring into the world. I just wish he could have experienced it himself."

"What about your partner – Michael? What does he have to say about you being pregnant with Will's child?"

"I am fortunate that Michael is such a compassionate and understanding person," Alice acknowledged gratefully. "We're a family, and he will treat this baby as if it were his own. We've been through a lot together, we're strong enough to get through the unusual circumstances. We'd like you to be involved in the baby's life – Will would have wanted that," Alice looked at him hopefully.

A smile formed on Scott's stony face and he blinked hard.

"Of course I'm going to be involved," he replied resolutely. "I have no family now. I go home and stare at the chess game that Will and I were playing; I daren't touch it. He was winning, but I never told him so. It's ironic that all I have now is work when all I want is my family back. When I had my family, all I did was work. Stupid fool."

"You're not stupid. You did the best with the knowledge you had at the time – that's all any of us can do," Alice reassured. "There's a blessing amongst this pain, don't forget that."

Scott looked at his son's gravestone and brushed his hand over the top of it, shaking his head.

"You look after your mother and sister now, son. I'm proud of you," he told the fresh earth of the grave.

Alice left him alone and walked back to where she'd left

Christopher sitting on a bench under a tree. He looked up and smiled, the sun glinting in his eyes.

"Have you left your flowers on their plaques?" Alice asked.

"Yes. Joanne, Toby and Emily are okay now – they don't want me to tie myself up in knots anymore."

"How do you know?"

"We're all linked by spirit, Alice," her father said wisely. "This is something I never realised before. They are in the trees, the breeze, the rain, the sun. They are all around me all the time, it's just that I can't see them. I feel them.

When we realise that we're not alone, but connected to everything else as one massive, energetic system, it doesn't feel like a loss, because energy never dies, it only recycles. I had a conversation about this once, and I thought the guy was nuts. Now I can see it and feel it for myself." Christopher smiled at the thought of the exchange he'd had with Father Oakley – an exchange that had buried itself in his psyche.

"I'm glad that you've found peace, Dad. I'm glad you are here," Alice returned her father's smile.

"I had my time in Asia – it was a crucial chapter of my life," Christopher continued. "Now, it is time for the next chapter: my daughter and my grandchildren. I know, I look too young to have grandchildren, you don't need to say it," he smirked wryly. Alice laughed and realised that her dad really had come full circle. Now, he was just Christopher – her father.

Christopher looked out over the open space thoughtfully.

"How is Michael doing with the new treatment?"

"He's doing great," Alice answered. "The new combination of drugs is working; he's like his old self again."

"That's good to hear. Did you resolve that issue with

his work colleague, the one that he told you he'd kissed?" Christopher asked.

"Elise, you mean? Michael was in a bad place mentally when it happened. He told her to go and fix her marriage. Besides, it's nothing compared to what I did." Alice said, putting her hand on her pregnant stomach.

"How are you both doing – you know, as a couple? It takes a real man to forgive and accept what happened and take on another man's baby."

"We're okay, considering," Alice rolled a blade of grass between her thumb and forefinger. "There are moments that are a bit strained, but we talk about them and get them out in the open. We're getting there. He's been very patient and tolerant while I've been grieving for Will. He's a one-off. I'm lucky to have him."

Christopher looked at his daughter meaningfully,

"Will is with you too, Alice. He will leave you signs to let you know he's okay, mark my words. I know I never met him, but I feel that he was a really special soul."

"He was," she agreed. "He was everything. I will never, ever be able to convey to anyone just how much he meant to me, or how strong the link was between us. That knowledge was something only Will and I understood."

"You never really get over it, Alice," Christopher went on. "You learn to adapt to the space that the person has left within you. It shapes you because it is supposed to shape you – like malleable clay. Humans are far too attached to things remaining unchanged; they want to be unbreakable, like a mighty oak tree. But the truth is, we are supposed to bend and break and go through the process of metamorphosis. We're like ink drops dancing and dispersing inside rainy puddles; the ink changes the water, and the water changes the ink."

"I know, Dad, but it hurts," Alice replied. "Changing, growing, evolving, losing people – it all hurts."

"I know it does, sweet pea," Christopher touched his daughter's arm and smiled. "You are a survivor, and your best times are yet to come. You have new life in your belly – that is truly a miracle. You and Will have given each other the world."

Alice looked down at her still-flat stomach and smiled. In that moment, she felt all the gratitude in the world for the life she carried within her. A new beginning was coming.

Acknowledgments

This novel wouldn't have come to be without some really amazing folks who have helped me along the way. I have the deepest gratitude for everyone who has shown enthusiasm and belief in me on this soul project – especially my mum for being my biggest supporter and believing I can do anything. Thanks to my beautiful children, who are the reason I work so hard, and who keep giving me reminders that life does not always have to be serious.

I'd like to give a shout out to my customers who have incessantly heard about my book writing process for the last few years, and have still continued to attend their sessions despite this!

For making my book presentable and professional, I'd like to thank Dark Raven Edits, Indie Author's Book Services, T.E. Black designs for the amazing cover art, and of course, my editor and generally lovely person – Fran at Eve Writing Services, who put up with me always sending chapters at the weekends.

A special mention goes to Nadine Galbraith, Joyce

Davenport and Jane Yigit for taking the time to read my novel and give me feedback before the book was finalised.

For picking me up when times have been stressful (there's been a lot of those!) I'd like to thank Victoria Wesson, Helen Louise Moore, Victoria Wilding, Dave Sinclair, and last but not least, for over twenty years of unwavering friendship even though I am terrible at replying to her messages – Amy Finch.

For those who helped me in my darkest times which inspired this book, I'd like to give thanks to Ziyana Abdalla and Louise Beh – I'll never forget what you did for me.

Finally, to the ones who hurt me the most – deepest gratitude to you for paving the way for this book, and for facilitating my highest growth in life.

About the Author

Asher M Israel was born in Lewisham, South East London. She has always been a highly sensitive soul who does not believe that anything happens by coincidence. She is fascinated by the human condition, and looks for the lesson in each situation or connection that comes her way.

As well as contemporary fiction, Asher writes self-development articles and comedy short stories. She is currently in the process of writing and illustrating her first children's book. When she is not writing, Asher is working at her tattoo studio and studying for her degree in nutritional therapy.

Asher uses herself and her life as an artistic expression in its most raw and honest form; she wears her heart on her sleeve and believes in love, above all else.

She currently lives in Manchester, England, with her

two sprightly children; who bring her the greatest lessons and the greatest blessings.

www.instagram.com/missravenspirit

www.facebook.com/missravenspirit

www.missravenspirit.com

Printed in Great Britain
by Amazon

60167538R00156